Wisconsin Vamp
Monsters in the Midwest, Book One

Scott Burtness

FREE Short Story

Get *Five Stars*, a FREE demonic horror comedy short story, when you sign up for **The Paranomedy Pint**, Scott's once-a-month email featuring a great book to read, a fun show to watch, something terrific to drink, and a little paranormal weirdness to enjoy!!

For Liz.

Contents

It Had to Start Somewhere...

W INGS NOW DRY, THE newly hatched Culex tarsalis took her first flight up from the brackish water that had pooled on the alley's cobblestones. Rising through the humid night air, she had no thoughts, no plans, no aspirations. Those were the burdens of more evolved creatures. For her, only one desire occupied the tiny ganglion of nerves that served as the mosquito's brain: the desire to feed.

• • • • • ● • ● • • • •

Amber and Jill made their fifth left-turn. While persistence is usually a virtue to be admired, in this case, it had simply made them lost.

When looking at a map, the New Orleans French Quarter seems like an orderly arrangement of opposing forces. Burgundy and Bourbon Street cross a multitude of saints; real ones like Louis, Ann, Peter, and Phillips, and hopeful impostors like Bienville, Governor Nicholls, and the Ursulines. This incongruous grouping of vice and virtue makes navigation look easy. Vice gets you across town, while following religion brings you to water. What the maps don't show is that buried deep inside this orderly arrangement of saints and sinners are winding alleys, by-ways, cul-de-sacs, and cubbies that could confound the savviest of French voyageurs. Rather than finding shrimp jambalaya and a good jazz club, Amber and Jill instead found themselves deep in the French Quarter's uncharted bowels, stumbling through a dark, narrow alley.

"Told you we should've turned left," Jill deadpanned after a long drag on the mostly smoked joint. The ensuing giggle fit found them doubled over with tears streaming down their cheeks when a deep, cultivated voice bled from the darkness.

"Good evening, ladies. What, pray tell, could be the source of your most delightful mirth?"

After yanking her heart straight up into her throat, the voice slid down Amber's gullet - all spoiled milk and sticky honey. It pooled in her gut, suffocating her laughter and curdling in her stomach. Jill merely yelped, burped, and laughed in rapid sequence, inducing a sudden and violent case of the hiccups.

"Oh, um. *Hic.* We just *hic*... should'a turned left," Jill choked out while laughing and trying to take a quick hit between hiccups. "Hey, weren't you in that movie?"

The stranger's smile turned mean and stretched to reveal two sharply pointed, impossibly long incisors. His arm lashed out cobra-quick, and his fingers twined tightly in Jill's hair. Something between a hiccup and a scream barely made it past her lips as the stranger wrenched her head and snapped her neck.

Amber froze in uncomprehending horror and watched her friend fall lifeless to the cobblestones. Her only lucid thought as the man turned and grasped her bare arms - fanged mouth moving toward her neck - was to wonder how his hands could be so cold. It was summer in New Orleans. Nothing could possibly be so cold.

. . . . ● . ● ● . . .

Moving erratically, the young mosquito descended upon the dark shapes below, drawn to the blood steaming upon a cool, smooth chin and running in rivulets down an alabaster neck.

. . . . ● . ● ● . . .

"You hear that?" Jerry interrupted. "That was a scream. A girl. C'mon! We gotta do something!"

Walter LaBauve, New Orleans native and Jerry's favorite client, shook his head, the movement loosening a deep, gravelly chuckle.

"You read too many scary books, mon ami. Is the French Quarter, no? People do all kinds of crazy here and usually not in private. Laissez les bons temps rouler! You go looking, you gonna see more than you planned for and probably get charged twenty bucks," he opined with a sage nod and sly wink.

Mostly convinced, Jerry let the humidity push him back into his seat at the small sidewalk cafe. It was true that people behaved very differently in The Big Easy compared to the folks back home. Trappersville was as different from New Orleans as day-old cheese curds from fresh jambalaya. Nestled in northern Wisconsin, just outside the

Nicolet National Forest and near the banks of the Wolf River, the tiny town was a tick-infested, cheese-infused, flannel-clad waiting room for the last train to boredom. He'd asked his wife a hundred times if they could pack up the girls and move. Before Katrina, Pam would say things like, "Maybe when the girls are a bit older." After Katrina, she'd just look at him until he sulked back to his Barca Lounger to watch cooking infomercials and dream of his next trip to the Crescent City.

"Speaking of books," said Jerry, picking up the dropped thread of their conversation. "I think she did justice to New Orleans. The books are good. You should just try one."

"Pah! Arrete toi. You just stop trying." Walter held his meaty palms out in front of him, forbidding Jerry to say any more. "Them couyons could'na find their own bumbos with a torch. Vampires. Why you read that stuff, mo pa konmprann! What nonsense. N'awlins has enough real stories to last a lifetime and you read about vampires. Pah!"

When Jerry started to protest, the bigger man rolled his eyes in exasperation.

"Maybe I send you some good books to read on your next flight down," he said, tone clear that the topic had been settled. "Speaking of, mon ami, you need to finish that drink and get to the airport. Red-eye leaving soon, ain't it so?"

Feeling the usual malaise that accompanied the end of his trips, Jerry opened his briefcase and shuffled some papers around. Both men knew that the idle busywork was a thinly veiled excuse to delay his departure. Walter sat with a patient grin, fingers laced over his ample belly. It was a fine evening, and neither man was in a terrible hurry to have it end.

· · · · ● · ● · ● · · ·

The vampire reveled in the blood flowing down his throat, pooling in his gut, leeching into his body. Engrossed with trying to drink back the life he'd forfeited centuries ago, he didn't feel the minuscule parody of his own dark thirst stab its proboscis into his flesh. He didn't hear when it screamed a tiny mosquito scream, or notice as it wrenched away from his neck and reeled back into the night air. And though he'd sired countless fiends since his turning, he did not recognize the beast as it died and was reborn undead while spiraling away, dizzy with a new hunger it could never slake.

· · · · ● · ● · ● · · ·

Had he not been so consumed with paper-shuffling stall tactics, Jerry might've noticed the peculiar speck of light zig-zagging down toward him, its bluish-grey glow contrasting eerily with the warm glow of the gas lamps. When the spark closed the final few inches to his face, it gave him such a start he near upended the table. Jerry grabbed a brochure from his briefcase and swung it in sharp, annoyed jerks at the luminescent nuisance. Half-uttered swear words, waving arms, and hopping legs waged a comical battle against the darting, gyrating glow until he finally connected, the force driving the bug clear out of sight. Jerry threw the brochure back in his briefcase and snapped it shut with a victorious *clack*.

"Laissez les bons temps rouler, indeed! Dat's one nasty bugger, yah?" exclaimed Walter, clapping in appreciation. "Never seen fire-bugs get so riled at someone."

"Well, not quite the way I'd planned to end the night, but it'll have to do," panted Jerry as he pulled at his sweat-stained and twisted shirt, completely unaware of the minuscule demon seething with unnatural hunger between brochures and invoices in his briefcase.

· · · ● · ● · ● ● · · ·

"Welcome to the General Mitchell International Airport and thank you for flying with us. Please remain seated until the plane has come to a complete stop and the fasten seat belt light is extinguished. It's a balmy night in Milwaukee, Wisconsin. The temperature outside is a mellow seventy-six degrees, there's a slight breeze from the south, and zero chance of rain. All in all, a perfect summer evening. There will be an attendant at the ramp directing people with connecting flights to the appropriate gates and also to the luggage retrieval area. Once again, it's been a pleasure serving you on our non-stop flight from New Orleans to Milwaukee."

Briefcase in hand, Jerry made his way through the terminal toward long-term parking. The red-eyes always took their toll, especially with the long drive from the airport to the middle of nowhere. At least his boss had agreed to let him work from home the next day. Leaving New Orleans always left him a little down. Hopefully, he could convince Pam to take the girls and the dog to the park for a few hours. Then he could queue up some good jazz, make the Cajuniest breakfast he could manage from the Get'n'Gobble's generally bland offerings, and acclimate himself to another few of weeks of small-town drudgery.

About three hours later, Jerry pulled into his driveway, quickly killing the headlights so they didn't shine into the kids' bedroom window. He groaned his way out of the car, sore and tired from a long night of travel. Halfway up the front walk, his briefcase latches gave. Brochures, invoices, and his new Jimmy Buffett gig poster from the '99 *Will Play for Gumbo* tour spilled onto the dew-soaked grass. Jerry stooped, muttering about rotten bosses and worthless anniversary gifts.

"If my poster's ruined, I'm gonna ram this dollar-store briefcase up his oversized behind like a greased petard," he promised, gently picking up the poster.

His world consumed by saving Buffet, Jerry didn't notice the sickly glowing gray-blue speck that buzzed past him into the pre-dawn sky. For its part, the tiny demon was so disoriented by its sudden release into the Wisconsin countryside that it completely disregarded the free lunch grumbling below and flew up, up, up, carried by a warm breeze into the fading night sky.

Chapter 1

H ERB'S ALARM CLOCK WAS a right bastard. A whiny, self-righteous twit. "Don't get mad at me," it buzzed. "You're the one that *set* me. Is it *my* fault that I can do my job at the exact right time - day in and day out - without fail? Maybe *you're* the one who's lacking here."

He really wanted to come up with a truly devastating response. If the damn thing would just *shut up,* he'd think of a zinger that would put that bleating piece of plastic in its place. But no, the noisy little nuisance wouldn't shut up. It just kept complaining and complaining and complaining...

A hand fumbled out from under the covers. Fingers moved across the top of a faux-wood nightstand and traversed bubbles and warps left in the veneer by countless glasses of water spilled while trying to silence the alarm. With past as prologue, Herb's hand knocked over an orange Tupperware cup. The remains of its contents soaked the nightstand while the cup itself fell to the floor, rolled in a lazy circle, and came to rest under the twin bed. A second well-placed grope landed the hand directly on the clock-radio, fingers working to decipher the complex code of a snooze button. For a moment, there was quiet, followed by a snore.

Know thyself, they say. No sooner had he silenced the monster on the nightstand than its dastardly twin started bleating. With an anguished groan, Herb rolled off the bed and stumbled to his well-used but seldom-cleaned living room, following the sound like a drunken moth to a whiskey flame. The second alarm clock perched between a daunting collection of 80s one-hit-wonder tapes and a Brett Favre bobble-head doll. Whacking Brett's noggin in the process, Herb switched off the alarm. His groan was suddenly and shockingly audible in the otherwise silent room. The groan trailed off to a sigh as his stubbled chin drooped toward his chest. Seconds before toppling over onto the couch, the kitchen alarm clock roared to electronic life.

Head snapping up so fast he almost tumbled into his cassette tapes, Herb turned toward the noise.

"Alright alright ALRIGHT!," he cried. "I'm up. Just stop! All of you, stop!"

Determined steps carried him around a battered coffee table and cracked leather recliner, past the front door and into the kitchen, and finally to an old stove that they probably built the 1970s rambler around. Perched on the back of the stove was alarm clock number three, which Herb dubbed the 'deal breaker.' One last swat of the hand, and blessed silence returned to Herb's humble home.

Mornings were usually like this. Herb often wondered if someday he'd be able to kick the three-alarm habit. Unfortunately, on the days when he set only two, or god forbid, one... well, he'd had enough warnings from his boss to know that being late again would mean a new cook at Ronnie's.

Coffee came first. Until the pot was set to brew, the rest of the world could take a number and get in line. While waiting for the slow, brown trickle to fulfill its promise of normalcy, Herb gazed out the window above the sink. The trees had that shadowy quality only pre-dawn can create, when the usual colors of the Wisconsin woods were stripped down to their black and gray essence. Hovering on sleep again, he imagined a glistening spark zigging and zagging among the pines, winding in and out of the million shades of gray, while a strange gurgle tugged and pulled at his awareness.

Herb's reverie snapped like a broken bowstring when the coffee pot proclaimed its job was done. The smell of brown, caffeinated water wrapped him in its promise of better things to come as he poured a cup and felt the ceramic mug warm against his fingers. While always a bit rough to begin with, Herb still enjoyed mornings best of all the hours in the day, especially in the late summer. His peculiar routine might seem chaotic to some, but for Herb, it was one he could no longer imagine doing without. Mug in hand and clothed in his favorite terrycloth bathrobe—a threadbare, dingy swath of green and gold he lovingly called Scary Terry—he stepped onto his front stoop and looked out upon the woods.

With thinning, rust-colored hair perpetually a few weeks past needing a cut, stubble smudged over round cheeks and a soft chin, glasses sliding down the bridge of a freckled and not-quite-bulbous nose, robe loosely tied below a gut more party ball than six-pack, and slippers decorated like cans of Milwaukee's Best beer, Herb didn't look well-suited to nature. Regardless, the serene woods of northern Wisconsin suited him. Like most of the homes in those parts, Herb's rambler squatted deep in the trees. The main road was a good seventy-five yards from his door and was only used by the occasional traveler en route to a real road that led to a real destination. His nearest neighbors,

Jerry and Pam, were about a half-mile away. On rare, still nights, he could sometimes hear the raspy bark of their little pug, but not much else penetrated the canopy of pine and maple. Not one for the hustle and bustle of the big cities like Madison or Milwaukee, Herb liked small-town backwoods living just fine. Provided, of course, that he could always have coffee in the morning and plenty of beer after.

As he breathed the warm scents of tree and earth and cheap coffee, a tiny spark spiraled down to the back of his exposed neck. Digging into the flesh, it began to feed, feed, feed. A hand lazily reached up in a gesture familiar as whacking a snooze button and came down just hard enough to crush the pest without slapping the back of his neck. Herb wiped the smooshed remains of the mosquito's body on the cowl of Scary Terry, and it fell unnoticed into his steaming mug. Floating on the brown liquid, the rolled up little lump of goo began to twitch and shift. Slowly, a crushed and torn wing unrolled, the shredded tissue re-stitching itself. A leg unfolded, then another, and another until six spindly limbs stuck out at jaunty angles from an abdomen that was inflating like a pigmy water balloon. Compound eyes sprouted and grew while a new proboscis unrolled and wavered around. As the minute demon worked its unholy way toward being whole, Herb took a healthy swig of coffee, sighed contentedly, and turned to walk back into the house.

"Damn skeeters," he observed softly, just like every other summer morning.

A short while later, Herb's Pinto—affectionately named The Pinto—motored down the highway, followed closely by a white cloud of oily exhaust. Inside the Pinto, portable Walkman speakers attempted to pit Fleetwood Mac against four poorly tuned cylinders and a rusted manifold. Smiling to himself, Herb dubbed the ensuing noise "Fleetwood Manifold." Since Ronnie wouldn't allow music in the kitchen, Herb had to make the most of his commute so it could carry him through the day. Sadly, Stevie Nicks was a little harder to hear than normal since he was pushing the little hatchback to its ninety-two horsepower limit. He didn't want to be late for work, and precious time had been lost trying to find some calamine lotion and a bandage for his neck.

Usually, he wouldn't have bothered. Like most Sconnies, Herb was pretty thick-skinned about the whole bug thing. It was a rare day that he needed a remedy to get over a few bites. The telltale pink blotches were a sure sign of a city slicker on his first real trip to the woods. If someone couldn't handle a few gnats, mosquitoes, wasps, flies, spiders, chiggers, yellow jackets, ants, centipedes or wood ticks, Herb figured they should either move or resign themselves to going clinically insane. When the mosquito bite on his neck started to burn, he'd finally caved and went in search of the calamine. Picking away the scabby coating around the cap, he'd lathered some on to the bite and rummaged for a bandage to hide the pink splotch. Most folks wouldn't give it a passing thought, but if Dallas happened by the truck stop, he'd never let Herb live it down. Bad enough that trying to find the bandages had Herb running late for work, and running late for work meant barely being able to hear Stevie.

The Pinto rode its classic-rock-and-exhaust cloud past town and out the county line highway past a whole bunch of nothing until Herb finally arrived at Ronnie's Famous Truck Stop, Grill, Bait Shop and Gift Emporium. Ronnie had been a long-haul trucker for about ten years before a wreck ended his time on the road. The lawsuit against the Amish couple that had been driving without proper buggy reflectors gave Ronnie enough money to buy a vacant gas station and diner on the outskirts of town and turn it into his own little kingdom. Now, almost seventeen years later, Ronnie claimed to have the best truck stop in all of Wisconsin, and maybe even the quad-state area. He never went into specifics, though. Best food? Best anniversary gifts? Best overnight cots and showers? No one quite knew for sure, and you certainly couldn't tell just from looking, but as far as Ronnie was concerned, it was *the best*. Anyone that thought otherwise was reminded by Ronnie that opinions were like assholes, rendering the need for empirical evidence moot. Same could be said for the 'famous' claim. Herb supposed it was just one of those little magics people could work. Call it famous and—alacadabra!—people decided it had to be famous for some reason or other. Maybe Capone had stopped by on vacation for some curds, or Elvis had performed in the parking lot, or the ghosts of lost hitchhikers had been seen in the windows at night. All it takes is one speculative tourist and, boom, your joint is famous.

Herb had been working for Ronnie off and on since he was a junior in high school. He'd quit a couple of times and been fired a few others, but Herb and Ronnie just seemed destined for one another. They would never call themselves friends, but they knew each other better than most, and with that came a level of understanding and acceptance. So when Herb parked his Pinto behind the truck stop and walked in the back entrance to the kitchen, he wasn't surprised that Ronnie was waiting and was even less surprised that Ronnie was pissed.

Which rant today? thought Herb. *Higher Calling, Engines of Industry, or God Hisself must be hatin' me to stick me with you as a line cook?*

"Damn it Herb. Damn it, damn it, damn it. We've got people out there needin' food, and who's gonna make it? Engines of industry just *sitting* out there, productivity dripping away like antifreeze from a busted hose, like air leaking out from eighteen God-gifted wheels. These boys gotta eat! Eat so they can drive, Herb. Drive! You look out there, whatdaya see?"

Oh goody, Engines, thought Herb as he looked obligingly over Ronnie's shoulder and through the serve-through window into the diner beyond.

"Old Hodge and Rob Gardner having coffee. Ned's got the Trappersville Times. Probably yesterday's 'cause the Johnson boy won't be around 'til eight-ish with today's. And um..."

Lois, he almost said. *Ah yes. Lois.*

"Oh, and Ronnie, it's only ten to. I'm on at seven," Herb added as an afterthought. "Bill's here 'til seven-thirty, right?"

Ronnie's face turned a shade of red not commonly found in nature. His squinted eyes pried themselves away from glaring intently at Herb's innocently blank face, shifted to the clock on the wall for all of a second, then jumped back.

"I know what time it is," he snapped. "I'm still trying to get over you being on time for once. Should'a had Bill call the ambulance. I could'a had me a heart'o'tack just now from the shock of it, and you'd be damn worthless. Probably just watch all stupid-faced with me twitchin' on the kitchen floor. And don't change the god damned subject. I'm trying—*trying*—to instill some sense of responsibility in you. You see Hodge and Gardner and Ned, and you think, 'Oh, isn't that nice? The fellas are back again! La dee dah, it's sooo nice to have a few fellas around sipping coffee and chewing the fat.' Idiot! Those men are engines of industry, and they need to eat!"

Ronnie's voice raised to a shrill note, one that Herb was quite accustomed to. He nodded, trying to look contrite as he tied on his apron and gave a wave to Bill, the diner's third-shift cook. Bill really wanted to be an Army guy who'd 'seen some shit.' Unfortunately, Bill was terrified of just about everything involved with joining the Army, such as getting shot at, eating MRE's, traveling, and not being able to shower every day. At thirty-six, he still lived at home with a mother who bought him camo pants and 'Army Strong' shirts and called him Sarge.

Yeah, Bill's a bit off, Herb often thought, *but he makes damn good onion rings, so there's that.*

"Order up! Eggs up where the sun shines, hash well, burn the pig, dry wheat, extra jam. Also need a Pope Benedict, holly on the side, hash soggy, fruit cup for two. And hurry up! These guys gotta get back on the road."

Herb would never understand how time could actually stop whenever he saw Lois. Maybe if he'd gone to college, or one of those science conventions with Stephen... Hawking? King? The really smart one. Maybe then he'd be able to make sense of it. Or maybe it was beyond science, something only pure faith could touch. Something Buddha and Jesus might chat about while taking a breather from the debate and drinking lemonade. Whatever it was, however it happened, Herb loved it. Lived for it. For that first moment of the day, when he got to drink in long fuchsia nails, powdery blue eyeliner, cherry red lips, and that hair. That lovely, golden hair pulled back in a sensible pony tail with a careless strand falling down across her cheek, waiting to be tucked back in place...

"Uh. Lois. Hiya. Hair. Nice, um. Sure thing," Herb managed.

Lois turned that confused look she always seemed to have waiting for him back through the serve-through window, causing Herb's heart to leap somewhere past his Adam's apple, plummet to his kidneys, and bounce back to tangle up in his lungs.

"... Thanks Herb. Oh, and I need a Sunrise Special and a Cheese Please with light toast to go. And please don't burn the light toast again."

"You see, Herb?" crowed Ronnie. "There's a girl that gets it. She knows these folks are in need, and our purpose, our *raison d'etre*, which is French for 'pretty damn important,' is to meet their needs. Even Bill, who's a couple spark plugs short in the engine upstairs–sorry Bill, no offense, just true."

"None taken, sir," saluted Bill with the spatula before flipping strips of bacon on the flat-grill.

"Even Bill knows that what we do here matters," Ronnie continued. "But you. You just float around with your shaggy head up your hairy ass. I can't take it. I just can't take it."

Ronnie's familiar rant faded as he stomped away toward the back office. Herb scratched absentmindedly at the bandage on his neck and picked up the order ticket Lois had left in the window. As he threw an English muffin in the toaster, he imagined for the millionth time that he was making her breakfast in bed. "Her favorite," she'd say. Then she'd smile, and that smile would be all his.

The hours passed in a blur as Herb served up breakfast all day and dinner any time. If he'd learned anything while cooking at Ronnie's, it was that breakfast, lunch, and dinner were in the eye of the beholder. Or mouth of the eater. Or whatever. Some people cling to the belief that eggs are breakfast, a Reuben sandwich is lunch, and walleye with mashed potatoes on the side is dinner. Ronnie's was a place where all such preconceived notions blew away like chaff in the wind. If it was on the menu, you could get it, be it sunrise, sunset, or some hour in between. Third-shift workers from the paper mill, tourists, truckers, college kids and families up camping during the summer, fishermen working their way up the Wolf River... Whoever found themselves at Ronnie's all found some strange common ground in the belief that breakfast, lunch, and dinner were the arbitrary constructs of less evolved minds. Herb didn't judge when an order for a Reuben with extra 'slaw and a Mountain Dew came across at eight a.m. alongside orders for corned beef hash and a rack of prime rib with potatoes. Truth be told, the chaotic variety of orders, sides, and substitutions made the days go by pretty quickly. The only mystery left was how - after all these years - he wasn't a better cook.

Herb finished cleaning up, threw his apron in the laundry basket, and made his way out of the kitchen. He balanced his turkey sandwich with coleslaw in one hand while filling up a glass of pop with the other. Multitasking accomplished, he pushed through the swinging door that led from the kitchen, slid onto a stool at the counter, and settled in to eat.

No sooner had he taken a mouthful of bread, turkey, bacon and mayo, than Lois came out from the ladies' washroom. Gone was the Ronnie's polo and apron. Instead, a striped tube top left slender arms and toned tummy on full display. A small diamond in her navel hypnotized as she wove around the counter. Low-rider jeans hugged hips kept trim by walking for a living, and stripy little sandals ensured that even the most casual of glances couldn't help but take in a full spread of perfectly painted toenails. Her hair, earlier pulled back in a sensible ponytail, was down and cascaded in golden blonde waves to crash against tanned shoulders. Dark blue eyeliner, bright red lipstick, a hint of blush on her cheeks... The result left Herb convinced that Aphrodite's personal stylist had taken up residence in Ronnie's bathroom. Lois had been working at Ronnie's since she rolled into town just after the New Year. Over six months later, his brain still short-circuited every time he saw her.

"Har, umm, Lois," muttered Herb around a mouthful of turkey. He forcibly swallowed and tried again. "Your hair is great. Again. I mean, at work. No, your hair's always great at work. But after work your hair is, um. Really great."

Silence hung for a few awkward moments before Lois replied, "Thank you, Herb. That's just, well, very nice."

Encouraged by how well things were going, Herb continued. "You working tomorrow? The schedule's up, but I didn't see you on it. Or me. I mean, I was just, not that I was looking at your, ah. I just saw the schedule."

Lois was almost at the door, but slowed to turn back and wave politely. "Nope, I'm out tomorrow. Probably going to stop by the bake sale at First Lutheran. You know, good cause and all. But I'll see you next week. Oh, and..." She paused while the line cook's heart swelled in his chest, then said, "You have mayonnaise on your face."

Herb managed to keep a smile in place until she was safely out of sight, then wiped his face and thunked his head on the countertop.

Chapter 2

HERB'S FOREHEAD WAS STILL pressed to the counter when Dallas barreled into the diner, his tall, muscular frame clad in flannel, worn denim, and unshakable self-confidence.

"Holy shipyards, Herb! Did you see Lois? Damn, she is on fire!"

The walking embodiment of manliness made his way through the diner like a king taking court, which, in a way, he was. Everyone in town knew Big D, since someone so much larger than life was hard to miss. Dallas was without question Trappersville's top dog. He even had a commercial on cable access for his HVAC service, That Blows HVAC.

"Broken thermostat? That blows. No A/C on a hot summer day? That blows. Think you can't afford to get that new furnace installed? That blows!"

Dallas was a natural for T.V.

Theirs was an unlikely friendship. From back in grade school when he was consistently picked first for kickball, to high school where he was the starting quarterback freshman through senior years, Dallas had always been 'the man.' Herb, on the other hand, was not. He had been terrible at kickball and spent most football games duct taped to something. It's not that he was unliked growing up. He just wasn't liked and made an irresistibly easy target for the other kids to practice their meanness. So it was really just another day in the eighth grade when Herb was surprise-wedgie'd by Joey O'Connell and shoved into the girl's bathroom. The commotion caused a handful of girls to run screaming to the hallway, including Denise Landry, who exploded out of a closed stall. Joey was using the leverage of Herb's hiked-up undies to shuttle him toward the recently vacated stall when Dallas stepped out, fist already heading toward Joey's nose.

"Whadaya think you're doing? I was gonna get to second base!" Dallas had yelled, punches punctuating his words.

Joey had gone down, red pluming from his nose, leaving Herb to wrestle with his underwear and watch in awe as someone actually stood up for him. When Mrs. Rafferty had burst in, she separated the pugilists and turned to Herb for answers. Still squirming in his skewed undies, Herb had blurted out, "Joey wedgie'd me and was gonna stick my head in the toilet when Dallas stopped him."

Joey got detention, Dallas got a gold star, and Herb got a friend. It worked out pretty well. Herb needed distraction from his own humdrum existence and occasional protection from bullies. Dallas needed an audience to endure hearing about his over-the-top escapades with an endless string of girls. They basically got along great.

"That Lois, I'll tell you what," Dallas continued after taking a stool next to Herb at the diner counter. "Ten minutes. If she'd just give me ten minutes, that girl would be stuck on me like white on rice, know what I mean? "

Herb nodded, uncomfortably aware that Dallas had no inkling of Herb's obsession with Lois, being too busy entertaining his own. Dallas looked past him, brow furrowed in deep thought.

"'Course, a guy like me could use a lot more than ten minutes, you understand. Sure, we both know that. I'm not implying that ten minutes is all I'd be good for. It's like… Well, here's a metaphor, Herby. It's like a train only needs a few hours to get from Milwaukee to Chicago, right? But that train, it could run all night and not even break a sweat. I'm the train, right? Damn right! I'm the train, I'm taking her to Chicago, where I'll bet she's never been, at least not with a dude, you know? Maybe she's gone a time or two for some girlie shopping weekend, but with a guy, a real guy? Hell, I'll bet she ain't even been to Pleasant Prairie," he finished on an authoritative note.

It took a moment before Dallas realized his own joke, but when it registered, he started to laugh. Herb knew that 'knee slapper' was just an expression, but also knew that whoever came up with it was referring literally to Dallas.

"Pleasant Prairie! Damn, that's good. I ain't gone down to Chi-town, but I've been to Pleasant Prairie. Ha!" Dallas sang out, slapping his knee in time.

Herb nodded again with what he hoped looked like enthusiastic support. Inwardly, he was having some trouble following Dallas, due in part to Dallas being rather long-winded, but more as a result of Lois. Herb was continually stunned by everything Lois. Even the mention of her drove him to distraction. It wasn't that she was the only cute girl in Trappersville. While not an avid dater, Herb had been known to have more than a few unrequited crushes in his day. Truth be told, Herb had been ignored, snubbed, or flat-out rejected by lots of girls over the years, starting with Wendy Jacobsen in third grade and ending most recently with Janis Lewinski last New Year's. Herb was still a little ticked at Dallas about that one.

"She's totally digging on you, dude!" Dallas had promised. "It's New Year's Eve, and she's been watching you for like hours. C'mon. Go show her some moves."

Dallas had poured encouraging words and shots of Wild Turkey in rapid succession until Herb actually thought that maybe, just maybe, Janis was *the one*. A nice girl, someone he would be happy to bring 'round on the holidays. She had such a nice smile, and Herb always wanted kids with nice teeth. Big D was right: he was a good catch. A job, a little rambler in the woods, four wheels ready to burn. Well, maybe not burn, but, by George, he had a car, right? And he liked good music. Maybe he was carrying a few extra pounds over the belt, but damn if he couldn't still shake a tail-feather when the mood was right. Yessir, Dallas was right. Janis was the one and Herb was the one and they were gonna be one happy couple. Or perhaps they would have been, until Herb had wobbled over, smiled, and puked on her lap. Sadly, after that opening move, Janis had joined the ranks of women that were anywhere from oblivious of to plain old repulsed by Herb.

Lois was different. Those other girls, minor crushes at best, while Lois was in a league of her own. A league that Herb knew he wasn't in. Dallas, sure. She'd go for a guy like Dallas. Tall, fit, good looking. He probably never burned light toast.

Everyone liked Dallas, especially the girls, he grumbled to himself, the thought a dark cloud across his mind. *Bet they wouldn't like him so much without a face.*

It was suddenly so clear. All Herb had to do was rip Dallas's face off and pull out his eyeballs. Then he'd see how lucky Dallas was with the girls.

"...with a feather. I kid you not, Herby, I am always going to use a feather from now on. Wow. A goddamned feather. Who'da thunk?" Dallas said, an expression of wonder on his face.

Herb blinked, realizing he'd completely spaced out. "Oh. Yeah, ah, me too. For sure," he offered, sending Dallas into a fit of laughter.

Reaching for his half-eaten turkey sandwich, he discovered his appetite was gone. Sliding the plate away, Herb leaned on his elbow and faked listened to Dallas, all the while thinking of Lois's smile and scratching his neck.

Chapter 3

HERB WAS ABOUT HALFWAY home when inspiration struck.

The bake sale, he suddenly remembered. *She's going to the bake sale.*

It was an annual affair that drew Trappersville's gerontological society into a mostly good-natured competition to raise funds for the church. Banana breads and lemon bars squared off against cupcakes and krumkake while the blue-haired bakers fake-fawned over each other's concoctions and caught up on town gossip. Herb had visited in years past, since it was impossible to skip a sale devoted entirely to dessert. This year was going to be different, though. This year, Lois was going.

Turning back toward civilization, he rolled into the local supermarket. The Pinto made a knocking noise every time he turned right, so Herb proceeded to turn left and head toward a space near the front door. As he drew closer, another car came in from the other direction and smoothly pulled into the spot Herb had his eye on. With a friendly smile and wave to cover a mumbled curse involving firstborns and explosive diarrhea, Herb headed past the spot and made a right turn to head for the next row.

Brong brong brong, the Pinto's wheel complained as Herb navigated the turn and headed down the next row of spots. One spot was too narrow; a full-sized pickup had parked diagonally, taking up most of two spaces. The next spot was blocked with abandoned shopping carts. Herb turned left at the end of the row and started heading up the next. Long, weaving minutes later, he finally settled for an open spot near the back of the lot, killed the engine, and headed for the store.

Herb bee-lined straight to the snicker doodles. Stacked like a shrine to all things good, he stood for a moment in hushed reverence before grabbing a large box.

So much easier than baking, he reasoned.

Realizing that he didn't have anything for supper, he wandered the aisles and add the essentials of bachelor life to his cart. White bread, squeeze cheese, cereal, a couple of pounds of ground beef, and other vittles slowly made a pile. It was a rolling testament to the fact that while he might cook for a living, Herb wasn't one to bring work home with him. As he rounded the corner into the snack food and soda aisle, he nearly collided with another shopper's cart right in front of the cheddar puffs. Herb hastily pulled up short, causing the contents of the cart to shift and crash inside the wire cage. Crisis averted, he reached for the last bag of puffs. Like an overstuffed boa constrictor with skin of worn polyester, the other guy's arm snaked out, meaty hand grasping for the same bag of puffs. A strange, ritualistic dance ensued. Both men reached for the bag and backed off simultaneously, politesse warring with the urge to eat puffed up balls of cheese-flavored air, and the aisle filled with the grunts and murmurs of stuttered apologies and excuses.

"Did you want those?"

"Sorry! My wife, she loves these..."

"I was just going to..."

"Why don't you just..."

Suddenly, unexpectedly, and with a half-spoken apology still hanging in the air, the other man's hand reversed and grasped for the last bag of puffs off the shelf.

It was too much. Herb never got the cheddar puffs. While the other shopper was surprisingly agile, his quick reverse was nothing compared to the speed of Herb's reaction. Instead of grabbing the cheese puffs bag as expected, the man's hand met Herb's. Their fingers intertwined, and the cook squeezed. Herb heard a low growl, vaguely surprised to identify its source was somewhere deep in his gut. He looked at the man, watched his eyes widen first in shock and then pain as Herb's fingers tightened like hydraulic pistons. Shadows encroached on his vision while indistinct whispers twined with the low growl. A voice he barely recognized rumbled its way up from deep in his throat, tumbled past his teeth, and fell from his mouth like rough-hewn stone.

"My. Cheddar. Puffs. Mine."

The other man gasped as Herb twisted his hand back further. "Geezuz, okay! Have 'em! They're yours! Awww crap, that hurts."

Maybe it was the genuine fear in the large man's suddenly boyish voice, or the tear that formed in the corner of his eye as he sank to one knee, wrist bent back at an unnatural angle. Whatever it was, it speared Herb like a giant shard of ice. Dropping the man's hand, he took a hasty step back into the shelves, dislodging the contested cheddar puffs and knocking them to the linoleum tiles below.

"Holy cow. I am so... I don't know what got into... Uh, here," Herb offered, picking up the bag and holding it out to the man.

Anger, wariness, and a fierce desire for sodium phosphate and yellow-number-five played across the man's face before he haltingly reached for the bag. Snatching it, he shoved the puffs between a dented box of snack cakes and some off-brand facial tissues and raced away down the aisle. Herb stood watching the man's receding back, the bite on his neck itching like the dickens. With a trembling hand, he grabbed a bag of French onion potato chips and continued down the aisle.

Once the cart had reached its limit of cholesterol, sugar, preservatives, and artificial flavoring, Herb headed for the checkout. There were only two lanes open, and both had lines. He pulled into lane number four behind an elderly woman with a full cart and a purse leaking crumpled coupons through the seams. As she haggled over expiration dates with the kid behind the register, Herb's gaze wandered the lip balm, tabloids, gum, and candy bars pressing in from both sides. After a few restless moments, his eyes finally came to rest on the plastic-wrapped ground beef in his cart. The meat peeked out from beneath the Lucky Charms like a bare ankle from under a long skirt. The beef was reddish-pink and moist, with that peculiar texture ground flesh packed for mass consumption always has. Mesmerized, his eyes traced each curl and swerve in the beef, each bit of fat and grizzle. Reveling in the rawness of it, Herb was drawn in like water flowing down a slow drain. The sounds of the store around him, the old woman's nasally voice, the creaking of shopping cart wheels, the chatter of sample ladies handing out crackers with a new flavor of preserve, all became hollow, as if someone had stoppered Herb's ears with soggy cotton.

Just past the corner of his eye, Herb discerned movement; threatening shadows that seemed to slide around him, encroaching with sly, malicious intent. He wanted to look, wanted so very badly to see what was casting such odd shadows, but the meat held his attention and kept him enthralled. The rest of the world peeled off and fell away like the blood-stained bandage from his neck as he scratched, scratched. As sounds continued to recede, whispers swirled into the void. Unintelligible, full of strange syllables, they wound around Herb's awareness and filled his ears the way the dead, ground up flesh filled his vision. A salty, iron taste tickled his taste buds, and his nose twitched with the smell of rot and decay. The whispers grew louder and became words he could almost fathom hanging just beyond his reach. Herb stretched his concentration gossamer-thin, straining to understand...

"... for choosing Get'n'Gobble. I hope you found everything you need. We're having a sale on bandages."

Herb's head snapped up. The old woman was rolling away, grumbling about expired coupons still being coupons, while the bland and pimpled face of a nihilistic teenager stared at Herb.

"I'm sorry, what was that again?" Herb asked as he unloaded onto the conveyor belt.

"Bandages on sale." The teen repeated as his half-dead eyes seemed to look at a spot somewhere to the left of Herb's nose.

"Oh... um. On sale? Really? Wow. Back in a sec."

Herb mumbled apologies as he pushed his way past the other shoppers, driven along by their annoyed grunts. Flustered, he jogged back and forth across the ends of the aisles looking for the bandages. Herb's frantic search was suddenly accompanied by the teen's monotone voice over the store PA system.

"Bandages on sale in aisle three. Repeat, bandages are in aisle three. For those shoppers with festering neck wounds in desperate need of a bandage, you'll find them on sale in aisle three."

Herb stopped his scurrying to stare in horror at the clerk, his face going bright red. The woman waiting behind Herb's cart loudly cleared her throat and glared. Grabbing two, then three, then four boxes of bandages, Herb scampered back to the conveyor belt.

"Sorry again, excuse me. Sorry, just wanted to... They're on sale, you know. I'll be outta here in a jiffy," muttered Herb as he scrawled a check for the cashier. Skipping bags entirely, Herb shoveled his groceries back into his cart and rushed for the exit as the clerk's voice followed him out.

"Hello ma'am. Thank you for shopping Get'n'Gobble. I hope you found everything you need. Any festering wounds? Bandages are on sale in aisle three."

Safely back at his car, Herb angrily tossed groceries into the back seat with one hand while scratching his neck with the other. His mind was far away, in a place where nihilistic teenagers were flayed with razors, deep-fried like cheese curds, and served up in neat, little paper trays with ketchup.

Chapter 4

T HE SUN LAZED ACROSS the horizon as the Pinto rode its
burnt-oil cloud to the bowling alley. *Brong brong brong* complained the little car as Herb turned into a parking spot next to a rusty
Cavalier. Stanley stood next to his car, rail-thin, restless and fidgety as
always. A bookworm back in high school, Stanley had been on track
for valedictorian and a full-ride scholarship to the college of his choice.
Then 'the incident in the soccer field' had happened one rainy day
after school. Everyone agreed there was a flash of bright light and that
Stanley wasn't quite the same after. Opinion branched after those
two facts, though. The locals said it was lightning hitting his umbrella
during a summer storm. Stanley swore it was alien abduction, and
carried the unharmed umbrella wherever he went to shake angrily at
the abduction nay-sayers.

Stanley had fallen in with Dallas and Herb some years ago. They
had needed a third to join the bowling league, so Dallas had taken
a gamble on Stan. By Dallas's logic, whether it was old-fashioned
lightning or little green men with a penchant for probing, Stanley had
probably come out of 'the incident' with some helpful super-powers.
Dallas had yet to be proven right, but was also not one to be proven
wrong. So year after year they drank, bowled, and generally had good

times aplenty, while Dallas remained convinced that next year Stanley was going to light it up.

Stanley's fidgeting was most likely excitement about their weekly night of beers and bowling. Or he'd been waiting awhile and had to pee. Or he knew the answer the prior night's Final Jeopardy question. Herb wasn't too worried about being kept in suspense, though. Stanley was incapable of not telling you what he was excited about. It was a trait common to most five-year-olds and the occasional adult like Stanley.

"Herb! Hey Herb! You sure aren't gonna believe this. You might be thinking you're gonna believe it. 'Stanley,' you'll be sayin', 'Stanley, I know you wouldn't lie about things like this, oh heck no.' You'll be all thinking you're gonna b-believe me, but nope, not this time. No sir!"

So he doesn't need to pee, thought Herb with a smile as he excavated his tattered bowling bag from the Pinto's landfill of a backseat. No stopping Stanley now. Better to just let it all come out or Stanley wouldn't be able to concentrate on anything else for the rest of the evening.

"There are over one hundred and seventy different kinds of skeeters," Stanley exclaimed. "D-did you know that?"

Herb thought a moment, shook his head, and replied, "Nope. I sure didn't Stanley. A hundred seventy, you say? Huh. I suppose I would've guessed maybe twenty or thirty, but one-seventy. Wow."

Stanley's head moved like a bobble-head toy. "I know. I know! Uff dah, I was darn sh-shocked to find out, too!"

Ever since the incident, Stanley tended to stutter a bit when he got excited, which was often, which meant Herb was also quite used to Stanley's stutter.

"I thought to myself, Stanley, that's g-gotta explain why you got all them bites. Sure, you use the DEET and the Deep Woods OFF, but you get all these bites, you know? Oh sure, that explains it then. That spray, it p-probably works on one, maybe two, maybe ten kinds of skeeters. But one-seventy? No way. No way. Guys like us, we don't stand a ch-chance when there's so many different skeeters. Not a ch-chance at all, that's for sure."

Herb grimaced sympathetically. "One got me this morning," he said, peeling back the fresh bandage and turning to show Stanley the angry welt on his neck. "Was a nasty bite, too. I've had plenty of bites in my day. Mosquitoes, ticks, gnats, horseflies. But this... It feels like the little sucker had a diamond-tipped drill bit for a nose. Itches like nobody's business."

As Stanley *oohed* and *ahhed* over the welt on Herb's neck and lamented the lost cause of defending the race against so many kinds of predators, Dallas roared up in Deloris: his V8, four-wheel-drive Dodge pickup. The steel leviathan boasted a custom electric blue paint job, chrome jaws on the grill, and matching chrome fenders, running boards, bed rails, and exhaust pipes. Its windows were tinted black as night, and a pair of chrome testicles hung from the trailer hitch. Deloris truly was a sight to behold. If Dallas died and was reincarnated as a truck, he'd be Deloris, no mistake. The strange gender-bending of such a masculine truck with the name Deloris never made much sense to Herb, but he also knew that asking Dallas for clarification would invite being told about some girl he'd boned in high school.

"Time to bowl, compadres!" the third member of the bowling trio announced as he stepped down from the truck. "I'm thinking we qualify for the finals tonight. You little turd-rollers just try to hit a couple of pins and let old Dallas do the rest and we'll be golden. Golden!"

Dallas continued to crow as he corralled Herb and Stanley toward the entrance to Bay City Bowlers, the town's only, and by default premiere, bowling establishment. While the architecture suggested nineteen-sixties and the interior screamed eighties remodel, the place felt timeless to Herb. He liked to imagine early settlers making their way up the Wolf River and stumbling upon a band of Sioux or Ojibwa braves hanging out by the bowling alley. There'd be a challenge, and the newcomers would head inside for a game of bowling. He also liked to imagine the natives rolling perfect games and stomping the settlers.

It was probably early November, Herb thought to himself. *That's the real reason why we have turkey on Thanksgiving. The natives kept bowling strikes.*

Herb's thoughts continued to wander as the trio made their way inside, swallowed whole by the dimly lit, smoky maw of the bowling alley. Herb's sneakers, Dallas's boots, and Stanley's duct taped loafers padded across the confetti-patterned, day-glow carpet. The distinctive smells of smoke, beer, disinfectant, lane oil, and halitosis flowed around the three men as they strolled past the lanes and welcomed them with its embrace. Dallas led the way, turning to and fro as he walked, looking like a politician about to accept his party's nomination. Smiles, waves, high fives, and fist bumps abounded as the denizens greeted Dallas. Herb knew most of the faces too and smiled as he and Stanley got a few greetings tossed their direction. Even though they were just catching stray rays of sun bouncing off of Dallas, it still felt good.

Something about bowling alleys, thought Herb.

There was definitely something magical about the simple ritual of having a beer and a game of bowling that brought out the best in people. His gait slowed as he took it all in. Over there was Marge Henderson, the dandruff on her bowling jersey sparkling in the track lighting. And there, Fancy Dan, whose artful blend of polyester and pleather threw mismatched patterns and eye-searing colors at anyone foolish enough to look. Slow Johnson moved with his measured gait, a regal dance across a ballroom all his own. The people Herb had seen for years were suddenly vivid, new, moving in perfect arrangement against a backdrop of wood paneling. Bathed in neon beer sign light, they appeared infused with all the colors of the rainbow.

Herb felt tears start to form as he took in the radiant beauty of it all. His heart ready to burst, Herb looked toward the bathrooms. Cheryl Dannigan glided out of the women's, a graceful ballerina with swooping hands and pointed toes. Jimmy Tibeaudeax followed a half-moment later, all reckless, impromptu jazz to her smooth steps, goofy grin smeared across his pimply face and still zipping his fly. They wended their way under NASCAR banners hung over mounted fish and game trophies, a celebration of victory and death that made Herb swoon.

Every amazing moment stretched the fiber of his being, wrapped him into a tapestry he'd never known encompassed them all. Cheryl teetered past Herb, following her thread in the weave of the world around him. His smile stretched as he breathed in her scent: sweat, beer, pot, coke, sex, nachos, hairspray, Neosporin... An unexpected redolence that was at once both intoxicating and arousing. Sound drained away as she passed in slow motion. Faint whispers tickled Herb's ears as he watched Jimmy hop along a few strides behind, trying to walk while tying his left Nike high-top. Every movement became an eternity of exquisite beauty, a study in form and grace with each step trapped in amber for him to admire. Herb's widened eyes caught the shifting light and glinted blue-black as they traced the line of Cheryl's brow, jaw, neck. He watched blood fill each capillary in her cheeks when she noticed his stare and began to blush. He could hear her pulse, a deliberate timpani urging him to dance, writhe, stomp in primal syncopation with that coursing rhythm of life, as she turned, mouth moving, tongue darting, hand raising, brows coming together, flecks of spittle flying...

"...hell are you staring at, you little pervert?" Cheryl's eyes tried to focus on Herb's. She wobbled to a stop, Jimmy catching up as she slowed.

"He botherin' you babe? I'll kick his ass!" Jimmy proclaimed. He swerved and leveled bloodshot eyes at whoever had been foolish enough to bother his girl, fists raised in front of his sunken chest.

The moment came rushing back with an almost audible pop. Herb's jaw worked like a guppy out of water while he tried to sort-out just what the hell was happening. One moment he was walking through the bowling alley, and suddenly Cheryl and Jimmy were yelling, screaming, pointing...

"I'm sorry. I didn't mean. Whatever it was, I didn't mean to," he sputtered, and then Dallas came round like a skidding semi.

"What the hell's going on here?" the much larger man barked at Jimmy's upturned squint.

"Oooh shit.. Hey Dallas!" Jimmy squeaked out, voice turned oily. "Didn't see ya there. Oh, and Herb?" Jimmy said with a squint. "Wow, I didn't recognize you! Sorry, guys."

Jimmy rounded on Cheryl and shook an angry finger. "Hell, Cherry. What's wrong with you? It's just Big D and Herby."

"Oh, hey there, Dal," she slurred, sidling closer to Dallas.

"Save it, babe," Dallas said over his shoulder, already strolling away. "I don't want it to burn when I pee. Have fun, Jimmy!"

Herb quickly followed Dallas, confusion giving way to indifference as they headed toward their lane. Now wasn't the time for distractions. They had a big game ahead of them, and Herb was ready to kick some bowling ass.

A game and a half later, frame four to be exact, Herb missed the spare, leaving him with a six. Turning back from the lane, he tried not to imagine what would happen if Dallas actually swung the fists that were clenched by his sides.

"I don't think I'm feeling too good," Herb apologized as his hand moved again to scratch the burning spot on the back of his neck. "Kinda bowling like crap."

"No shit, Captain Obvious. Any other stunning revelations you've been keeping from us? Next you'll be sayin' the ocean's wet and bears shit in the woods. Geezuz, Herbert! We're trying to make the finals here. What the hell?"

Stanley was kinder. "Tough spare, Herby. Tough spare," he offered, patting his teammate on the shoulder.

Dallas threw up his hands in disgust, looking at Stanley like he'd grown a second head.

Eager to avert disaster, Herb made a show of his empty pint glass.

"Just lemme grab a fresh beer, okay? I'll get this game back on track," he promised, backing away from the lane.

"Ten bucks says I kick your ass if you don't," Dallas replied, waving calloused hands over the air vents. "Now don't be a cheapskate and a shitty bowler. Bring us a round. Least you can do after blowing that spare."

Chapter 5

S INCE MOST FOLKS WERE on the lanes, the karaoke bar wasn't too full. As the saloon-style doors swung shut behind him, Herb took in a handful of regulars and followed their stares toward the back of the room. Standing behind a mic-stand on a small, elevated stage, round face lit from beneath by a T.V. monitor, a woman stared zombie-like at the screen and absolutely butchered "The Rose." After recovering from the shock at how bad the lady's singing was, Herb quickly made for the bar, intent on getting in and out before a very indignant Bette Midler crashed through the ceiling with a machete. Rhonda, the bartender, flipped her mullet as she turned toward Herb, smiling around cigarette-stained teeth.

"Another round a 'Waukee's Best? Jus'a'minute, sweetie. Gotta re-fill Jasper's Cosmopolitan," she drawled like a third-grader in a spelling bee, "before Jennie there finishes. My little Jasper, he's such a natural showman. Isn't he just a darlin? Drinks Cosmopolitans like a real gentleman."

Rhonda beamed at the scruffy thirty-something sitting by the karaoke soundboard. The bartender's son was a chip off the old mul-let-block, hers iron grey while his was dark brown and dappled with reds, yellows and purples from a portable disco light. Hands dramatically cupped as if he were yelling, Jasper mouthed, "Hi mom!" followed by the international sign for 'get me another drink.'

As Herb waited patiently for the proud mother to mix her KJ baby another Cosmo, his gaze drifted up toward the Budweiser chandelier hanging over the bar. A wonder of plastic and light, the fixture was ringed by a team of little Clydesdales pulling a tiny Bud wagon round and round. Herb's eyes followed the red wagon, trapped by its endless circling. Unable to blink, his eyes began to water, his tears making the colors swirl. Eddies and currents formed and shifted as the slowly spiraling red filled his vision, and faint whispers, words he could almost hear, brushed his ears.

Breaking glass and a curse snapped Herb's attention away from the chandelier and refocused it on a drop of blood. Shards of broken martini glass lay haphazardly around the ice bin and pink vodka dripped to the floor while a thin stream of red dripped down Rhonda's finger. Without realizing he had moved, Herb found himself standing across the bar from Rhonda, watching the blood drip to the ice bin below. As she turned to get a napkin, Herb's hand snaked out adder-quick to snatch a bloody ice cube and pop it in his mouth.

"Damn, that stings," Rhonda muttered. "Lemme get a bandage, Herby. I'll be right back with the beers."

Herb stood transfixed at the bar, ice melting on his tongue, the tang of fresh blood an avalanche of sensation so intense it near rendered him senseless. His pupils dilated, nostrils snuffled, fingers twitched. Time stretched, slowed, bent as he felt himself expand and swell like a water balloon.

I'm going to explode, he heard someone say. *Explode into a million ice cubes, a million bloody cubes.*

The words wove in and out through the barely audible whispers. Recognizing his own voice was perplexing. His lips hadn't moved, had they? Herb's breath came in shorter and shorter gasps. Trying to calm the influx of sensations, he breathed deep, suddenly smelling more than seeing Rhonda as she returned with his drinks. The sharp, metallic, tangy scent of blood twined amongst the smoke and booze, cheap perfume and antiperspirant. It curled around the smell of adhesive from the bandage on her finger, the preserved cotton of dry gauze slowly saturating as the blood trickled and soaked. The scent crawled up his flared nostrils and turned his once amiable smile into a devious, devilish grin. His eyes, faintly glowing with a preternatural light of their own, caught Rhonda's, holding her gaze as easily as a mantis holding a moth, drawing her in like the moon pulling on the tide. She set two cans of beer on the bar. The third she brought to her throat, sliding the cool, glistening aluminum across her jugular, down her trachea, toward the low-cut collar of her top.

"Here you go, Herby," she whispered, her eyes never leaving his. The can of Milwaukee's Best slid up and down her bare throat and across her chest, drips of condensation moving from can to neck to cleavage. Her low, asthmatic voice rasped huskily. "On the house, 'kay sweetie?"

Herb collected the two cans from the bar in one hand. The other reached out and caressed Rhonda's neck before taking the third beer from her trembling fingers. Exhaling softly, he turned and glided from the bar, the final words of a tone deaf drunk butchering "The Rose" filling the space behind him.

Gliding? Not quite. Floating? Perhaps. Water on a Rain-X'd windshield beading up and rolling gently across the glass. Like that? Almost. Did he know where he was going? Did it matter? Moving like air, carried and caressed by whispers, he wafted across polyester carpet, past smoke-stained paneling and glowing neon. Herb couldn't tell if he was moving himself or becoming movement itself. Each step wrapped in velvet, each stride made of the finest silk. The air itself barely stirred with his passing. Gleaming eyes roved, head turned. Dallas and Stanley, mouths moving, words irrelevant. Herb heard only whispers, smiled, took his ball, rolled. Was that music? Who invited a choir? It was beautiful. Beautiful. Herb rolled again. Pins crashed, robotic arms pushed them into the maw of the lane. Herb rolled. Was the lane smiling? The lights above the pins winked, shared their secrets. Roll. Laughter, high-five's, each ridge of each fingerprint resonating with the contact of flesh, blood infused flesh. Herb rolled again and again. Beer, Milwaukee's Best. Its finest. The pinnacle of beerness, cold and crisp. Swallow, savor the hops, roll again. The pins shatter, bounce, fall like raindrops on a newly dug grave. Drink deep, recall each grain in the field drenched in sun, stretching, rotting in the heat, putrefying and wilting toward the ground.

Herb coughed and spit up his beer, suddenly nauseous. Stanley held him steady and pounded his back while Dallas laughed.

"Holy shit, buddy. That was like only your third beer. When'd you become such a lightweight? Although I seriously don't care. You roll like that in the finals and you can puke on your shoes as much as you want. That was insane, dude!" Dallas whooped. "If you'd rolled like that for the whole game, instead of just showing up in the middle, hell... You might've even beat me!"

Dallas paused, celebration forgotten as he eyed Herb skeptically. "Ah, who we kidding? That will never happen. But damn if you didn't come close, Herbster. Damn close. Now even Stanley's shitty game won't hold us back. We're goin' to the finals for sure!"

Dallas continued to crow as he scooped up the score sheet and jigged toward the counter. Stanley stayed with Herb as the last of the beer came up and dribbled down his chin. Face drawn, sweaty hair clinging to his forehead, Herb rocked back onto the bench.

"You okay'den, Herby," soothed Stanley. "You okay. Jus' let it settle. That's the way. Think of them cool tiles by the toilet. Think of your face pressed all up on them c-cool floor tiles. That cooling' sensation ..."

"Um, Stanley," Herb croaked, looking up for the first time since releasing the beast onto his shoes. "What are you talking about?"

Stanley's head bobbed up and down like a Tourette's-plagued puppeteer held its strings.

"I was watching this hypnosis show on the T.V.'s. You know, you can make yourself c-cold on one side, warm on the other? All in the mind, he says. You were sick, you needed to leverage the power of your mind, convince yourself you ain't so sick. Convince yourself you're all nice and cool, right? So I thought, Stanley, what's nice and cool? Drinking too much always sends us to the bathroom. That b-bathroom floor's sure nice and cool. So I hypnotized you, made you feel better. Yessir," Stanley finished and leaned back with obvious delight in his newfound abilities.

Hypnotist or not, Herb couldn't deny that he felt a little better.

"Thanks Stanley. Who'da thunk I'd be so easy to hypnotize? But you're right, I feel better already. Hey, how'd we do?"

Stanley's beaming smile fell to a confused frown as he asked, "Whadaya mean, Herb?"

"Oh, uh. I guess I must've been a little out of it, you know. I guess I," he managed before Stanley's confusion caught and became his own. "Huh. Well, I don't really remember what I've been. Um. Doing." Herb's face screwed up as he tried to remember the evening. "I know I got you guys some beers, but then..."

Stanley shook his head and *hmph'd*.

"Oh, sure. You j-just go act all like nothing happened. Geez!" Rolling his eyes theatrically, Stanley helped a wobbly Herb to his feet.

"So... we did good?" Herb asked again as they moved past the lanes toward the exit. Dallas joined them as they passed the shoe rental counter.

"Yeah, ya dumb ass," he whooped with a triumphant grin. "We did good, and we are going to the god damned finals!"

Chapter 6

THE PINTO SPUTTERED AND smoked down the highway while Herb reflected back on the evening. The details were a bit sparse. He clearly remembered meeting Stanley and Dallas in the parking lot. He had then rolled the best game of his life, but try as he might he couldn't remember any of it.

Figures, he lamented. *I can't remember being a bowling rock star, but vividly recall yacking Milwaukee's Best all over my only pair of bowling shoes.*

Now, though, he felt like a million—no, two million—bucks. Any trace of the nausea that claimed him earlier was completely gone. Too bad the same couldn't be said for the smell clinging to his shoes. He tried to make sense of it all. Between getting a beer and puking, he'd bowled better than ever before in his life. When had Herb ever bowled a turkey? Kung Fu master of the bowling world, that's what he was. He grabbed his copy of their score sheet. Could he have been dreaming? Was he dreaming still? Would his three alarm clocks snap him back to reality, relegating this strange night to a heap of other odd and mostly forgotten dreams? Well, dream or not, the Pinto needed gas. He imagined running out of gas in a dream would be just as much of a drag as running out of gas in real life.

Pulling into Petro Patterson's gas station on the side of the highway, the Pinto *brong brong brong'd* as he turned and pulled up to the pump opposite of a well-used pickup truck. As Herb got out and pulled the hose toward the Pinto's gas tank, he waved amicably at the truck's driver.

"Nice looking dog," he commented to the driver, referring to a large, old golden retriever standing ramrod-still in the truck's bed. "Hi boy! Who's a good dog?" he called. In response, the dog just stared, tail straight out, unmoving.

"Name's Bo. Had him since he was a pup," grinned the truck's driver while leaning back to pat the dog's head. The man chuckled and scratched Bo's ears, but the retriever stood statue-still, eyes locked on Herb.

"I'll tell ya, golden's gotta be the best dogs in the world," the man remarked, unmoved by his dog's strange behavior. "You a dog fella, too?"

Herb's smile was tenuous as the dog added a low-throated snarl to its unyielding stare. "Uh, no. Pet rocks are about as much responsibility as I can handle. But I'd have to agree, if I got a dog, I think a nice fella like Bo there would be just great. Ain't that right, Bo?" Herb offered and tried a step toward the truck.

Bo's low snarl ratcheted up a notch. The dog leaned back, dipping his chest toward the bed of the truck. The snarl escalated in volume to a growl that, in turn, became a series of raspy barks. Tail down tight, ears back, Bo barked and squirmed against the far rail of the truck bed, eyes never leaving Herb.

"Easy Bo. Easy. What's the matter there, boy?" the driver said as he tried to grab the dog's collar. "He ain't usually like this. Friendly as a kitten, this one. Sorry, mister! Bo, calm down now!"

Herb backed away, embarrassed. As he did, Bo's snarls and barks turned to pathetic whines.

"No, it's no problem," stammered Herb. "I guess old Bo there doesn't like bowlers."

"That's enough, Bo!" the driver snapped at the dog's continued whines and barks. Bo finally cowered down, quietly whimpering in the truck bed as the owner waved an embarrassed apology and climbed up in the cab. "Sorry mister, guess he's in a mood. We'll be on our way then."

The old pickup sputtered to life and turned onto the highway, Bo's eyes reflecting the sodium lights of the gas station as he stared over the gate at Herb. Repressing a shiver, Herb fished a crumpled wad of bills out of his pocket and headed inside to pay.

There's a certain sameness to roadside gas stations in rural America, which Patterson's embraced. Tchotchkes clung to every inch of available space, encouraging shoppers to empty their wallets and walk away with nothing of value to show for it. Snow-globes with a Packers helmet or Vince Lombardi statue inside, Wisconsin-themed shot-glasses and decorative spoons, foam-front baseball caps proudly displaying NASCAR heroes or catchy sayings like, "Gun control means hitting your target," Milwaukee Brewers bobble-head dolls, singing plastic fish, radar detectors guaranteed to "Beat the fuzz without killin' your buzz," sunglasses in every shade of neon, key-fobs, hip-pockets, monogrammed money-clips, cheap cigarette lighters shaped like beer bottles, tiny grenades, or buxom, bikini-clad babes next to expensive Zippo lighters stamped with bold American eagles, evoking the heart and soul of America itself.

So many wonderful things, but the tchotchkes were just a fraction of the splendor. Aisle after aisle offered a plethora of crunchy, artificially flavored, olestra and sodium-packed, heavenly delicious snacks. Beer nuts, corn nuts, mixed nuts, corn chips, tortilla chips, potato chips, Doritos, Tostitos, Fritos, Lays, Pringles, Cheez-Its, Peanut-butter Cheez-Its and on and on. There was an honest-to-god candy land, shelves piled high with everything from Almond Joys to Zagnuts. The entire space was ringed with brightly lit coolers. Sodas, beers, juices, and weird combinations of all three glowed in the fluorescent light, beckoning thirsty travelers to slake their dusty throats in a hundred different ways, or at least to grab something to wash down those corn nuts.

Herb was convinced that if the rest of civilization fell and only roadside gas stations survived, everyone would pretty much be okay. He strolled past the aisles, comforted by the hum of the coolers and the nineties pop music trickling through the ceiling speakers. The stress from a few moments ago melted away as Herb gazed longingly at thirty different varieties of beef jerky. There was definitely something comforting about so many kinds of jerky. Something beautiful.

America the beautiful indeed, his stomach gurgled happily.

A young teenage girl leaned against the counter, watching reruns of what Herb thought could be either *Dawson's Creek* or *The O.C.* on a small television set. A quick glimpse of Pacey looking pensive cleared up that confusion. The girl ignored Herb in that special way only teenagers can, chewing gum and painting her fingernails... fuchsia, pink, bright coral? Herb couldn't quite tell, but was certain that the color shouldn't exist.

"Gas on pump two," he said. A sudden craving for meat snuck up and punched him in the paunch. "Oh, and two, um. Three of the teriyaki beef sticks."

Without looking up, the girl punched a few keys on the register, fingers splayed to protect the still-drying polish.

"Twenty-six-oh-three. Will that be all?"

Herb scratched his head and looked around the gas station interior again before adding, "Um, maybe a small cherry Slurpee and, oh. Lemme grab some beer."

Quickly returning with a six-pack in one hand, Slurpee caught in the crook of his elbow, and jerky sticks in the other hand, he juggled his impending diabetes, heart attack and liver disease until he finally got enough cash on the counter to cover his essentials.

"Okay-den. That ought'a do it," Herb said with a nod at the crumpled pile of bills.

"Uh huh. Here's your change," the girl intoned, attention never wavering from Pacey's image.

Well, he thought, *I always thought Pacey was the better catch of the two.*

Herb collected his sundries, turned toward the door, and glanced up toward the closed-circuit monitor showing a camera's view of the entrance. He stopped and stared at his image: a smooshy thirty-something with bedraggled hair, glasses sliding down his nose, one arm cradling a cherry Slurpee, jerky sticking out from the corner of his mouth. A too-familiar malaise settled over Herb as he inevitably thought of Lois. Whether Lois was a Dawson girl or a Pacey girl, one thing was certain. She was most definitely not a Herb girl.

Herb's image flickered. He blinked, shoved his glasses further up his nose, and looked more closely at the monitor. Again, his image flickered in and out. Not his glasses, tee-shirt or the stuff he was carrying. Those all stayed put. Just him. His face, arms, hands flicked out of existence for the tiniest of an instant, and then returned. An uncertain smile tugged at the corner of his mouth as he turned back toward the girl at the counter.

"Glitchy camera?"

The girl looked up and stared at Herb for a moment, then shrugged and returned her attention to her nails. Embarrassed, Herb walked toward the door when the same phenomenon happened to his reflection in its glass. One moment he was all there. The next, everything else was there except him. Clothes, food, glasses casting a blurred reflection in the glass, but no Herb. Then, just as quickly, his reflection was back, staring at him in dumbfounded shock.

"Who you calling crazy?" he muttered, glaring at his reflection as he pushed through the door and hurried toward his car.

The Pinto rolled through the pines and up the drive to Herb's little house in the woods. Killing the engine, Herb gripped the steering wheel, a thin sheen of perspiration on his brow causing stray hairs to stick to his forehead. His neck itching something fierce and his earlier nausea returning with a vengeance, he exited the car and pushed his way toward the front door. Once inside, he ran to the kitchen sink as the dry heaves set in. A few convulsions later, the nausea passed. Trembling, he rinsed his face in the sink and collapsed into a chair at the kitchen table. His mouth felt stuffed with dirty cotton, and his lips pulled back like two dehydrated worms left on the sidewalk in the sun. Herb couldn't remember the last time he'd been so thirsty. Grabbing the closest beverage, he took a long pull of cherry Slurpee. Before he could even swallow, he retched and spit cherry-colored slush all over the table. Hands shaking, he popped open a can of beer to wash away the vile taste of spoiled Slurpee. Nausea tornadoed through his guts. With a surprised groan, he added a mouthful of beer to the melting, sticky mix on the tabletop.

Fighting back an involuntary gag reflex, Herb grabbed a jerky stick and bit down hard. As the dried, salted, artificially flavored dead animal settled on his tongue, the nausea receded. Slowly, he chewed once. Again. Swallowed. Another bite. Chew. Swallow. The first stick gone, he grabbed the second, hungrily grunting as his teeth tore off chunk after chunk of meat. Too soon, the three sticks of jerky were gone. He stood so quickly the chair flew over behind him. Still grunting like a feral wolverine, each grunt adding a strange counter-beat to the pulsing whispers clamoring behind his burning eyeballs, he stalked toward the fridge. The door swung open, and he pulled out the package of ground beef. The torn plastic wrap fell to the floor as Herb scooped up handfuls of raw ground meat and crammed it into his mouth. Had his eyes been engaged in seeing, he might've noticed his reflection in the window above the kitchen sink, blinking in and out, in and out, in... and out.

Chapter 7

T HE MORNING SUN PUSHED its way through the windowpane, and slight distortions in the glass cast ripples of light across the bedspread. Inch by slow inch, the line of sun advanced until the rays reached a carelessly exposed hand. As the light touched the fingers, a soft sizzling underscored the faint snores coming from beneath the covers. The sizzling grew louder as the skin turned an angry red, and thin trails of smoke rose up from the singed flesh. Snores gave way to groggy whimpers as the hand pulled back into the shadows. Moments later, the sunlight closed the gap, dissolving the shadowy sanctuary the hand had crawled into. Thin tendrils of smoke appeared again as the hairs on the back of fingers scorched and burned, and the whimper grew into a genuine groan. Herb swept the covers back and swung his feet to the carpeted floor. When he stood up, the sun slapped him full in the face. An incoherent sound, more zombie than English, burst from his throat as he staggered back from the light into the safer shadows of the bedroom. Semi-conscious, he lurched down the hall and into the bathroom.

Twenty minutes later, Herb emerged from the shower. He was clean and a tad more aware, but a hangover worthy of a page in the Guinness Book split his skull. Light was too bright, sounds were too loud, and a sea-sick pelican had apparently visited his mouth during the night. Leaning in toward the bathroom mirror, he pulled down his lower eyelids, staring at the bloodshot whites of his eyes and sighing at the stubble that always seemed to mar his cheeks and chin. Herb bent down toward the sink and splashed cold water on his face in an ongoing attempt to wake up. Raising back up, he watched his blurry reflection flicker in the mirror. Translucent for a moment, gone, back. Translucent, back.

"Murphle. Awbuss shooey," he chided as he reached up and jiggled the bulb above the mirror.

Reflection stabilized, Herb flipped off the light, pushed his glasses onto his face, and slouched back to his bedroom. The morning sun was waiting and slapped him across the face again. Reacting on instinct, he grabbed the curtains and yanked hard. Blessed shade descended on the little room, allowing him to begin the morning excavating that constituted getting dressed. Shove, dig, flap, sniff test, repeat. Soon, Herb was clad in worn blue jeans and a red, short-sleeved flannel shirt that added up to his Sunday best. In preparation for a big day ahead, he tucked in the flannel, threw on the lesser worn of his two belts and his favorite rope tie, and double-checked to make sure his socks matched. Satisfied that the ritz had been put on successfully, he headed back down the hallway toward the kitchen.

It took a moment to process the scene. Sticky-dry beer and Slurpee coated the table, splattered the cupboards and puddled on the floor, congealed around pink bits of ground beef. Always industrious, a colony of ants had arrived and were busily trucking minuscule bits of grossness to present to their queen. The fridge door hung open, compressor struggling and failing to keep a steady forty degrees. Stepping across the line of ants and swinging the fridge door shut, Herb thought back on what little he remembered from the previous night.

Obviously, had a few too many, he concluded when the details failed to surface. He probably shouldn't have driven home, but there weren't many cabs in Trappersville. *Must've been one helluva night. Need to ask Stanley how we did bowling.*

Herb surveyed the overturned Slurpee cup, jerky wrappers, shreds of ground beef on and around the table. Wheels turned, but slowly. Very slowly.

Oh yeah, Patt's. I stopped for gas. The memories that finally percolated up felt borrowed. He reached around them, felt their edges, trying to decide if they really were his. *Raw ground beef?* he wondered. *Geez, how drunk was I?*

Shrugging at the perplexities of inebriation, Herb resigned himself to a long span of cleaning. That would have to wait, though. Returning to the fridge, he pulled out the box of Get'n'Gobble snicker doodles. Cracking the cover, he dumped the cookies onto a plastic tray and arranged them in concentric circles. After stretching Saran Wrap over the top, Herb looked appreciatively at the result.

"Herby's home-made snicker doodles coming right up!" he chuckled. Grabbing his coat and heading for the door, his mind danced with thoughts of Lois while the trashed kitchen was demoted to 'I'll-deal-with-that-late" status.

To say the drive to First Lutheran was uncomfortable would be a poor accounting of the experience, but excruciating might've been overstating things a bit. Suffice it to say, the drive was unexpectedly unnerving and definitely unpleasant. The light was too bright, washing out all the colors of the world and causing Herb's eyes to squint and tear up. Every time the sun found exposed skin, it felt like a tiny cattle prod jolting away. The closer he got to the church, the harder it became to drive in a straight line, since getting to the church required driving into the morning sun. He must've been more out of sorts than he thought, because Herb drove past the entrance to the parking lot three times, only realizing he'd passed the entrance moments after he'd missed it. When he finally directed his Pinto into the parking lot, the hangover headache reached a crescendo. He was early and there were plenty of parking spots to choose from, but the closer he got to the church, the more severe the pain in his temples. *Brong brong brong* complained his car as Herb swerved away from a spot in front and headed back toward the road. Once his car was moving away from the church, his headache immediately receded from a thirteen to a comparatively pleasant eleven on a one-to-ten scale. Giving in, Herb finally parked in the farthest corner of the lot, panting and squinting at the blindingly bright world beyond his windshield.

Brewers cap pulled down as far as it would go, and snicker doodles platter clutched tight in his hands, Herb exited his car and started across the inferno that had once been a parking lot. Guts twisting, eyeballs melting, throat caked in chalk, he suffered forward as each step added a spoonful of misery. When he forced himself to look up, Herb was horrified to realize he hadn't headed toward the church at all. Instead, he'd veered in a circle and was approaching his car. Turning back toward the church, he set out again, leaning forward as if walking against a stiff gale. After losing count of how many steps he'd taken, Herb looked up again and discovered he still wasn't any closer to the church. Redirecting yet again and sweltering in the morning sun, he set his eyes on the church doors and moved inexorably toward the entrance. With each step, the church seemed to bend away from him, veer to the side, stretch further beyond his grasp. Mirage-like, it didn't appear any closer despite holding it in his sights and refusing to blink the boiled eggs he was using to see. Despite taking step after tortuous step, the church kept sliding away until, suddenly, the mirage popped like a bubble and Herb found himself at the entrance.

He ducked into a patch of shade near a 'No smoking' sign and stood panting. Herb had been hung over plenty of times before, but never had he felt like this. His muscles screamed like he'd just run a marathon, and each pump of his heart sent jagged bolts of pain arcing across his temples while hammers whammed the backs of his eyeballs. As he collected himself, an elderly couple stepped up, glared at him, and looked pointedly at the 'No smoking' sign. The gentleman cleared his throat while the woman scowled.

"Oh, I don't smoke," Herb offered, following their pointed looks.

The couple harrumphed and went into the church. Herb could smell it too, and turned to see who the culprit was. Looking around, he didn't see anyone nearby. He could smell the burning, though, could smell the smoke. Confused, Herb turned his head once more, sniffed deeply, and realized that he was smoking. Literally. Curls of white, sooty smoke rose from every patch of his exposed and angry red skin. With a yelp, Herb grabbed the church door and pulled to get inside, fighting the urge to stop, drop, and roll. Had the old couple barred the door? It didn't want to budge. Unwilling to drop the snicker doodles, Herb adjusted his grip on the platter with one hand and placed the other on the brass handle. Ignoring the scorching of his palm, he braced a foot against the wall and pulled, pulled, and pulled some more. Sure that his arm was about to be wrenched from its socket, tears turning to puffs of steam as they ran down his flushed cheeks, Herb pulled on the church door to no avail. It didn't budge. Not an inch. Panting with pain, fear, and exertion, panic rising up his gorge and threatening to choke him, Herb recoiled to the shadows as another elderly woman came walking up toward the church entrance.

"Oh, is that you Herbert? You poor fellow, trying to do too much at a time. Young people, all the same. Let me get that for you. Here you go now. Come on in. I suppose I'll be helping you cross the street tomorrow, do you think? Heh! Oh, are those snicker doodles? I didn't know you baked."

Smiling, Mrs. Devereaux pulled open the door and gestured Herb inside. Desperate to get out of the scorching sun, he ducked inside the foyer, Mrs. Devereaux puttering along behind him.

Crossing into the church felt like someone turned Herb inside out, poured lye on his exposed innards, rolled him in shards of broken glass and razor wire, and then flipped him right-side in again. For a moment, the only sensation in Herb's existence was wholly consuming pain. So lost was he in the unexpected torment that he completely forgot about everything else. Sheer momentum carried him into the church foyer as Mrs. Devereaux walked beside him, gibbering on about the weather, how much coriander to put in lemon bars, and other trivialities, oblivious to Herb's excruciating torment. Once he'd made it a few steps in, though, the torturous sensation suddenly evaporated and left him feeling weightless and unsettled. While the words 'right' or 'good' or 'fine' didn't quite apply, he didn't feel like the inside of a nuked hotdog, either. Panting, Herb stared at the entrance to the church's main chapel.

"Herbert? Are you okay?" Mrs. Devereaux's face scrunched up at his, sniffing? "Oh Herb, did you start smoking? Shame on you. Disgusting habit. No wonder you don't feel good."

"Oh, no," he stammered, coming back to himself. "Um, I don't smoke, Mrs. D."

She clucked her tongue in the way only old women can. Turning left, Mrs. Devereux walked with Herb across the foyer and toward the stairs that led to the gathering hall in the basement. Herb followed, lost in his own confused thoughts and trailing wispy tendrils of smoke.

Chapter 8

THE GATHERING HALL IN First Lutheran was a testament to the no-nonsense functionality of fluorescent lighting, cinderblocks, and linoleum tiles. An austere space, it was a blank canvas that could easily transform to suit any occasion. With the addition of some folding chairs, tables and tablecloths, the right felt banners, and a couple of colorful signs done up by the youth group, the bare room could become Santa's North Pole workshop, a St. Patty's Day paradise, or an Easter emporium. Wedding receptions, funeral receptions, baby showers, Bible studies, bingo or a bake sale, the space could accommodate it all. Just swap out the felt banners, throw the appropriately themed tablecloths on the folding tables, and *wallah*, it was perfect.

Herb admired the effort that had gone into the event. A wide sign over the entrance proudly proclaimed the 27th Annual First Lutheran Bake Sale. On one wall, a giant construction paper Cookie Monster chased giant cartoon cookies. Across the hall, a mural on large sheets of butcher paper showed Jesus in the parable of the loaves and fishes, passing out strudels and pumpkin bread instead of the more traditional bread and fish. The folding tables had picnic style red-and-white checkered tablecloths, rolls of paper tickets were neatly stacked in anticipation of the big raffle, and small wicker baskets sported signs proclaiming that 'every dollar helps,' and that this year's proceeds would be putting 'more pads on the pews.' Herb couldn't personally attest to whether the current padding was sufficient or not. He wasn't a regular church-goer, a fact that made his sudden entrance into the bake sale stick in the craw of more than a few devout Lutheran blue-hairs. But he supposed pew-pads were as good of a cause as any. Last year, the proceeds had gone toward buying azaleas for the church garden. Why azaleas were so important for the church garden, Herb wasn't sure, but he supposed that was a good cause, too.

Herb checked in and wound his way toward the table marked Number Seven, instinctively ducking and weaving to avoid the stray beams of sunlight that pushed through the ground-level windows. By the time he reached his spot, he felt dizzy and short of breath. As luck would have it, the window directly behind his table had an old curtain drawn across it, filtering out most of the light. Settling in to the relative safety of the half-shadows, Herb peeled the plastic wrap off his snicker doodles and took a deep breath to settle his nerves. Soon, anticipation of when Lois might stop by had eclipsed any worry about his strange reaction to the sun.

The widower Mrs. Lowry was next to him at Table Six, setting out her signature cinnamon wheels. Ever since old Mr. Lowry passed away, there wasn't a charitable event in town that didn't include Mrs. Lowry's cinnamon wheels. This correlation wasn't lost on the general population of Trappersville. Despite being a well-liked man, there were more than a few bake sale aficionados who found themselves guiltily wishing dear old Mr. Lowry had met an earlier demise.

"Hiya Mrs. Lowry. Cinnamon wheels! They, um, smell delicious," Herb offered politely. Usually, a buttery pastry buried under cinnamon and sugar would've made his mouth water. Today, each whiff churned his gut and threatened him with the dry heaves.

Mrs. Lowry turned to look at Herb, her smile stopping well short of her eyes. Squinting ever so slightly, her faded blue irises flicked down to look at his platter of cookies, then locked onto Herb's, glinting in the fluorescent light and sending icy chills down his spine.

Unbeknownst to Herb, this particular bake sale marked the official beginning of bake sale season, and all the blue hairs were chasing blue ribbons. A strong start at the First Lutheran afforded bragging rights. More importantly, enough blue ribbons virtually guaranteed the best table at the county fair in the fall, and that's where the real money was. All of Trappersville's old ladies were in attendance, pious and giving and ready to do their part for a good cause, while secretly hoping that their lemon bars, krumkake, or brioche would pave the way for some fat cash at the fair.

Herb had overheard a few comments when waiting to check in. It was hard not to, since the gossipers were hard of hearing and whispered louder than most people shouted. Apparently, Mrs. Lowry came in second place last year and was pretty salty about the whole thing. As a result, this year was all business. So while she smiled politely and thanked Herb for his kind words, her eyes made it clear that this year—this year—she would win first place, even if she had to go Tonya Harding on everyone else in the room. The elderly woman continued to smile her piranha smile as she moved behind Herb to pull back the curtain covering the window.

She was quick for an old lady. When Herb realized what she meant to do, he was far too slow to stop her. Rays of light that had been smashing ineffectually against the curtain were suddenly free to invade the room and splash across his face with all the heat of boiling oil. Jerking away, he backed into the table, scattering snicker doodles from their platter. He recoiled and pressed his back against the wall, sinking down below the torrent of sunlight.

Mrs. Lowry's barracuda smile grew a tad wider. "Nervous Herbert?" she asked. "Oh, I can't imagine why. Those snicker doodles of yours look so tasty, I'm sure the judges will just love them. In fact, I was talking with Judy Macintyre—you know Judy, she's judging this year with Bill Homestead and Clarice Goodman—and Judy just loves snicker doodles. She gets them from the Get'n'Gobble all the time. But I'm sure yours are much better than some store-bought excuse for a home-made confection. Although, the resemblance is striking. Hmmm. Maybe they stole your recipe? Wouldn't that be something?"

Oblivious to Mrs. Lowry's thinly veiled threats, Herb reeled in pain-induced shock. Despite being in relative shade, his face still felt like a thousand red-hot pins were being pressed through his forehead, cheeks, lips. Sweat ran freely down his back, plastering his shirt to his chill-wracked spine. Sure he was going to vomit, he staggered his way toward the back of the hall where the bathrooms were. He made it past Mrs. Lowry and past Table Five, where another contestant was building pyramids from marshmallow treats. At Table Four, where Miss Devereaux was putting the finishing touches on her display, a stabbing pain wrenched through his gut, causing him to stumble and catch himself on the edge of the table.

"Goodness Herb! Are you okay?" asked Mrs. Devereaux. "Um, Herbert, dear," she continued a moment later, as confusion warred with concern on her elderly face. "I do think... Well, I do think you're getting a tab bit of sunburn. You really should be more careful with a complexion like yours. Maybe you should be getting some aloe on that."

Malcontent wasps wriggled under his skin, and his brain felt like microwaved Cheez Whiz. He stared at Mrs. D. and tried to make sense of what she was saying. Other blue-hairs began to gather around, nodding and clucking their agreement about the benefits of aloe and sunburns, one even going so far as to espouse the anti-inflammatory qualities of hemorrhoid cream. All fell silent, though, as they got a better look at Herb's face.

Skin red, raw, and starting to blister, eyebrows singed black, eyes wide with pain, Herb stammered out between burnt and peeling lips, "Yeah, us redheads gotta watch out for the sun." He gasped in rapidly escalating pain before adding, "M-M-Mrs. Devereaux. Could you… Aaaaahhhhh… Could you maybe take over my table? I think…" he grimaced again, drew a ragged breath, and yelled as he ran from the hall, "I think I need to get some aloe!"

Herb ran beneath the burning sun, blood running freely from his ears, nose, and eyes. Reaching his Pinto, he fumbled with his keys, yanked open the rear hatch, pulled out a worn blanket, and wrapped it around himself. Half-rolling across the side of the car, he flopped into the driver's seat, arm grasping at the glove compartment as the skin on the back of his hand smoked and blistered. The catch finally released, and he pulled out a large pair of sun goggles, the kind old farts wear over their regular glasses. Shoving them onto his face felt like he was ramming toasting forks fresh from the campfire along his temples, but his eyes stopped boiling like poached eggs. Slamming the door, he reached for the steering wheel, only to realize that his still-exposed hands were literally sizzling like bacon on a flat-top grill.

He shoved a nasty curse through blistered lips and kicked open the door. Swearing all the way back around the car, he reached the back and dug in again. Finding what he was looking for, he wrapped a long woven scarf around and around until his entire face was swaddled and hidden from the sun and pulled leather choppers onto his hands.

Panting and hunched over, Herb leaned against his car as the pain slowly subsided. Despite being bundled to the hilt, his skin cooled from turkey fryer to Easy Bake Oven. A small crowd had gathered just outside the church door to watch his antics. Slowly, he waved, gave a double-thumbs up with his Chopper-clad hands, and climbed back into the Pinto's driver's seat. He gently shut the door, waved again, started up the Pinto, and carefully reversed out of his parking spot. Still waving, he drove at a snail's pace through the parking lot, down the row of cars to the lot exit, and turned onto the road. Once clear of the church parking lot, he stomped on the accelerator. The Pinto's balding tired spun madly on the pavement and rocketed the car forward. Herb watched the church and small crowd of spectators recede in the rearview mirror. Flexing still-sore hands in the now-sticky fleece lining of his choppers, Herb fought back confused tears as he drove toward the sanctuary of his little home in the woods.

Chapter 9

EVERY WINDOW OF HIS ramshackle home was covered. Newspapers, blankets and quilts, cushions from the couch, a place mat from the kitchen table, even a flattened-out empty cereal box, were all held precariously in place by no less than three rolls of duct tape. Here and there, little slivers of sun managed to slip through cracks in the haphazard defenses that Herb had erected, illuminating dust particles in thin shafts of diffused light.

Herb wove around the bright slivers as he paced across the living room, thermometer sticking out of the corner of his mouth. When he reached the entrance to the kitchen, he pulled the thermometer out and looked at the thin silver line. Seventy-three degrees. He turned and wove back through the living room again and continued down the hallway. At the entrance to his bedroom, he stood for a moment and stared unseeing at the Packers flag taped upside down across his bedroom window. Eyes unfocused, chewing his lower lip, thermometer still jutting out from his mouth, Herb turned and retraced his steps back down the hall and through the living room. Once again, at the entrance to the kitchen, he checked his temperature. Seventy-three degrees. Herb had been pacing like that for close to an hour, checking his temperature again and again. The drive home from the church bake sale had been a mad, confused dash. Convinced he had typhoid fever or malaria or Lyme Disease or some other malady, he'd grabbed the thermometer to see how severe his fever was. All he'd determined since was that his thermometer must be broken, and that he now felt just fine.

Stopping suddenly, Herb listed to one side to avoid a tiny beam of sunlight. He reached a hand back to scratch at the scabrous wound on the back of his neck. His other hand, he slowly, timidly moved forward until the little ray of sunlight fell across the backs of his fingers. The burning was immediate. The hair on the backs of his knuckles started to smoke and the faint scent of scorched hair filled his nose.

Herb turned and sprinted back down the hall and into the bathroom. Flipping on the light, he grabbed the edges of the sink and leaned in close to the mirror. For a moment, all he saw was an out of focus blur where his face was supposed to be. Squinting, a strange reflection suddenly leapt out in stark and exact detail. Unruly, rust-red hair fell across his brow. Bruise-dark circles wallowed under bloodshot eyes, once-soft and rounded cheekbones and chin now jutted out at harsh angles beneath pale skin pulled taut. Scabs still hung where the blistering had been the worst, but for the most part, the burns had healed just as inexplicably as they had appeared. The face in the mirror's mouth hung open, oozing disbelief and bewilderment. The lips were dark red and freckles bright orange against the pale surrounding skin. The teeth were pearlescent white and extended further than they really should; two sharp incisors framing a slightly protruding tongue.

The thermometer balanced precariously for a moment and then fell with a small clank into the sink. Herb didn't notice and simply stared at himself, transfixed by the stranger's face gazing back. Suddenly, the reflection flickered, and Herb gasped in shock. In and out of focus, solid and overwhelmingly detailed for a moment, fuzzy and translucent the next, Herb's reflection sputtered like the silent cries of a dying firefly for the next few moments. Finally, the reflection diminished until only the faintest image gazed back from the mirror, a ghostly face that floated above his shirt collar and overlaid the patterned wallpaper of the bathroom wall behind him. Herb raised a hand and watched its specter appear in the mirror, as translucent as his face. A slight whimper escaped his lips as he backed away from the mirror and pressed up against the opposite wall. Herb slid down, rolled over on his side, pressed his face into the peeling linoleum of the bathroom floor, wrapped his arms around his chest, and drew his knees up tight below his gut. His mouth worked like a guppy out of water, and from somewhere far off in the distance, he could hear a voice whimpering.

"No, no. Please, no."

Chapter 10

Herb's head snapped up. Lost in a deep and dreamless sleep a moment before, he was suddenly awake. Wiping the drool from his chin and sitting up against the bathroom wall, he took a deep breath through his nose and exhaled slowly through his mouth. Turning toward the bathroom window, now covered with the shower curtain and duct tape, Herb realized that he could *smell* that the sun had gone down. No dusty slivers of light crept in through the cracks, but that wasn't how he'd known. He could actually smell the night, and it was that smell that had awakened him so abruptly. Like the ozone smell after a spring rain, or the smell of newly turned earth beside a grave, night had a scent. While his depression and confusion from earlier hadn't entirely gone away, they had been mostly replaced with a sense of calm and the faintest twinge of hunger. Pushing his fingers through the lank strands of his hair, he thought long and hard about what to do next.

Just to be safe, Herb waited until the sun had been down for about an hour. Recent memories of being deep-fried still fresh in his mind, he peeled back a piece of newspaper covering the kitchen window to make absolutely sure the sun was good and gone. Before he could lose his nerve, he picked up his car keys, slipped out the door, and walked purposefully to the Pinto. Once inside the car, he flipped down the visor and gazed hard at the ghostly reflection in the little vanity mirror. With a sigh and a shake of his head, Herb flipped the visor back up, revved the engine, whipped the little Pinto around, and headed for the highway.

About ten minutes later, he pulled into Petro Patterson's. Patt's, as it was called by the locals, offered more than just a wide variety of beef jerky and three grades of gas plus diesel. Patt's had movies. Not many, and most weren't very good, but there were a few that Herb remembered seeing on the shelves.

"Knowing is half the battle," he muttered, hoping to fool himself with false bravado. Fixing his Brewer's cap firmly on his head and pulling up the hood of his sweatshirt, Herb walked inside and immediately turned his back to the closed-circuit camera covering the front counter and door. With a quick wave at Patterson's daughter Molly, who was sitting behind the counter, he headed toward the back, where two shelves overflowed with VHS tapes.

Herb scanned the tapes for a moment and quickly found what he hoped he wasn't looking for. The black-and-white photo of Bela Lugosi stared directly at him as he reached out to take *Dracula* off the shelf. Nodding in approval, he selected *Lost Boys* next. A quick, guilty look-around later, and *Buffy the Vampire Slayer* found its way between the other tapes.

Always good to have another perspective, Herb reassured himself. This was research, after all. Just research.

"Wow. Theme night, huh?" Molly took stock of his selections, nodding appreciatively as Herb laid them on the counter.

Suddenly self-conscious, Herb looked at the tapes spread across the counter and shrugged.

"I get that. My friend Dustin watched all three of *The Godfather* movies in a row. Director's cuts, too. Says he only got up to pee and order pizza. That's like, wow."

As the chatty teenager rang up the total, the side of her neck filled Herb's vision and wiped away every thought. He watched perplexed as her neck moved closer, and realized in a fuzzy way that it was in fact he who had leaned forward, palms flat on the counter, mouth opening wider. As the inches between his mouth and her exposed neck dwindled, the ringing of the register faded, replaced with whispers and the sound of a heart beating faster and faster.

"Herb? Hello!? Earth to Herb, come in Herby!" Molly had finished tallying the costs of his rentals and was holding out a plastic bag. "You in there?"

Herb rocked back on his heels like he had been slapped, but couldn't pull his eyes away from the smooth skin of Molly's jugular. Forcing his mouth to cooperate when his eyes wouldn't, he said, "Um. Yep. I'm here. And those are mine. Right."

The girl's growing discomfort was a wet blanket on his smoldering hunger. She self-consciously pulled at the collar of her shirt with one hand while she handed the bag of videos to him with the other. Herb reached for it awkwardly, convinced there was at least a gallon of water in each of his armpits. Tearing his gaze away from Molly's neck, he pulled a twenty out of his wallet, slapped it on the counter, and proceeded to fidget. As the girl counted out his change, Herb forced himself to look elsewhere, anywhere, just not at her neck. A moment later, he realized he was staring directly at the closed-circuit camera screen. Molly noticed the direction of his gaze and automatically turned to the monitor by the door. As her mouth dropped open in shock, Herb shoved his change in his pocket and dashed for the door. Petro Patterson's had long vanished from his rearview before his hands stopped shaking and his panicked gasps subsided to something resembling regular breaths.

Chapter 11

Full night draped the Wisconsin countryside like a dark cloak adorned with a pale crescent brooch and a million twinkling buttons. Light clouds drifted by, casting pale shadows on the small house nestled in the trees below. Inside, Herb sat hunched forward on his sofa, absorbed in the flickering T.V. perched in the room's corner.

Just days before, his collection of movies would have been mere entertainment. Now, they were vital survival guides. Unfortunately, the films produced as many questions as answers. According to Hollywood, he could have a really ugly face when he 'vamped out,' or not. He might instinctively know Kung Fu, be able to control people with his eyes, turn into a bat, or possibly fly without sprouting leathery wings. Did he need a coffin, or could he just sleep underground? What about a cape? Required or optional? Lots of questions with a range of answers, but despite the variations, some things were consistent from film to film.

Avoid daylight? I think we can give that one a check. Herb thought. *No reflection?*

He strode resolutely to the bathroom, flicked on the light, and stood looking at... not much. He cast a faint reflection in the glass, but it was so weak and translucent that he could barely make out his features. Herb squinted, trying to will himself to show up better in the mirror. Surprisingly, it started to work. His reflection swam into existence like a body floating up from the depths of a murky pond until he could only faintly see the patterned wall paper reflected through his head.

Huh, he thought. *I guess sort-of a half check. Okay. Last one. Blood.*

His stomach growled, low and insistent. Unbidden, Molly's neck sprung into his mind's eye. As he stared at his translucent reflection, his eyes glistened.

Blood, he thought. *Bloooooood.*

The whispers started to build, followed by a head rush and shivers that coursed from the top of his skull all the way down to the soles of his feet. He felt more than heard a soft *snick* and opened his mouth to display two long, gleaming, sharp-looking fangs. He reached a finger up and poked first one pointy tip, then the other. Rotating his head side to side, he took in the whole image. Stubble covering a weak chin, unruly hair, pimple next to his nose, shiny eyes, and fangs. Genuine, honest-to-God, one-hundred percent real fangs.

Turning from the mirror, he walked back to his living room, lost in thought. He was still Herb, an overweight, under-groomed cook at a truck stop. But for the first time in his life, that wasn't all. He, Herbert Knudsen, was something more. Something special.

He was a vampire.

It had been a long time since something akin to resolve showed on Herb's face. It was an uncomfortable sensation that pulled his cheeks and forehead into awkward shapes. Gritting his teeth, he tried a couple of kicks, chops, and punches. Was it his imagination, or did he actually feel something? When his arm sliced through the air, was he moving faster? He side-kicked his leg three times, each snap bringing his foot higher and higher. After the third kick, he jumped up and turned to bring his other foot around in a wide roundhouse kick. A soft *whoosh* followed his swiftly moving foot. Following the momentum of the roundhouse kick, Herb pivoted gracefully into a crouch, rotated his body, thrust up with his legs, and swung his arm toward the wall. Palm up, hand held in a rigid claw, his fingers raked up the wall and shredded deep grooves into the sheetrock. No sooner had his hand finished raking the wall than his other fist shot straight-out and punched a hole clean through like it was tissue paper. A picture of Herb, Stanley, and Dallas holding recently caught fish rattled and fell to the floor with a crash.

The vampire looked at his hands in disbelief. Not a scratch, not even a nicked cuticle. His gaze moved to the wall, to the four parallel grooves and the hole directly above them. A laugh bubbled up, turning to a whoop as Herb cavorted around his living room.

"I know Kung Fu! I'm badass. Badass! BADASS!" Herb chanted as he fist-pumped the air around his head. Bringing his hands down and resting his fists on his hips, he started a jig around the living room.

"Badass, badass, beedelie boodelie badass. I'm. A. Bad. Ass! I'm. A. Bad. Ayek!" Herb exclaimed as his foot hit a stray beer can, causing his legs to shoot straight out. For a moment, he lay across the air, perfectly horizontal, mouth wide in shock. The next moment, gravity pulled him back down, landing him solidly on his back, knocking his breath out with a sharp, "Hooff!" followed by a pained sigh. Herb lay still for a moment, working the taste of humble-pie around his mouth, face screwed up in thought.

"Okay. Maybe a little stronger, faster. Still kinda clumsy. I'm fine with that. But what else can I do? Holy crapola! What else can I do?"

The night air was electric on Herb's skin. Each and every hair on his forearms tingled as the breeze shifted and ebbed. His terrycloth bathrobe rippled around him like the cape of an unassuming super-hero that just happened to like the Green Bay Packers. Looking down from the peak of his rooftop, Herb giggled again. Getting up on the roof had been no effort at all. He'd scampered out the front door and up the chimney, landed on the pitched roof, slipped slightly as his slippers found purchase, and then moved with feline grace. Herb had never felt so alive. Each move felt so sure, so right. He looked up again at the night sky, still dark. He knew that dawn was still about two hours off. He could do this. He knew it. The fangs, the Kung Fu, climbing his house like a monkey on loan from the Milwaukee zoo... He could do this.

Breathing deeply, Herb raised up on the balls of his feet. His arms rose up slowly to each side, his chin lifted toward the treetops. Like DiCaprio on the Titanic, Herb leaned forward, felt the breeze quicken around him, catching him, lifting him. For a moment, he wondered what it would be like as a bat. Then he turned his thoughts to *blood, blood, blood!* A slight spring of his legs and Herb was free of the roof, floating, rushing toward the night sky.

When he belly-flopped on the ground about two seconds later, it knocked all the air out of his lungs, and Herb both heard and felt at least two ribs crack. His teeth bit down when his chin was jammed up, impaling his tongue on one of his new, sharp incisors and dislocating his jaw. Judging from the lacing pain in his hip, Herb was pretty sure he'd cracked his pelvis, too. Immobilized by the pain, Herb lay face down in the grass. A single bloody tear welled up in his eye, rolled sideways down to drip into the grassy dirt pressed into his cheek. Fangs? Yup. No reflection in mirrors? True. Ugly? Not yet. Kung Fu? Sorta. Fly? Not so much...

Wracked with waves of pain and hovering on the edge of consciousness, Herb still somehow managed to sense the rabbit. He felt the impossibly fast thrumming of its tiny heart, heard its rapid breaths drawing the night air in and out of its sensitive nose. It must've startled when he fell from the sky, but didn't run far. Herb lay in the grass, surrounded by small patches of clover. With a cautious hop followed by another, the rabbit slowly made its way back toward its evening snack. Each hop was followed by a pause, nose working to test the night air for danger, ears rotating back and forth, alert for the slightest noise. Hopping closer and closer, the rabbit nuzzled up to a bit of clover and started to munch. One leaf down, it turned in a slow circle to sniff out the more tender leaves. Herb's hand snatched out and grabbed it by the neck so quickly that the rabbit didn't even have time to scream. Two white-hot needles ripped a nasty gash and sent splashes of red onto the green clover, both turned shades of gray in the night's dark palette.

The vampire drank the rabbit in hungry gulps. Whispers roared in his ears and every inch of his being sang. Broken ribs snapped back together. A shattered cheekbone knitted, muscle and skin forming over the new bone. The enamel of a chipped front tooth slowly regrew to take the shape of the original. With each gulp of blood, a scar vanished, a blemish smoothed. Old fillings drilled their way backward out of molars, and Herb felt each eyeball stretch and reform.

Too soon, the rabbit was sucked dry. The thing that was Herb looked out upon the moonlit forest around his home. Blurry shapes resolved into crystal clarity when he slid his cracked glasses from his nose. A slight inhalation caused his head to spin as he recognized the scent of each blade of grass, each leaf on each tree. And he could smell—actually smell—the blood. Countless sparks of life teemed around him. All that warmth and vitality rushed up each nostril, coursed down his spine, settled in his gut with sickening weight. Urges to rend, tear, and feast roiled through Herb and brought him to his feet. Crouching in the cool night air, head tilted slightly, moonlight reflecting off silvery eyes, a growl escaped Herb's blood-stained lips. A flicker of movement just past the tree line snapped his head around. Like a sprinter from the gate, he launched himself into the night. To hunt. To kill. To feed.

Chapter 12

H ERB SWAM. LONG, SMOOTH strokes pulled him through the red, viscous fluid. Tiny air bubbles slipped down his body, down his legs as they kicked with an easy rhythm. He'd been under a long time and wondered absently when he might need a breath of air. Still his arms pulled, his legs kicked, and stars flickered through the deep red like a school of minnows far above. Shark-like, he glided, dove, turned. His mouth opened to breathe, and heavy blood flowed deep into his lungs. It filled him up to burst, flooding through his chest, saturating every organ. The more blood he absorbed, the deeper he sank. Before, he could see the stars. Now, all he could see was red, red, red. Deeper he fell, gasping, suffocating, each gulp filling him with more blood. The taste spoiled in his mouth, curdled on his tongue. He tried to wretch, to purge...

The vampire woke coughing, rolled onto his side, and promptly fell ass over teakettle to the floor. He had been sprawled upside down on the couch with his legs up its back cushions, heels against the wall, while his head hung back and down near the ottoman. Landing awkwardly, his cheek pressed against the scratchy carpet. Deep, shuddering breaths helped slow his racing heart. His mouth was full of a foul taste and he could smell... something. Sluggish thoughts crawled through the steel wool stuffed between his ears. The last thing he remembered was falling off his roof. There was a brief memory of agonizing pain and then... nothing. Herb's hands slowly pulled in, patted his face, chest, thighs. He was filthy, covered with what felt like sticky mud and grass, but nothing hurt. He cracked open one eye, then two, rolled onto his back and slowly sat up. As his eyes focused, he was mildly surprised to recognize his living room, strangely lit by the T.V.'s static and slivers of sunlight that filtered in through the haphazardly covered windows. Disoriented and dizzy, he listed to one side, and a tiny beam of sunlight hit his eye like a white-hot needle. Hissing in pain, he lurched away to avoid the offending beam and plunged his arm up to his elbow in a cow's stomach.

The high-pitched scream of a young and obviously terrified little girl brought Herb halfway to his senses. Realizing that the scared, screaming child was actually him brought him the rest of the way there. For a few incoherent moments, all he could feel was the slimy guts of the dead cow lying in front of him. He sucked in a ragged breath. Exhaling slowly, he shifted his weight and extracted his bile-covered arm and hand from the cow. Careful to avoid the sunlight, Herb's head turned in a slow arc and took in the mayhem around him. The cow sprawled on its side, tongue protruding, once-liquid brown eyes now very dead and staring at the Favre bobble-head doll on the credenza. Herb's arm had pushed through a large rent in the bovine's side. Some wild beast had torn skin, muscle, and bone asunder, leaving a gaping wound. Strewn around the rest of the living room was a macabre collection of other dead creatures: a fox, small leftover pieces of what might've once been birds, a goat, and easily half of the squirrels in Wisconsin. Jammed up on the back of the sofa, little fuzzy head pointing toward the cushions where Herb had been lying upside down mere moments before, was a raccoon, its tiny paws curled in like a prizefighter, its slowly congealing blood dripping to the floor. It was horrible, monstrous. The guy that shot Bambi's mother was a saint compared to what Herb had done. Bloody tears were already forming when he saw the final and most heart-wrenching victim of his bloodlust. Folded in the corner, its tan coat mottled red with gore, was an all too familiar, scrappy little pug.

Horrified, Herb crawled on his hands and knees through the mostly dried pools of blood and clumps of skin and fur toward the dog. Its smooshy little face was untouched, bug eyes glassed over, flat nose still slightly damp, and tiny pink tongue protruding from its dark muzzle. A sequined collar sparkled bravely through the gristle and blood-matted fur, adorned with a purple tag proudly proclaiming the name Lady. Never mind the gruesome Disney slasher flick that covered the rest of the room. Herb had eaten the neighbor's pug.

Red tears flowing freely, he sat in the middle of the carnage, trying to sort-out just how in the hell he managed to get half a petting zoo into his house. At some point, an almost-familiar noise pressed in on his limited awareness. The phone rang and rang again, causing Herb's head to swing in a dazed circle and bringing his eyes to bear on where the phone stuck out from beneath most of a dead grouse.

"Um, hello. You've reached the Knudsen residence. Um. The Knudsen, Herb, I mean me, well, it's a recording of Herb. Me. Oh crap. Does this rewind? Uff dah. Ah, crap. Oh, okay. Sorry! Can't take your call! I'd sure love to and I hope I can take your call again. Later. When I call you back. Um. Okay'den, thanks! So wait for the beep... um, the beep. It should be this one. Oh for chrissakes..."

Beeeep!

It had been a long time since Herb had listened to his answering machine greeting. He found himself wondering when the suave and self-confident message he remembered had been replaced by a drunken Ole impersonator.

"Herb? Herb! Are you there? Why aren't you at work? Ronnie's furious and Hector is exhausted 'cause he's been here since like five o'clock last night." Lois's voice floated from the tinny speakers of the RadioShack machine, leaving Herb in awestruck wonder.

She called me, thought Herb. *She's worried about me and she called.* A smile cracked the caked blood around Herb's mouth as he leaned toward the voice.

"Ronnie's making me call since you haven't picked up your phone all morning. He's been calling and calling and thinks you're trying to ruin him or something. You'd better call back or get your ass in here pronto, ok Herb? Seriously, it's like quarter to eleven in the morning. Just..."

Herb knocked the remains of the grouse off the phone and grabbed the receiver. "Lois! Hi, Lois. Um. Wow. Hi there. It's Herb. Me. I'm Herb. Um..."

He squeezed his eyes shut, slowly pounded his forehead on the lifeless grouse, and took a deep breath.

"So. I'm here. You called. Me. Lois. Um, how are you?"

"How am I? Oh, just peachy, thanks so much for asking. It's busier than heck here, but our morning cook has apparently decided to take the morning off, which means the exhausted overnight cook can't leave since Ronnie only knows how to make Rice-A-Roni."

"Ronnie."

"That's what I said."

"No, Ronnie calls it 'Rice-A-Ronnie.' He adds cilantro, dill, some mayo. Thinks it makes it fancier."

"Roni, Ronnie, whatever. Hector burned his hand when he dozed off near the deep fryer half an hour ago. Seriously, I don't know what your deal is, but you really gotta get to work."

For a few treasured moments after the phone at Ronnie's was slammed into the cradle, Lois's voice flittered on Cupid-wings through the fog in Herb's brain. Gone were the dead animals, the blood-soaked couch, the gore-spattered Brett Favre bobble-head doll. Even Lady, Jerry and Pam's poor little pug, flew from his conscious mind like dandelion fluff on a warm summer breeze. Herb bobbed in a sea of bliss, looking at the phone that had recently held her angel voice. Gently setting the receiver down on its cradle, he caressed it with a grimy finger.

A red 'eleven' blinked at him from the answering machine, a stark reminder of the ten angry Ronnies and one blissful Lois waiting for his attention. Herb stumbled to his feet and hit play and delete in rapid sequence, turning Ronnie's messages into a staccato of angry reproaches.

"Come on, come on!" Jittering with anticipation, he hit play, delete, play, delete. Reaching the final truncated message, he stopped, quivering in anticipation, and then gently, reverently hit play. Lois's voice again filled his senses, buckled his knees, and sent him sliding back to the floor. Oblivious to the fact that he was sitting in a half-congealed puddle of blood, Herb smiled, contentment incarnate. She had called him. Called his phone to talk to him. And she was waiting for him. All he had to do was get in the Pinto, go to work and...

Reality clattered down like kitchen knives from an overturned drawer.

After taking in the farmhouse slaughter scene lit by slivers of burning sun, Herb fumbled for the phone and quickly called back Ronnie's. No angelic Lois on the phone this time, though. The voice that answered was Ronnie himself, the soul of small town courtesy turning *Wrath of the Titans* the second Ronnie recognized the caller. Herb held the phone away from his ear for a moment as a torrent of expletives ruptured through the receiver.

Halfway through the tirade, Herb yelled a quick, "Sorry Ronnie! I'm really sick."

Ronnie's screaming ended abruptly as the Herb slapped the phone back into the cradle. With a shaky sigh and a slow turn, Herb took a measuring look at the carnage strewn about what had once been a simple living room. There was little doubt that he was out of a job again. However, before he could worry about that, he had to deal with more immediate concerns. Apparently, he'd gotten hungry the prior night, and he had to clean up the leftovers.

Chapter 13

WHAT STRUCK HERB AS odd wasn't the fact that he was burying assorted woodland creatures, farm animals, and the neighbor's dog in his root cellar. The root cellar was a logical choice. He had first thought to bury them outside, but the freight train of sunlight that slammed into him upon opening the back door was a stark reminder that he was home-bound until nightfall. And he certainly couldn't leave all the critters in their varying states of repose in the living room. That was just gross and would probably violate some code or ordinance or whatnot. No, burying the animals in the cellar wasn't really the weirdest part. It just made sense. What had him perplexed was how ungodly tired he became while doing it.

He'd started out well enough. Never one to lift a weight or push in any direction, up or otherwise, Herb had wondered how he'd gotten the cow home until he grabbed a hoof and pulled. With a wet, ripping, slurpy sound, the carcass slid easily across the carpet before the whole haunch pulled clean off. Herb stumbled back, only to catch himself with cat-like grace. The cow must've weighed a few hundred pounds at least, but he'd dragged it and ripped a leg off with hardly a tug. Something that started as a giggle and ended as a belch slipped out as he took a firmer hold on the cow's back end and hauled it across the room, through the kitchen, and finally to the top of cellar stairs. Reversing his grip, he gave a shove, and the cow flopped end-over-end to sprawl in a gory hump at the bottom of the steps. Herb followed, hopping lightly over dead Bessie, and took in the space. Since he'd never acquired anything of real value or significance, the cellar was mostly bare. Furnace and water heater, laundry machine and a washtub, an old weight bench he'd picked up at a garage sale years back, and a ten-speed whose tires resembled the cast-off skins of molting snakes. Plenty of bare, hard-packed dirt floor and an old railroad switch-shovel leaning conveniently in the corner.

Herb had crossed the room, grabbed the shovel, and moved a small mountain of dirt before he realized he'd forgotten to turn on a light. Stopping briefly and leaning on the shovel, he turned his head, first left, then right. Things did look a little different. Everything he saw stood out in perfect clarity, despite it being almost totally dark in the cellar. With no windows, the only sources of light were the few rays brave enough to come down the stairs from the kitchen and the glow of the pilot light under the water heater. But Herb could see *everything*. Every crack in the foundation wall, every cobweb in the joists. With a grin that would've sent a jack-o'-lantern scurrying, Herb finished excavating a hole big enough to accommodate the cow, goat, and raccoon for sure, and probably more than a few of their smaller compadres if he squished them in. The cow settled in the hole with a wet *schlup*, followed by a deep thud. Dropping the shovel next to the pit, he turned to head back toward the stairs, only to swoon and collapse to the dirt floor. A ginormous yawn stretched his jaw so wide the tendons in his face popped and cracked. Smacking his lips while simultaneously reaching around to scratch his behind, Herb felt himself drift down, down…

… and shook himself awake. Dragging himself up the stairs, he emerged into the relative brightness of the kitchen. Despite the covered windows, his sensitive eyes reacted to the dim glow, like he'd stumbled in front of a spotlight. Squinting as his eyes adjusted, Herb moved into the living room and scooped up the goat in one arm and poor little Lady in the other. Turning to head back through the kitchen, he wondered who had snuck in and stuffed the animals with lead. While the cow had felt light as a feather, each step with the goat and dog felt like he was pulling cinderblocks through a field of mud. Another huge yawn stretched his mouth, but he continued to move purposefully toward the stairs.

What ensued was a tortuous endeavor. Each step threatened to be his last. His muscles burned, and he couldn't stop yawning. Red rivulets streamed from his eyes, down his cheeks, and out of his ears to trickle down his neck. Blood-sweat smudges covered his face like war paint, with matching marks on the backs of his wrists. Finally, after what seemed an eternity, every little creature, critter, and fowl was safely in the pit and covered with a thin layer of dirt. A few final pats of the shovel to level it with the rest of the floor did Herb in, and he collapsed onto the remaining pile of earth. Within moments, the only sounds disturbing the final resting place of Herb's dinner were snores.

Waking was a sudden thing, not the arduous, torturous, Herculean task he was accustomed to. One moment he slept, dreamless and deep. The next, he was awake, alert, finely tuned to the still air around him, and uncomfortably aware that he'd somehow covered himself in loose dirt. Sliding out from the earthen blanket, Herb sat up and rested his arms on his knees.

Sunset, he realized.

The vampire raised his head and looked up toward the stairs leading out of the cellar. His preternatural eyesight confirmed what he already instinctively knew; outside night had fallen. Herb rolled his neck, shrugged his shoulders, and flowed gracefully to his feet, at which point his stained and blood-caked jeans promptly fell down around his ankles. Despite being completely alone in a dark, underground, windowless cellar, Herb still squeaked in embarrassment and quickly doubled over, spontaneously covering his briefs with one hand while grasping for his jeans with the other. Hiking his Wranglers back up, he went to tighten his belt and pulled it in past the last notch. The waistband of his jeans bunched and gathered in front of where Herb's beer gut used to reside. Both hands flew to his stomach as his jeans pooled down around his ankles again. Experimentally, Herb curled one hand into a loose fist and rapped on his abdomen like knocking on a door. Instead of the smooshy paunch he was accustomed to, Herb felt a leaner... well, not toned expanse of muscle, exactly... but definitely less-smooshy gut. Scrabbling, he pulled up the front of this shirt, yanked it over his head, and ripped it in the process like it was no more than tissue paper. Standing in the dark on a packed dirt floor in nothing but a dingy pair of tighty whities, jeans in a pile around his tube sock-wrapped ankles, Herb looked down at himself in complete disbelief. He'd always thought of his physique as 'unfortunate.' Stooped shoulders, scrawny arms, flabby chest. Beer gut and love handles that caused the waistbands of all of his pants to be permanently rolled over. Neither obese nor svelte, Herb often felt that he looked like a wax statue that stood a little too close to the oven. Dallas was less kind and had once called him cheese curds and gravy poured into a medium flannel and jeans. But now...

Almost tripping over his jeans in his haste, Herb launched himself across the cellar, up the stairs and into the bathroom. Flicking on the light, he stared at the uncooperative mirror, slowed his breathing, and concentrated until a faint reflection coalesced in the glass. What he saw took his breath away. Quickly turning on the faucet and grabbing a washcloth, he scrubbed at the gore on his face and used his fingers to tame the rat's nest of hair on top of his head. Concentrating again, he willed his reflection back into being. Where before he'd been a pasty, pudgy walking testament to the effects of Midwestern bachelordom, he was now... Herb struggled for the right word... *Hot.* Never in a million years would he have dreamed he'd be able to wear that particular adjective.

Well, if the shoe fits, he thought with awe.

The extra pounds that had previously rounded his face and softened his chin were gone, exposing his cheekbones and defining his jawline. The stubble that still covered his cheeks now gave his face a rugged cast instead of a 'geez, that guy should probably shave' look. Eyes that had always been a lackluster brown now glowed indigo blue, so dark as to be almost black. He had passed out an unremarkable, squishy, beanbag of a man and woke up... different.

No, he thought with a devilish grin. *Not just different. Special.*

Chapter 14

BY THE TIME THE last of the carpet was scrubbed and the spatters of blood had been wiped off the plastic picture frames on the walls, Herb was hungry. Weaving a path through his home like a caged beast, opening and closing the fridge, pacing, opening and closing the cupboards, pacing, opening and closing the fridge, Herb contemplated what to do next. He tried to think objectively about his situation. He couldn't go to Ronnie's. Not yet anyway, and what was the use besides? While the thought of a turkey bacon melt and cheese curds or some syrup-drenched French toast and a hot cup of Folgers would've made his mouth water a handful of days ago, Herb couldn't think of a single thing on Ronnie's not-insubstantial menu that he wanted to eat.

Dark, unbidden memories rumbled in his stomach and bubbled to the surface: snapping the goat's neck, slinging it across his shoulders, and running through a moonlit field, a bead of bright red blood welling up from the cut on Rhonda's finger, holding a grouse above his head by the feet as he sucked at the gash in its side, the way the side of Molly's neck glowed in the fluorescent light. Every recollection spurred another rumble in his stomach, and each rumble ratcheted up the volume of the ever-present whispers. Herb could feel the sun making its way around the far side of the globe, drawing inexorably closer to his little abode. If he was going to eat, he'd better do it soon. But what to eat?

No, his mind whispered. *Not what. Who...*

His first thought when the phone rang was *Dinner calling!* followed by an immediate wave of guilt. Not trusting himself on the phone, Herb waited for the machine to kick in.

"Um, hello. You've reached the Knudsen residence. Um. The Knudsen, Herb, I mean me, well it's a recording of Herb. Me. Oh crap. Does this rewind? Uff dah. Ah, crap. Oh, okay. Sorry! Can't take your call! I'd sure love to and I hope I can take your call again. Later. When I call you back. Um. Okay'den, thanks! So wait for the beep... um, the beep. It should be this one. Oh for chrissakes..."

Beeeep!

"Crap on a cracker, Herby! You really need a new message. Anyway, where you at? Heard you was sick and stuff yesterday, and I thought you'd maybe be feeling better today and figured you'd wanna shoot some pool and grab a couple beers. Pick up. Pick up pick up pick up pick up. Hello? Okay, fine. I'll just grab Stanley. We'll be at Steinknockers in an hour or so."

As if in direct response to Dallas's invite, Herb's stomach rumbled with a plaintive growl. Maybe a night out would be just what he needed to help him make sense of all of this. He'd never tell Dallas or Stanley he had recently turned into a vampire, not in a thousand years. Stanley might believe, but Dallas? No way. Regardless, he figured he should get used to the idea before bringing anyone else into the fold. But some time with the guys and a game of pool sounded so normal. After the past couple of days, normal would be a nice change of pace.

Maybe after bar-close you could grab a little snack, the whispers suggested.

Herb turned the thought in his mind, looked it over appraisingly. It seemed like a reasonable suggestion. Not someone he knew, that was for sure, but maybe a tourist. Some Joe Schmo from Michigan or Minnesota, or a little international cuisine from Canada. There were usually more than a few out-of-towners hanging around. He'd just grab a little sip. Just the littlest of sips.

After a short spelunking expedition into his closet, followed by a quick archaeological dig through a few piles of laundry, Herb unearthed a pair of faded denims from his high school days. He used a penknife to punch a new hole in his belt to make sure the jeans stayed in place, pulled on a Foghat tee-shirt, and headed back to the bathroom to gussy up. But when he flicked on the light, all that showed up in the medicine cabinet mirror was an empty tee-shirt sitting on top of a pair of jeans. Not one scrap of Herb looked back.

"Crap," complained Herb. "How the hell am I supposed to comb my hair?" He usually spent more time putting on his socks than fixing his hair, but tonight he felt different. Something akin to self-confidence was starting to poke and prod at his insides. It was just rotten luck that when he finally decided to give a damn about his hair, he couldn't see it.

He slowed his breathing and tried to concentrate on the mirror, but to no avail. His thoughts kept drifting to shooting pool and eating tourists while his reflection remained M.I.A. Stifling a 'that figures' sigh, he pushed his fingers through his hair, followed by a black plastic comb. Judging by touch that he'd finally pulled most of the tangles out, he parted it in near the middle and patted around his head for good measure. Herb thought briefly about the razor and shaving cream sitting next to the faucet and weighed shaving without a reflection. Deciding that he'd rather live, he let the stubble stay.

Stepping back from the mirror, he looked down, pulling in vain to get the wrinkles out of Foghat. Skinny felt weird, like a wallet in the wrong pocket weird, or forgetting your glasses were on top of your head weird. But that insistent little kernel of self-confidence jabbed him hard in the ribs and he smiled.

The guys aren't gonna believe it's me, he thought with pride.

"Oh, Christ on a stick," he exclaimed.

Realization struck like a needle to a balloon. Some things could be explained. Shedding thirty-odd pounds in a couple of days, though? Not so much. Grumbling about the injustices of the world, he pulled off his tee-shirt and replaced his jeans with a looser pair. Next, he used his belt to secure a lumpy throw pillow where his paunch used to ride carefree above his waistband. Pulling *Foghat* back over his head, he finished the ensemble with a light flannel over the tee-shirt to better hide the belt-cinched pillow. Scoping himself out as best he could sans mirror, he added a few smooshes, tweaks, and punches, shaping his torso into a reasonable facsimile of his former physique. As long as no one wrapped him up for a hug or punched him in the stomach, they'd probably never notice. Probably.

Chafing a bit at having to hide the new washboard under a pillow, Herb still felt better. And just because he was wearing a pillow under a tee-shirt didn't mean he wasn't a badass. As he stepped out of his house and turned back to lock the door, a strange elation took hold.

Hunting, he thought. *I'm going hunting.*

Chapter 15

Herb pulled up to Steinknockers and glanced around the parking lot. There were a couple of bikers smoking by their Harleys, but it was otherwise void of people. Mondays were always slow, which suited him just fine. Herb slid out of his Pinto, realigned his stuffing, and glided toward the door, instinctively keeping to the shadows and avoiding the bug-filled pools of amber cast by the few lights in the lot. His ears perked at a variety of sounds: a car backfire far off on the main highway, the feathery swoosh of an owl descending upon a field mouse, the snick of an old Zippo as one of the bikers lit a second cigarette. The scents were even more pronounced: smoke, warm rubber from his car's mostly-bald tires, a cornucopia of olfactory overload from the dumpster behind the bar, and the sharp tang of urine where the occasional patron would let loose in back when the bar's bathroom was occupied. Oddly, Herb didn't find any of the smells to be bad or off-putting. They were just smells, and they painted a picture of the night more vivid than anything he could have ever imagined.

Having reached the entrance, he quietly cracked the door and peered into the dimly lit bar. A handful of regulars, many of whom Herb had already recognized by smell from the parking lot, occupied the space. They were clumped up at the far end of the bar by an old television mounted in the corner. Since the T.V. didn't have highly trained men chasing a ball, the regulars were occupied with grumbling to Stein, the grizzled owner, about bad sinus weather and the best way to clear a jammed-up butterfly valve in a Chevy carburetor.

Herb's cautious eyes took in the mirror running the length of the wall behind Stein. Panic rose up and strongly suggested fleeing back to the shadows of the parking lot. Without the surefire distraction of a game on T.V., Herb wasn't sure he could make it inside completely unnoticed. But damn it, he wanted to play pool, see the guys. After the past couple of nights, he didn't think he could handle another one at home. Firming up his resolve and cinching it into place like the pillow around his gut, he eased forward over the threshold, letting the door swing shut behind him. Another step, then another, each as careful as walking on thin ice.

Please, no one notice me, he thought. *Nothing to see here. I'm not the droid you're looking for.*

A glance at the mirror showed an empty, floating flannel walking into a bar. The seeds of a joke had just sprouted in the vampire's mind when Stein glanced up. Fear constricted Herb's chest and sharpened his senses, and time slowed to a molasses trickle. Herb saw the stubbly chin of Stein's broad face turn in his direction, skin crinkling at one corner of his mouth, making way for his easy smile. He watched fabric start to wrinkle and bunch as Stein's shoulder came slowly up, precursor to the inevitable wave and head nod Stein shared with every new patron.

Their eyes connected, and someone vacuum-packed their brains together. There was no other way to describe it. All that was Herb and all that was Stein were suddenly sucked in to the same narrow, shapeless space. There was a sound, like surf rhythmically pounding a distant shore. With each pulse, Herb created form from the void. He inhaled. Stein exhaled. He slowly let out his breath. Stein breathed in. As Herb's brow furrowed, Stein's gaze went slack. Both men stood motionless, Herb a few steps inside the doorway, Stein with his shoulder still in a half-shrug.

Please don't see me! Herb's panicked thought raced through the void, and Stein's eyes slipped out of focus to stare vacantly toward a spot somewhere above and to the left of Herb's head.

Afraid to move or even breathe, Herb waited, his inner mantra running in loops. *I'm not the droid. Please don't see me. I'm not the droid.* Amazingly, Stein turned back to the grumblers across from him at the bar, seemingly unaware that a newcomer was standing in the doorway.

Mightily confused, but not in the mood to push his luck looking for answers, Herb released a shaky sigh and cat-stepped through the bar to the back room. He instantly relaxed as the familiar space embraced him. Steinknockers was one of his favorite haunts in Trappersville, second only to the bowling alley. It was an easy place to like because Stein had simple rules. Drink and behave yourself, and you could stay as long as you wanted. Drink and misbehave, and Stein tossed your ass out. Easy as that.

Two bar sized pool tables occupied the back third of the bar, framed on three sides by the juke box, bathrooms and the back door where deliveries came in and unruly drunks were shoved out. A couple of guys in purple and white Vikings jerseys with smart-looking mullets occupied one table. Dallas and Stanley leaned against the wall near the other. Stanley was in the middle of a story that Dallas was obviously not listening to, seeing as how Dallas was actively engaged in surreptitiously watching the Vikings guys play pool.

Helen arrived with a tray full of beers a moment before Herb walked over and moved to the table where the mullet twins were finishing a game. The woman worked the bar a couple nights a week, Nekked's strip club up the road on the weekends and, according to Dallas, put the 'knockers' in Steinknockers. Herb had heard that she went by the stage name Helen of Troy at the strip club. Trappersville was a land-locked town, so it would be hard to prove whether her face could actually launch a thousand ships. But truth be told, most of those engaged in speculation had probably never looked up far enough to see her face.

"Look who made it to the party!" Dallas hollered to Herb. "Welcome back to the living. Sounds like you must'a been pretty sick yesterday. The way Ronnie told it, you'd better have had the gee'damn Bubonic plague if you still expect to have a job. And don't you dare lose your job. I ain't about to start paying for my meals, no thank you!"

Stanley's head bobbed up and down in agreement as he stammered, "You feelin' better, Herb? I sure hope so. I got the shingles once, and them-there sh-shingles, they had me feeling pretty awful. You don't got sh-shingles, do ya Herb? You gotta watch out for chocolate and nuts and take a buttermilk bath, and that's not ch-cheap. No, sir."

"Uh, thanks Stanley. Nope, not shingles. Had a, um… fever, though. Yeah. Uh, a nasty one. But I'm better now. Right as rain." Herb smiled, politely averting his eyes from Helen's shapely form as she slid around their pool table like a mermaid at a water park.

As Herb took in more sage advice from Stanley about holistic treatments for shingles and the best brands of shea butter skin creams, Helen deposited two cans of Milwaukee's Best on the ledge running the length of the wall.

"Five bucks. Hey new guy. Lemme know whatcha need, 'kay?"

Herb blushed. "Oh, um. Hi, Helen. It's Herb. Again. Still. Um. I've been here. A lot. I uh..." was about all he could manage while struggling mightily to not look at her cleavage.

It felt like Herb's eyes were made of metal and someone had placed a really strong magnet in Helen's shirt. His sense of propriety was still struggling with his hormones when Dallas flourished a crisp ten-dollar bill in front of the waitress. She moved to take it a few times, only to have Dallas flit the bill to the side, up, over, always just out of reach of her grasping fingers.

After a few unsuccessful swipes, Helen's fist dropped to a shapely hip as she glared up at Dallas from under long lashes. "Cute, Dal. You ever heard the expression, 'Just pay the lady?'"

In response, Dallas flourished the bill one last time before plunging it down the front of her strained V-neck tee-shirt and into her ample cleavage. As Helen stepped back in shock, Dallas winked and flashed a wicked grin.

"Ever heard the expression 'Pay to play?' Whadaya say, sweetums? Wanna play with old Dallas?"

"Sorry hon. I'm not real interested in Little League. Although the next time you push something down my shirt uninvited, I might just take a swing at a couple of balls," Helen growled, her voice all honey-dipped razor wire.

"Oh, c'mon now. We're just playin' is all, ain't we Herby?" laughed Dallas.

Oh crap. Herb turned to look at Helen, acutely aware that she still hadn't taken the folded bill out from between her bosom.

Eyes, eyes, eyes. Look in the eyes. Not down, look up. Good! Okay, smile. Smile.

"Uh, s-sorry Helen. Um, I'll make sure Dallas behaves." As Herb spoke, he looked straight into Helen's eyes.

They're hazel, he thought. *Huh, never knew she had hazel eyes.*

His gaze went deeper into the liquid pools flowing around night-black pupils. Glints of light caught, flashed, and disappeared, minnows catching the moonlight, swirling and drawing him into, around, through Helen's mind. He was vaguely aware that time had that molasses-slow quality again, like when Stein saw him walk in. He could detect the movement of the world in his periphery vision: Stanley's finger crawling inevitably toward his nostril. Dallas's mouth stretched mid-laugh. Over his shoulder, one of the Viking mullets was in the process of drawing back his pool stick. Herb acknowledged, pondered, and dismissed these minutiae. Ants crossing the sidewalk carried more significance. Of sole and tantamount importance in this infinite moment of time was the quivering candle flame of Helen, wavering in the steadily building gale of his attention.

A single puff and she's gone, he thought.

Gone, she sighed in agreement, her thoughts the purr of a post-coital lover wrapped deep in the covers, drifting down to satiated sleep and warming dreams.

It's all right, came his thought, a warm blanket enveloping her, holding her close.

"It's all right," he heard a strange voice say, a voice he almost recognized as his own, gently plucking the bill from her cleavage and pressing it into her palm. "You're doing a fine job here, that's a sure thing. A gem like you shouldn't be bothered by the likes of him, isn't that so?"

When Helen returned the slightest of nods, he added, "Tell you what. I'll have a Bloody Mary."

A flush had crept across her chest and up her cheeks, and her breath was coming in shallow gasps.

"One Bloody Mary coming up," Helen sighed. She blinked a few times, pushed a stray lock of hair back behind her ear. Smiling, she turned and wove a lazy zig-zag between the tables back toward the bar, casting surreptitious glances back toward Herb as she walked.

Herb watched her go and slowly fell back into himself. Two sharp points of pain in his lower lip brought him suddenly back to his senses. Snapping his hand up over his mouth, he whipped his attention back to Dallas and Stanley. Neither was paying any attention to him. Stanley was surreptitiously picking his nose, while Dallas was not-so-surreptitiously watching Helen's swaying behind.

"God almighty, I gotta hit that again. You know we hooked up, right?"

Stanley's attention strayed from whatever was in his nose to Dallas, and Herb shrugged. Sure of an attentive audience, Dallas's voice dropped to a conspiratorial whisper.

"Yeah, it was after homecoming, junior year. I'd just thrown over two-hundred twenty yards for three touchdowns. I didn't even have a chance to hit the showers. She grabbed me as I was coming off the field and pulled me into the equipment shed. Coming off the field indeed!" Dallas guffawed. "Holy hell, that was a night," he sighed, lost in a memory you'd never find in the front room of the video rental store.

Herb nodded politely, but his attention was still on the curious sensation of having fangs. Suddenly, Dallas turned his attention to Herb.

"Wait a 'sec," the larger man demanded. "Did you just order a Bloody Mary? A god damned Bloody Mary?"

Huh, thought Herb. *He's right. It's not like there's actual blood in there.* As he thought the word 'blood,' his stomach growled long and deep.

"Oh crappers, Herb. You ain't gonna hurl, are you? I thought you said you felt better," Dallas remarked, stepping back.

Still trying to hide his fangs, Herb quickly turned his back on the guys. "Oh yeah. No, I'm good. Feeling great. But yeah." He forced a quick laugh as he started to walk away. "Bloody Mary. What was I thinking? I'll, ah, be right back."

His attention caught up in hiding his fickle fangs, Herb walked right into one of the Vikings fan's pool stick, causing the stick to knock a beer off the rail of the table.

"What gives?" the man snapped. Chest puffed like an absurd purple and white rooster, he shoved his chin toward Herb. "You gotta problem? god damned cheeseheads."

With a soft *snick*, Herb's fangs were gone. Well, not gone, but just regular teeth again.

"Holy cats! Sorry guy. I wasn't paying attention. Not trying to start anything," Herb stammered. "How about, hey, I'll grab you a beer. What were you drinking?"

"Beverages shouldn't be on the tables," offered Stanley. "N-not your fault that guy put his beer on the table, Herb. If Stein saw that, he'd b-bounce his head off the dumpster, he would. Beer ruins the felt. Screws up the English on the b-ball. I lost twenty bucks to Fancy Dan last month 'cause I couldn't get the English."

Mullet-guy turned his ire toward Stanley. "Something to *s-s-say*, retard?"

Dallas took that moment to make his presence known. Stepping up and placing himself squarely between Stanley and the Vikings fan, he held out a meaty palm and turned his head back toward Stanley.

"It was ten bucks, not twenty, and you lost because one, Fancy Dan's a hustler and I told you that, and two, you suck at pool." Turning his ice-blue eyes back toward the angry mullet guy, Dallas loomed.

There wasn't another word for it. He technically was leaning, but that description didn't do it justice. A lean is just sort of being at an angle. But a loom... There's violence suggested in a loom. Danger. Herb always knew Dallas was a big guy, but it never ceased to amaze him when Dallas decided to show that he was a big guy, and looming did just that.

"Call my buddy a retard again and I'll use your front teeth to scrape the mud out of my boot treads. Herby here spilled your beer. Not intentional, and he apologized, so quit your posturing. Besides, the beer here's really cheap, so you're only out like what, two bucks?"

The mulleted Vikings fan started to bristle, but Dallas ratcheted up his *loom*, bringing his nose to within a few inches of the ruddy-faced Minnesotan.

"Now, Herb here made a right nice offer to replace your beverage, and he's gonna follow through on that, ain't you Herbert? Not 'cause he needs to, but because he's just a swell guy that way. And when he gets back with that beer, we'll all toast to accidents and happy endings. Sound like a plan? Hell, maybe we'll end up such good buds that we'll play a few games of pool." Leaning back, Dallas's face broke into a welcoming smile. "Whatdaya say?"

And just like that, crisis averted. The guy shook his head, dislodging a few dandruff flakes in the process. He grumbled, "Sure," to Herb, and added a begrudging, "Thanks," after catching a glare from Dallas.

Herb stared at Dallas for a moment in awe. Dallas had something, no doubt about it. Loud, crass, egomaniacal to a fault, sure, but there was definitely something. As Herb made his way back toward the bar, memories bubbled up. Dallas tying Herb to a tree, but then bloodying the nose of the kid who took Herb's Trapper Keeper. Dallas daring Herb to eat a bunch of Pop Rocks and slam a can of Pepsi and then laughing 'til snot ran in long gooey rivulets down his nose, but being the only one to stand up and clap when Herb tried to do David Copperfield at the 10th grade talent show. Dallas getting half the football team to help him prop Herb's car up against a tree like the space shuttle preparing for take-off, but then paying for the tow truck to get it back down safely.

Dallas was a strange one to be sure, dishing out mockery and mayhem at every chance, but there was that weird protectiveness, too. Herb couldn't count the number of times Dallas had pranked him, punk'd him, or embarrassed the holy hell out of him. But he also couldn't count how many times Dallas had picked him up when he was down or saved the day when Herb had made a mess of things.

Those thoughts still working their way around his brain in well-worn ruts, he reached the bar, mindful to stay far at the end so as not to land opposite the back wall mirror. Helen had just filled a glass pint with ice when Herb placed his hand on hers.

"Uh, sorry Helen. I changed my mind. Nothing for me and a Coors Light for the purple guy over there."

"You sure?" Helen purred, leaning forward, ample breasts resting on the bar. "Could be that this round's on the house. If you want it." Still leaning forward, she reached over to the olive dish, nimbly plucked one with cherry-tipped fingers, popped the olive between her lips, and proceeded to use her finger to slowly push the olive all the way in. Full lips closed around her finger as she slid it further into her mouth and then slowly drew it out again. "You want it, don't you?"

Flustered, Herb giggled nervously and rocked back for a moment, worried that if she leaned any closer, he might need to slide the pillow a little further down. Swallowing hard, he forced himself to look at the worn surface of the bar and think of old men playing hockey. That usually worked.

"No, I'm, ah. I'm okay. Thanks though. Just a, um."

He flicked his gaze up for a moment, a habit of human interaction. That brief moment of acknowledgement and apology he engaged in a thousand times a day. Just a quick glimpse followed by an apologetic bob of the head or small wave of the hand, one that let the other person know that it was okay, he didn't mean to be a bother and in fact, it was all most likely his fault, anyway. It was so second nature, so very Herb, that he couldn't do anything else. Smiling wanly, he glanced up and in that fraction of a fraction of a moment, their eyes met.

The sensation was nothing Herb could ever have ever expected. In that perfect simpatico moment, Herb knew two unalienable truths; that Helen was his completely, and that he was *hungry*. Inundating her with his gaze, Herb slid through the server opening in the bar and glided forward. She stood and followed him, caught by a strange gravity. Stein and the townies at the bar were oblivious to the building maelstrom of hormones and pheromones mere feet away, but Herb felt like he was stepping into the center of a tornado. Violent forces spun and whirled all around, yet he and Helen stood in perfect, crystalline stillness. It was more than the eye of the storm. It was the thinning ice before the first crack, the mountainside before the avalanche. Herb reached out a hand, took Helen's, and closed the distance between their bodies. She guided him through the swinging door to the bar's modest kitchen, past stainless steel and Formica countertops, past cases of beer stacked next to boxes of corn nuts and pretzels. They moved as one toward the only place that might offer some privacy, the walk-in cooler. Helen slid Herb's hand down her hip, around her back, drawing him in. Even the forty degree air couldn't cool the fever burning between them. Eyes still locked, Herb pushed her back against the shelves, leaned in, and kissed her hard. His fangs cut her lip, the thin trickle of blood touching his lower lip like a match to dry tinder. Breath quickening, he kissed her cheek, ear, neck.

Helen gasped when his teeth cut into her flesh. As his lips melded to her skin, she moaned, a deep, primal sound welling up from deep inside her, the sound driving her body tighter against his. The pillow separating them compressed as she clung to him, fingers grasping, nails raking hard into his back. Herb sucked and swallowed, felt the blood flow from her neck across his tongue. The harder he sucked, the louder she moaned, shudders coursing through her body. His other hand pushed up through her hair to grip the back of her skull, holding it tilted slightly to the side as he drank deep from the well of her neck.

"Oooohhh, kinky..." It was barely a whisper, her lips brushing his ear. The faintest sigh of a ghost caressing a still-warm lover's cheek in the middle of a long and lonely night.

Her body convulsed again, her hips thrusting forward as she wrapped a leg around his waist. For a moment, Herb lost his balance and shot out a hand to catch himself. The side of his hand snagged on a sharp piece of metal shelving, leaving a wide, shallow cut. He pulled his head back and sucked in a deep breath at the sudden pain.

Helen's wide eyes latched on to his again. Hips still moving convulsively, she took his hand, pulled it to her mouth, licked at the blood on his palm. "I like kinky," she intoned in a throaty whisper.

Herb's fangs *snicked* back to their normal size as he drew back and inhaled loudly, a newborn taking its first real breath. Still holding his hand, Helen sagged against the shelves of the walk-in cooler, a dizzy, devilish smile on her face. Herb watched her pupils swell as her gaze went far, far away. In a distracted sort of way, she lapped at his bloody hand like a child with an ice cream cone. Still holding her, Herb gently lowered her to the floor, ecstasy doused by his sudden panic. Helen sat on the floor of the cooler, eyes focused on something no one else in this world could clearly see. She'd stopped licking his hand when he pulled it away, but now her breath was coming in short, fast pants. One finger traced indeterminate patterns across the skin above her breasts, while the other started to slide up and down her inner thigh. Twin rivulets of crimson ran down the side of her neck toward the v-neckline of her shirt. Still connected in some intimate, unexplainable way, Herb could *feel* her gentling bobbing on a sea of contentment, every conscious worry washed clean, leaving a shell of herself, a lingering image on the back of an eyelid after staring full-on at the sun.

He rocked back on his heels, senses whirring, thoughts racing. Shifting forward again, Herb searched for a way to bring her back. The cut on his palm had closed, but so too had the bite on her lip. With dawning realization, he gently bit his fingertip until fresh blood welled up, then lightly circled the punctures marring the otherwise unblemished expanse of skin on her neck. Helen's body convulsed again, shudders finally subsiding as she looked at him with the eyes of a drunken lover. Where Herb's finger had been a moment before, unbroken skin now stretched, marked only by a smudge of crimson.

Unsure of what to do next, but sure the guys would notice something was up if he didn't get back there soon, he wracked his brain for ideas. Suddenly, he remembered Stein looking toward him and then past him and then not seeing him at all. Was that just dumb luck? Or maybe, just maybe...

"Um. Helen? Hey, Helen?" Her eyes met his and once again everything fell to nothingness around them, a vast, empty space they moved through in perfect isolation, perfect union. Resisting all manner of urges and trying to block out the incessant whispers, he pushed on.

"Maybe you should, um. Huh. So. We had a nice time, it was very, um, nice. But you really shouldn't remember. Us. This. The, well, the sexy-like stuff and the biting. Definitely forget the biting. Okay. So just. Um. Forget that you and me, that I ever, well. You came back here for some. Ah. Corn nuts for Stanley. But you won't remember us being back here? Okay, Helen?"

Helen smiled, nodded. Standing, she moved with the careful steps of a sleepwalker to grab a bag of corn nuts. Hoping for the best, Herb quietly reversed out of the space, crept back behind the bar. Surreptitiously grabbing a couple of cold beers out of the cooler, he worked his way toward the pool tables in the back. Stein and the handful of regulars still jawed about the weather that one year when it was really bad, the T.V. still spouted worthless ads for worthless things, and Herb crackled with raw energy. The whole incident had taken less than five minutes, but everything had changed.

Chapter 16

"NICE OF YOU TO join us." Dallas took the beers from Herb and handed one to the Vikings fan as agreed upon. "We were gonna start without you."

Herb frowned. "Oh, sorry. Didn't realize we were playing cutthroat. I'll rack." Herb moved around to the change slot, fishing a few quarters out of his pocket.

"Not us. Them. We're playin' doubles, Herby. You and me versus the purple super fans here. You can still rack, though. Probably be the best part of your game." Dallas grinned like a hyena and threw a conspiratorial wink at the Vikings fans, followed by a long pull of beer.

"Oh, uh. Sure. You betcha." Herb shrugged, slid the quarters into the slots, and jammed the slide hard into the side of the table. The released balls started to drop and roll to the far end with the sound of distant thunder, a sound that always preceded the hustle.

Dallas loved hustling, especially Vikings fans. The usual routine had Herb playing his heart out while Dallas half-assed it, putting on a show of getting more and more irate. Since Herb playing his best was just slightly worse than Dallas half-assing it, the other guys would usually run the table on them. Then Dallas would swear and kick and double down on the next game, only to win by a hair, setting up a third game. If the other guys weren't actually good enough to run the table, Dallas could usually ensure he botched the first game with a well-placed scratch shot, followed by a shocked, "Sonofabitch! How the Sam hell did that happen?" All things considered, it was a pretty good show, one that had paid their bar tab more than a few times in the past.

Herb liked the hustle. It always made him nervous, living on the edge like that. The kind of nervous like when you get back too much change at the drive-through, or when the light slips from yellow to red when you're halfway through the intersection. It was an exciting kind of nervous, getting something you probably shouldn't. Also, playing a hustle with Dallas meant Herb was part of something bigger than just a few guys shooting pool. He was part of a team. It was a team on a mission, a mission that required a covert plan, and that plan required flawless execution from everyone involved. He liked that feeling, being on the inside of the covert plan. For the plan to work and the team to emerge victorious, it was imperative that Herb contribute one-hundred and ten percent and do what he was really good at, which in this case happened to be sucking at pool.

Herb finished the rack and walked back around the table to stand near Stanley, while Dallas spread his arms wide and bowed to their opponents.

"Gentlemen, be my guests. Break away."

"It's Stu and Donnie," said the one Herb had bumped earlier, turning a thumb first to himself and then his partner. "And don't mind if I do."

"Hope you shoot better than your boys catch." Dallas offered politely.

"I shoot better than your girls can tackle," Stu snipped in reply.

"Uh huh. Like you tackled those Super Bowls you got into. Remind me, how many did your purple pals win again?"

The vein in Stu's forehead started to throb. "Shut up," he grumbled, lining up his cue for the break.

"More like shut out," Dallas added thoughtfully.

Stu slapped his cue down on the table, prompting Donnie to put a hand on his arm. "Relax Stu. Don't let him get to you. It's just a game of pool, right?"

Stu shook off Donnie's hand, giving Dallas one last glare. Dallas returned the look, all innocence. As Stu and Donnie turned their attention back to the table, Dallas tossed a quick half-smile and wink toward Herb before letting his face go blank again. Stu reared back on the cue and rammed it forward. The cue ball shot across the felt, impacting the triangle of balls with a satisfying crack, sending stripes and solids haphazardly around the table. As a handful of seconds ticked by, first one, then two solids and a stripe rolled into pockets around the table.

"Solids," called Stu, lining up for his next shot. An easy tap, and another solid jumped down a pocket to join its friends.

"Guess the Vike's ain't off to such a bad start, huh," Stu observed smugly. He worked his way around the table, lined up his next shot, and snapped the cue forward. The five made an orange streak off the side rail, only to catch the corner of the pocket and spin off to the side.

"Shit," muttered Stu, returning to his beer.

Dallas turned to Herb and belched loudly. "Go for it, dude. Dude? Um, Herb?"

It was beautiful. The minuscule threads of the felt, the light dusting of chalk, like the moors on the first frost of autumn. Each ball a splash of eye-searing color thundering across the pristine expanse of green, boulders of import crashing in chaos and violence while thin, invisible threads of physics tied them unwilling to this plane, forced them toward their destiny. Each spinning, crashing journey a product of violence and intent, pushed onward by the incomprehensible hand of fate toward an endless descent into darkness. Creation lay spread out before him, beauty and terror so complete that Herb knew his heart would burst trying to take it all in.

"Herb!" Dallas's cue whipped by, whacking Herb's shoulder and snapping him out of his reverie.

Herb grimaced, feeling like something terribly important had just slipped his grasp. Lining up, he took a shot and watched, mystified, as the balls seemed to take on lives of their own. The cue ball made clean white lines and perfect protracted angles as the nine, fifteen and twelve-balls all dropped. A split second after finally coming to rest, the cue ball moved again, and the thirteen went down. The cue ball rolled gently past the eight-ball, leaving a hair's breadth between them. Next the eleven, perfect leave. The ten-ball dropped with a satisfying *thunk,* and the cue ball rolled unencumbered across the felt to a gentle stop.

Dallas stood in silence. The Vikings fans were purple statues; Stu with his fingers pushed halfway back through his coarse mullet, and Donnie with his beer forgotten mere inches from his slack mouth. Even Stanley couldn't find the wherewithal to stutter. It was an exquisite lie. Mathematicians, engineers, architects would have wept at the perfect alignment of the cue ball, eight-ball, and pocket. A soft swoosh, clack, and thump, and the eight rolled through the table's intestines while the cue ball coasted to a gentle stop at the lip of the pocket. Five men signed in unison, with three of the sighs becoming whoops of laughter while the other two devolved into curses of disbelief and disgust.

"Sonofabitch, Herb." Dallas slapped his friend hard enough on the back to knock him off balance for a moment. "Son. Of. A. Bitch." He shook his mane, face caught between a grin and a grimace while Stanley hopped back and forth from foot to foot, so excited he couldn't make actual words. Instead, each step was punctuated with yips and grunts.

Donnie and Stu exchanged a glance, Donnie's amused, Stu's much less so.

"Nice run," Donnie offered as he fished a handful of quarters and a crumpled twenty out of his front pocket. "Twenty bucks and a round of beer says you can't do it twice. Wanna go again?"

"Now we're talking! Rack 'em, bitches, and my distinguished associate and I would happily teach you the finer points of billiarding." Dallas made a half bow, gesturing grandly toward the table.

"Billiarding ain't even a word. Maybe you should'a stayed in school instead of going into cheesecurdery."

Stu laughed through his nose at his own joke, a sound that made Herb think of an aardvark snorting a snail, while Donnie shoved fresh coins into the slot and dropped the balls. While he was racking, Dallas turned his back to the Vikings fans, picked up the appetizer menu from the table, and made a show of studying the contents. While doing so, he leaned imperceptibly toward Herb.

"Holy shitballs, Herbert. I don't know where that run came from, but don't you dare do it again. WHADAYA THINK, STAN? MOZ-

ZARELLA STICKS? Play good, but if you all of a sudden feel like Paul Frickin' Newman, try to hold back a little, okay? OR MAYBE THE BEER BATTERED GREEN BEANS? NEED ME SOME VEGGIES! Don't make it too obvious, but we gotta let them win, okay?"

Dallas finished with a pointed glare at Herb and turned back toward Stanley. "You're no help. I'm getting French fries and wings. Oh, and Stanley?"

Looking like a neglected hound dog about to get a treat, Stan's ears, eyes, and chin perked up. "Y-y-yeah Dallas?"

"You can't have any. Now where are those gorgeous double-D's when you need them?" Dallas called out, scanning the bar.

"You guys ready?" Donnie asked, standing to the side of the table and casually chalking his cue. "I mean, unless you want to call it off. I got twenty bucks says flannel boy over there can't run the table again."

"Me too," said Dallas. "Herb, I'm betting twenty you can't do that again."

"Wait! You can't bet against your partner! That's bullshit. He's gonna throw it, Donnie. He's gonna just throw the whole game." Stu was so worked up he was starting to sound like a purple-clad version of Stanley.

Dallas and Donnie just laughed, Dallas whacking his new buddy on the back a time or two.

"Just effin' with you guys. But we're still gonna mop the floor with you. Unless we don't, in which case we'll call it a draw and go for a third. Now, who wants to play some pool?"

Stu and Donnie grunted their assent, and the game commenced.

Chapter 17

IT WAS HARD. EVERYTHING was backward, mixed up, out of sorts. Herb was used to trying to overcome his mediocrity, striving and inevitably coming up short. He had never been good at anything, but now Herb felt like he was intentionally shoving square pegs into round holes. He'd line up a shot, instinctively adjusting each muscle from the pressure of his index finger on the side of the cue to the amount of weight on his left big toe, pose in statuesque grace, ready himself to execute perfection, a direct challenge to an imperfect world... and then he'd catch Dallas's eye and crumble. Shift his grip a fraction of an inch, bring his other foot forward just a tad, lean a bit further to the left, belt holding the pillow under his shirt pinching his back, and just like that, perfection would shatter. The cue would slide forward, the cue ball would streak across the table, meet its intended mate in a brief, shocking kiss, only to have both careen off in opposite directions. The cue ball would wind its way inevitably toward a terrible lie, while the other ball would narrowly miss the intended pocket and spin off to rest some place worse than where it was before. Herb would curse, his frustration genuine if for reasons other than what the guys expected. He could've made that shot. He could've made them all and finished this game ten minutes ago if only Dallas would let him.

But no, he had to play his part, be his little piece in Dallas's hustle. He had to play badly while Dallas cursed, rolled his eyes, and said bits like, 'Oh thanks, Herb. Why don'tcha gift-wrap it for them while you're at it,' and other disparaging remarks. Then Dallas would drop one or two himself, just enough to keep the game close.

Donnie turned out to be a decent player, dropping two or three and always leaving Dallas a tough lie, but Dallas wasn't a schmuck when it came to bar pool. He'd been shooting at Stein's since Helen was in a training bra. To the outside observer, in this case Stanley, it looked like a really close game with Dallas and Herb always chasing the lead but never quite getting there. Finally, Stu dropped the eight-ball, narrowly avoided scratching, and started strutting around the table, cockle-doodle-doing like a rooster.

"Beers! Beers! Beers!" Stu and Donnie chanted, exchanging high-fives.

Dallas made a show of kicking chairs and complaining about the slope of the table. Herb just stood glowering, fingers clenching the cue stick like the Boston strangler practicing for a night on the town. Stanley looked at him, an odd expression on his face, but Herb hardly noticed. Watching Stu and Donnie grin and Dallas muck around like a bad soap opera actor was making his blood boil. Visions of taking the seven-ball in his hand and cracking it against Stu's temple made his breath come fast and stomach clench. He could see, smell, *taste* the blood and bits of crushed skull in that greasy mullet, like ripping the skin off a dog with your teeth and getting bits of fur and grass and sandy earth in your mouth, each giving its own flavor to the rush of life and power as it runs down your jaws, coats your tongue.

Gonna rip that mullet right off your head, Herb salivated. *Bet you won't be feeling so prancy then.*

He'd suck him dry and watch those dumb, arrogant eyes go blank, and all that life, all that blood, would be his where it rightfully belonged.

"Upset stomach, Herb? You g-got the acid refluxes?"

Stanley appearing in Herb's field of vision was a bucket of ice water on the fire building inside of him. He realized that he had been growling, actually *growling* like a feral beast, and quickly coughed and forced a burp.

"Oh, uh. Yeah, I had some…" visions of the neighbor's dead pug flashed across his mind, "…bad goulash earlier. Must be repeating on me." Herb rubbed his pillow-clad stomach for effect.

"Seltzer. Soda crackers. A tuh-tablespoon of Pepto, maybe a piece of white toast unbu-bu, dry. That'll fix you right up. Sure will." Remedy proclaimed, he smiled and clapped Herb on the shoulder. "You w-watch that, Herby. Chronic acid reflux can cause throat cancer, and that's a n-nasty way to go."

"Thanks Stanley." Herb was struck by how much he meant it.

Crisis narrowly averted, Herb walked over to the table and readied himself for the next round. He and Dallas would play the hustle. They'd squeeze a few bucks outta the Vikings fans and call it a night. And Stu, with his puffy mullet and stupid Vikings jersey, would never know how close he'd come to falling a few links down the food chain.

Chapter 18

DALLAS HAD AN ARM around Stanley's shoulders, the two stumbling in unison while Herb lingered a few steps behind with Helen. The Vikings fans had left a while back with darkened moods and lightened wallets. Dallas had put the resulting cash to good use cleaning out Stein's beer cooler. He and Stanley, now both thoroughly drunk, were singing "Go You Packers, Go!" so loud Herb was sure it was going to wake up Lombardi himself.

"Hail, hail the gang's all here to yell for you, And keep you going in your winning ways,

Hail, hail the gang's all here to tell you too, That win or lose, we'll always sing your praises!

Packers! Go, you Packers, go and get 'em, Go, you fighting fools upset 'em,

Smash their line with all your might, A touchdown, Packers, Fight, Fight, Fight, Fight!

On, you Green and Gold, to glory, Win this game the same old story,

Fight, you Packers, Fight, and bring the bacon home to...

Oooooooold Greeeeeeeeeen Baaaaaaaaaaaaaaaay!"

Anyone dragged from their slumber by that ballad would probably assume it was a state holiday with a parade. They'd jump up, rouse the green and yellow jammie-clad kids, grab their pennants, and head for the streets, only to be sadly disappointed and stuck explaining to the kids that, no, it wasn't a Packers parade after all, just two guys with the right priorities, but bad timing. Herb decided it was probably for the best that the state's two drunkest Packer fans were safely away from the sleeping residents of Trappersville. The only real downside was that Herb needed to drive them home.

Dallas and Stanley serenaded half of northern Wisconsin while Herb was trying to disengage himself from Helen. As far as he could tell, she didn't remember what had gone down in the cooler. Even so, she'd been all over him the whole night. He'd never had a girl express any kind of interest before, especially not one that looked like Helen. The experience was more intoxicating than a double shot of Wild Turkey with a 'Waukee's Best chaser. Herb had enjoyed the smiles, the lingering stares, her brushing against his arm or touching his shoulder whenever she passed, but he was uncomfortably aware that she showed zero interest in Dallas. It was weird. Dallas was certainly trying, all cheesy one-liners and drunken gropes, but Helen wouldn't even take his drink orders. Herb had to repeat each order, after which Helen would slip him a seductive smile and say, "Anything for you, sweetie." When the bar tab finally came, there were far fewer drinks on it than there should've been.

"Told'ya she's into me," Dallas slurred. "I tapped that, and she wants it again, but she's playing all hard to get. But she's into me. Look! Sh'didn't charge me for my beers. Not a single one! Stanley. Stanley! She charged you. Pay up."

Herb was relieved that Dallas was too drunk and conceited to pick up on the fact that Helen wasn't 'digging his vibe,' and instead was ready to surgically attach herself to Herb's hip. It was something else he had to process. On top of everything that had happened in the past couple of days, he was trying to reconcile the hot waitress being more into him than Dallas. Having his fangs pop out repeatedly wasn't helping things, either.

"Um, so, you have a good night, too, Helen. Um. Thanks for the beers!" Herb ducked his head to once again hide the fangs and stepped backward, Helen matching his step back with a step forward.

"Anything for you, sweetie. Hey, how long you been coming here, you sweet little thing?" Her brow furrowed and her eyes tried to search his. "It's almost like... I kinda feel like we've just met..." Shaking her head, which resulted in her bosom shaking, which resulted in Herb turning an even brighter shade of red, she continued, "Must've been lovers in a past life, huh stranger? Seriously though. When did you get so cute?" She batted her long eyelashes and sidled in closer. "But you know, this isn't really the best place to come see me. You should stop by Nekked's sometime. Maybe this weekend? So you can, you know, really *see* me."

Nekked's again. She'd brought it up more than a few times throughout the night. While cognizant of the fact that he was an adult and could go to a strip club any time he wanted, the thought still made him distinctly uncomfortable, like when he was fourteen and his mom found the JC Penny lingerie ad under his mattress. He'd been to Nekked's once. Dallas had dragged him there for his eighteenth birthday. Herb had barely made it through the door when he saw the girl on the stage, plunged headlong to the bathroom, and then ran for the exit a few minutes later. Dallas had called him *Premat-Herb* for weeks, and Herb hadn't been to a strip club since.

Finally disentangling from Helen with a mumbled, "Oh yeah, sure. Um, probably see you naked. Ah, I mean at Nekked's. Sometime...," he scurried off after the guys. Helen just smiled, watching him the entire way.

Chapter 19

I T TOOK THREE ATTEMPTS for Dallas to fish his keys feat his pocket, the usually manageable feat complicated by a staggering volume of alcohol. Finally freeing the keys, he whooped in delight, belched, and fell over, causing the key ring to skitter across the pavement like a frightened, shiny critter.

"I got this," said Herb, scooping up the keys. "I'll drive. You two climb in the other side."

Dallas stared, then squinted, then laughed. "Holy shit, Stan. Herbert's drivin' Miss Dallas! I'm a goddamned celebrity."

Stanley burped amicably in response, and the two of them stumbled around the back of Deloris. En route, Dallas kicked Deloris right in the chrome testicles.

"Take that, you purple sonsabitches. You suck! We whooped you good, huh? god damned right we did. Go you Packers, go!"

Getting the pair into the raised up truck was tougher than Herb expected. He wasn't used to being the sober one trying to do responsible things. Using an improvised recipe of two parts cajoling and one part brute force, Herb had pulled first Stanley and then Dallas ("I don't ride bitch in my own god damned truck!") into the front bench seat.

Cranking up the diesel V8, he dropped Deloris into gear and rolled out of the parking lot.

"Who, um. Whosgunnagetyourcar *hic* Herb?" Stanley forced out before another long belch.

"Don't sweat it Stanley. I'll be okay."

"But who. Ugh. WhosgunnagetmycarHerby?" Stanley burped out as Dallas launched into another round of "Go You Packers, Go. "

"Why don'tcha crash on Dal's couch tonight, Stan? I'm sure he'll be able to drive you back over to Stein's in the morning."

Stan's head bobbed in what could've been assent before it flopped back onto the headrest. Claustrophobia squeezed, and suddenly Herb couldn't wait to get out of the truck and into the night air. He pushed the accelerator down, and Deloris roared in response. Scrub and ditch flashed by on either side, caught in the headlights for a brief moment as the truck flew past. A few miles, a few blown stop signs, and a few belches from Stanley and Dallas later, Deloris skidded around the final bend, the centrifugal force shoving them against the door.

"Sheeeeee-yit! Where'ja learnin' drive like that? Woooo-hooo!" Dallas whooped like a rodeo star.

Herb glanced at his drunken friend. "Guess there's a few things I've picked up lately."

Dallas snorted a semi-coherent response and Stan belched yet again. Bringing Deloris back down to a reasonable speed, he drove up the driveway to Dallas's rambler and killed the engine. He jumped to the ground and quickly circled the truck, arriving just in time to help catch Dallas and a near-unconscious Stanley as they fell out of the passenger side door.

"Whereshelen? Helen! I thought she was in the back?" Dallas squinted at Herb, all suspicion and sour beer breath. Dropping to his knees, Dallas peered under the truck. "Where's my girl? Here girly-irly-irly! Where's my..." Dallas's voice mumbled off as his eyes lost focus.

Still on his hands and knees, he wavered back and forth, throat working like he was about to give back the Steinknockers fries and wings. Instead of revisiting his late night bar food, he let out a long groan instead.

"C'mon out babe. It's me. It's big D! Why you... why you gotta be like that. It's me. It's D... Me dee me dee." Another belch and Dallas's head dipped toward the ground, eyes drooping.

Herb stared as Dallas flopped over on his back, muttered gibberish devolving into deep snores. Sighing, he dragged Stanley to the front of the truck and hung him on the fender rail by the arm. Stanley sagged against Deloris's bug-spattered grill and muttered something about shampoo while Herb sorted through Dallas's various keys. Finally settling on one that seemed like a winner, he untangled Stanley from Deloris's bumper, flipped him over his shoulder and fireman-carried him toward the house. When he reached the front door, he shoved the key in the lock, gave it a twist, and was rewarded with a nice *thock* as the deadbolt pulled back. Pulling the key out, he pushed it into the handle lock, gave another twist, and pushed the door open. That was it, though. He couldn't move any further. He wanted to. Hell, he definitely didn't want to spend the rest of the night hanging out on the stoop with Stanley draped mink-like over his shoulders, but despite a sincere desire to move from *outside* to *inside*, Herb stood frozen. He tried leaning in, letting Stan's weight drag him forward, but his body simply stayed in place.

"What the hell?" Herb grumbled, shifting Stanley's weight to a slightly more comfortable position.

The rhetorical question briefly roused Dallas from his stupor. "Sally ho, you bastards!" he called out. Pushing himself up onto his elbows, he cast a squinty glare in their general direction. "What're ya doin', Herby?"

"Oh, ya know. I just figured I'd take Stan for a carry," Herb snipped back in annoyance. "I'm trying to get you guys into your house so you can pass out and I can get on with my evening. *That's* what I'm doing, Dallas."

"Oooh," Dallas nodded sagely. "S'a good plan. You get in there. Go right on in. Hey, when yer in there..." Dallas settled back down onto his back. A lengthy belch, followed by an "uff dah" preceded the rest of Dallas's thought. "S'beer inda fridge. Have a beer on me. Since Stanely's on you. Hah! Stan's on you. Beer's on me. Deedle-leedle-dee. Hash've.... buurrrr..." Another deep snore sawed the night air as Dallas passed out again.

Herb glowered. Shifting Stanley again, he walked into Dallas's home, careful to avoid cracking Stan's head against the doorjamb. After dropping him on the couch in the downstairs living room, sliding off his loafers, and flipping a worn quilt over him, Herb headed back to Deloris. Pulling Dallas up and slinging him over his shoulders, he trudged back toward the house. Dallas grunted with each step as Herb carried him inside and up the stairs, finally depositing him on the king-sized bed occupying the home's master bedroom. Taking a moment to absorb the absurd awesomeness of Dallas's bedroom, which included zebra print sheets, lots of mirrors, deep shag carpet and, a quick double-take confirmed, a pair of fuzzy handcuffs hanging from a nightstand drawer knob, Herb placed Dallas's keys square on the center of his chest. He took a mostly clean glass from the kitchen, filled it with cold tap water, and set it on the handcuff-bedecked nightstand. For a final touch, he slid a wastebasket over next to the bed in case the fries and wings decided to come back for a visit.

Burdens deposited, Herb closed the rambler's front door, checked to make sure it was locked, and turned to look up at the night sky. He basked briefly in the memories from the previous few days, and wondered at the strangeness of the world. From the Vulcan mind-trick on old Stein to drinking Helen and having her cling to him like Saran wrap to running the table on those two Vikings wankers like he was auditioning for *The Color of Money*, this was by and far the best night Herb had ever had in his life. And it wasn't over yet. There were still easily three hours or so until sunrise. Time for anything to happen. Buoyed by his thoughts, Herb began to jog down the drive toward the highway. Reaching the highway, he lengthened his stride.

Chapter 20

THE NIGHT AIR WAS crisp against his face and his red hair rippled. Maybe he couldn't fly, but damn if he couldn't run like the wind. Losing himself in the sensation, Herb felt an uncoiling inside. All the years of being average, overlooked, overshadowed were evaporating behind him like the dashed lines stretching down the highway. He knew that no normal human being could run like he was running. Only something extraordinary, something amazing could run that way. And that was him. Finally—finally!—he was something truly special.

"Intoxicating, isn't it?"

The question hit Herb like a cable stretched across the highway, followed a split second later by a grasshopper splattering across his forehead. Half blinded by bug guts and shocked by the unexpected voice, Herb's newfound agility faltered, spilling him to the ground. He hit the pavement with a bone-crunching thud and half-tumbled, half-skidded ass over tea kettle for a good fifteen yards before friction finally trumped momentum and dragged him bleeding and sore to a stop. For a few seconds, all he could think about was the excruciating pain coming from all over his body. Elbows were bloody and torn, his left kneecap felt like it had been clipped by an aluminum bat, and blood flowed from a gash in his forehead through the remains of the grasshopper and down his chin to join the dirt stains on his shirt. As he took stock of the various pains, he also became acutely aware of their diminishing. Turning his palms toward his face, he watched the gashes mend, leaving unbroken skin beneath smears of dirt, gravel, and blood. He wiped an unsteady palm across his brow and felt unblemished skin beneath the blood and bug guts. He pulled at the tear in his jeans and watched the last bit of a nasty scrape close up right before his eyes.

Like Wolverine, he thought. *This is so awesome. I'm an X-man!*

As he marveled anew at his super powers, he failed to notice the shape moving languidly to position itself just in front of him. A soft clearing of a throat broke through his reverie, and Herb looked up to see,

"Hey, weren't you in that movie?"

"Oh, for the love of... No!" The stranger shuddered for a moment before he visibly regained his composure and spat words down at Herb, spraying him with derision. "I swear, I should've never consulted on the casting for that infernal film. Do you have any idea how annoying it is to have my intended victims asking me for autographs and photo-ops?"

When the words 'intended victims' crawled into his ears, Herb's insides turned to ice, and his stomach flipped inside out. It took an immense effort to squeak out a, "Sorry." While he cowered before the obviously upset stranger, Herb's mind whirled in confusion. He was sure he'd never met the man glaring derisively at him before, but had the distinct impression that he knew him. Like *actually* knew him, not just 'he looked like a movie star' knew him.

The stranger stood quietly, staring down his nose and offering no answers to Herb's unasked questions. Dark hair fell around his face, bringing his pale skin into sharp relief. His black slacks, black shirt, and black vest trimmed in deep red blended with the nightscape behind him. A matching short cape stretched from his shoulders to his waist and shifted languidly in the gentle breeze. He looked like he had come from an evening at the opera, only there were no opera houses within a hundred miles of Trappersville. Even when the local community theater put on *Guys and Dolls,* most folks just wore their nicest flannel and cleanest jeans. The stranger obviously wasn't from town and probably wasn't from Wisconsin. He looked *exotic.* It wasn't just the formal attire that set him apart. The fear he instilled with those cold, stabbing eyes made him seem less, or possibly more, than human. Plus, he had just matched Herb stride for stride, running at inhuman speeds down the night highway in those fancy clothes and wasn't even breathing heavy.

Neither am I, thought Herb, *but that makes sense because I'm a vampire. But this guy...*

Never the sharpest tool in the shed, it took a moment before the pieces clicked in Herb's brain, and he realized he was looking at one of his own kind.

The stranger's lips curled in a mirthless smile at Herb's dawning comprehension. He extended a pale hand with perfectly manicured fingernails toward him. "Yes, that's right. Now, please forgive my manners. Allow me to help you up."

The hand looked so fragile, like carefully crafted porcelain, but the grip that closed on Herb's palm was a vice sculpted from a glacier. The pull that followed would've dislocated the shoulder of anyone else.

Fortunately for Herb, he'd toughened a bit since *the change*, otherwise he might've ended up the only one-armed bowler in Trappersville. He stood, massaging his aching shoulder as the stranger scoured him with a disapproving examination.

"How is it that I don't know you?"

Before Herb could even make sense of the question, the stranger closed the distance between them, and two molten spears pierced the flesh of his neck. The sensation defied description. Pain, yes. Pain like he'd never experienced, pain that he was sure couldn't exist in this world, but there was something beyond the pain. Something greater, something he craved. The pain became an afterthought, a gnat buzzing near his ear. It was there and vaguely annoying, but otherwise inconsequential. He moved beyond it, grasping for that elusive thing, desire pulling him further, further...

The stranger pulled away and Herb fell back to the road. Gasping, his hand flew to his bloodied neck and stayed there long after the two holes had closed and healed.

"As disgusting as it is for me to admit it, you're definitely mine." The pale stranger turned his head and spat into the dirt, wiping blood-red lips with the back of his hand. "But where in the seven hells did you come from? I know all of my... *creations*. Despite centuries of roaming this pathetic plane, I know every single soul I've condemned and claimed as my own. So how is it that you, *you*," the sneer returned to his face as the question trailed away on his bloody lips, "are one of *mine*?" Rising up, the stranger filled Herb's vision, blotting out the night sky. "Who are you?"

Self-preservation finally kicked in, causing him to stammer in response, "Please. I don't... Please don't kill me. I'm just Herb. Knudsen.

I work at Ronnie's. You probably, um. Yeah, you might've seen me behind the window. Kitchen. Um, the kitchen window. Where the food goes. I put it there when it's ready." Desperation poured forth like water from a broken main. "Oh, please, mister. I'm just a cook. I make French toast. Ever get the French toast? I make pretty good French toast... Please don't kill me. Please. I'll... I can... do you like French toast?"

Herb's voice ran dry, followed by an eternity of silence. The unexpected laughter that sliced out of the stranger's mouth cut the tension, and the sounds of the night came rushing back. Herb sat staring up at the man as he laughed a deep, throaty laugh. Head thrown back, mouth stretched wide, two long, gleaming fangs caught the moonlight and glistened in the dark. Blood-red tears began streaming down alabaster cheeks as the stranger snorted and coughed. The laughing fit continued, doubling him over. One hand across his midsection, the other outstretched to ward off Herb's confused and imploring expression. His terror melting, Herb began to chuckle as well.

For a few minutes, the stranger huffed and guffawed while Herb chortled and chuckled without getting the joke. Then, as suddenly as it began, the stranger stopped laughing, straightened, and pierced Herb again with those eyes.

"Well met, Herb Knudsen, who makes pretty good French toast. Well met. But no, I have not been a patron of... Ronnie's. Perhaps I shall, though. Perhaps I shall." He smiled before asking, "Is the service good?" Again, that stare.

Herb shrugged, and he drew himself back up to standing. "Sure, um. Yeah. I guess so."

"Excellent. Most excellent. Perhaps I'll partake of the excellent service one day, but back to more pressing matters. You and I, we have much to discuss. Specifically, how is it that I am your Maker, and yet I did not make you? Walk with me, and tell me all."

And so it was that Herb found himself walking alongside the oddly dressed stranger with the dangerous eyes and wicked fangs, telling without hesitation or omission his tale of the past week. The mosquito bite that felt like a pterodactyl got a piece of his neck, the bowling alley, the bloody ice cube, and the dog at the gas station. The freaky flickering of his image in the security camera screen, the bake sale at the First Lutheran that nearly set him on fire, his reflection's refusal to act like a normal reflection, and his growing suspicion that something wasn't quite right.

He told of his research, his improvised Kung Fu and ill-fated attempt at flying. He told about how he woke up among the remains of a farmhouse slaughter in his living room, minus twenty or thirty pounds, but with new night vision. About meeting Dallas and Stanley, putting the whammy on Stein, and seducing and sucking on Helen. Like a Chatty Cathy with an endless string, he spoke of hustling pool, driving the guys back to Dallas's place, running across the countryside to get his car, getting hit by a grasshopper and scared shitless by a stranger running at warp speed alongside of him...

"Yes, yes. That's quite enough, thank you Herb. As you may recall, I was present for those most recent bits, but your attention to detail is quite astounding."

The stranger had stopped walking and looked askance at Herb. He reached out, grabbed the back of Herb's head, and twisted his neck, causing Herb to yelp in surprised pain. The stranger pushed Herb's lanky hair aside to get a clear look at the back of his neck, where a small dot showed stubbornly red against the surrounding white.

"Will wonders never cease? Truly delightful, to be my age and still surprised. A mosquito?" His eyes took on an inward look for a moment as he brought his nose down to the back of Herb's neck and *snuffed*. "Ah, yes. Yes, I recall. That was a lovely meal. I barely even noticed the pest was sharing. Amazing that it not only survived, but was able to carry it on to you. Truly, truly amazing. Although why you'd swallow a mosquito that bit you is quite beyond me. And yet, I'm the monster," he huffed indignantly.

The stranger turned Herb back to face him, placing both hands squarely on Herb's shoulders like twin blocks of granite. His eyes bored relentlessly into Herb's once again, while a dangerous smile touched the farthest corners of his mouth.

"Listen well, Herb Knudsen, who works at Ronnie's and makes pretty good French toast." Each syllable came out clipped to razor-sharp edges. "You are a mistake. You should not be. I would never have knowingly, willingly given this immeasurable gift to such a pathetic creature as yourself. I would not have even considered you an appetizer. Rats that have fed on syphilitic sailors would be preferable to drinking from you. I swear, I can smell Krispy Kremes and cheese curds oozing from your every pathetic pore." The stranger paused, a calculating look in his ancient eyes. "Be that as it may, I have a whim."

He drew even closer, until his Aquiline nose bifurcated Herb's vision like a knife, and the faintest smell of roses and decay and raw meat filled the millimeters between them.

"I can see you, Herb Knudsen. I know you now. Mediocrity is drawn to you like a moth to a consummate loser's sputtering flame.

I see this in you, and I despise you. Be that as it may, Fate has plucked a thread, and that thread has found itself looped, however unlikely, around you. You." Again, the sneer followed by a resigned sigh.

"You have received an unintended gift whose value you will most likely never appreciate or understand. For the fortunate children I choose to sire, I give guidance, even love, if you can believe me capable of such. But you," again, that calculating stare summed up all that was Herb and deemed it worthless. "No, I cannot—I will not—give you that. I will, however, give you life. You are more than you should have ever been, Herb Knudsen. Do with it what you will, and perhaps I'll be amused. And now, you may go."

Herb's eyes pulled back into focus as all his breath rushed out of his lungs. He sagged and found himself resting against the rust-spattered side of his Pinto. Of the stranger, there was no sign. Herb pushed a shaky hand through his hair, fished his keys out of his pocket, and drove home, his mind carefully blank. The sun was painting the pre-dawn sky with soft, ominous colors when he pulled into his front drive and killed the Pinto's engine. He moved woodenly through his home to the cellar stairs, down to the hole he'd dug before. Peeling off the remnants of his shirt, releasing the belt that still held the pillow lopsided against his midsection, and sliding off his torn and blood smudged jeans, Herb stretched out on the dirt bottom of his impromptu grave. His eyes stared into the luminous dark for a long time before he exhaled a tremulous whisper.

"Holy shit."

Chapter 21

ERB'S EYES OPENED, GUMMY and raw. The nightmare faded into the cobwebs dressing the corners of his home's dark root cellar. He remembered people, mobs of faceless, screaming people pounding to be let in, words unintelligible, but intent clear. Nothing would satisfy but the destruction of the demon within. Despite his impending demise, Herb remembered laughing. Mouth stretched, head back, the moon shining on his brow while the flicker of firelight reflected on his chin. Laughing as they banged on the door below, a rhythm of hatred, a drumbeat of retribution...

Knock knock knock

Herb sat up so quickly, he spilled forward onto his hands and knees. He listened again, just to confirm he wasn't still in the fog of a dream.

Knock knock knock

Nope. Not a dream. Someone was definitely at the front door. Which was weird, since no one in Herb's neck of the woods lived close enough together to make door-to-door visits very practical. Even the local Girl Scouts just set up shop in front of the grocery store instead of pedaling guilt and sugar door-to-door.

Besides, Herb mused, *it wasn't Girl Scout cookie season, was it? If it was, what could I get? I love Tagalongs, but they're just going to make the trip back up as soon as I swallow. Too bad they aren't meat Tagalongs. Raw meat Tagalongs. That would be awesome. Dipped in blood, too. Oh, heck yeah! Meat Tagalongs Girl Scout cookies dipped in blood. Or maybe just Girl Scouts...*

Knock knock knock

Herb hadn't even realized he had closed his eyes and reclined back down into his dirt bed. Jumping up, he reached for the clothes he'd had on the night prior and was half-dressed before belatedly realizing that answering the door in dirty, torn, and blood-caked attire might not be a great idea. Wearing only his boxers, he climbed the stairs and wove quickly into his bathroom. Judging by the angles of the sunlight slivers slipping through the cracks in his window coverings, it must've been about three in the afternoon. He wrapped himself in Scary Terry, tied the cloth belt firmly around his midsection, mussed his hair, and crept to the front door as the visitor outside knocked again.

Putting a squinted eye to the peephole, Herb surveyed the front stoop. A middle-aged man stood with his back to the door, looking out across Herb's property, then turned back toward the door as if to knock one last time. Herb's heart plunged into his bowels. Jerry, his nearest neighbor, paused before rapping knuckles on wood. Instead, he reached into a backpack and pulled out a photocopied flyer. Herb couldn't see the contents, but in a leap of intuition, he envisioned a picture of Lady, Jerry and Pam's dog. Before he could think better of it, he twisted the doorknob and swung it open, hissing softly in automatic response to the light from outside.

"Jerry, hey. Hi. Um, how are you?" Herb managed with forced nonchalance, squinting first one sweltering eyeball, then the other.

"Oh, hi Herb. Gosh, I'm sorry. I saw your car and figured you were home. I didn't mean to wake you up. I do the same thing when I'm staying at hotels."

"Huh?"

Jerry gestured toward the living room window beside the door. "The windows. Sometimes I need to black out the windows too, or I can't get any sleep."

"Black out the windows?" Herb was trying to concentrate, but the glaring light and guilt of eating Jerry's dog were making it a little hard to focus.

"Sure. Lots of folks do, I guess, but, look. I am sorry I woke you. I just, well. It's just that our dog, our pug Lady's been gone since Sunday night, and Pam and the girls are devastated. She was outside, and we don't usually bother to tether her. I mean, she's never run off before. But she wasn't there Monday morning and didn't come home last night. So I took the day off work, and I was just going around this side of town to see if maybe anyone's seen her. The girls, oh man. They loved that dog, and they're just devastated. Anyway, I know you know what she looks like, but here's a flyer, anyway. Pam helped the girls make them."

Herb took the offered sheet of paper and drew back into the safer shadows of the entryway. Turning it right-side up, his guilt grew razor-sharp talons that rummaged around in his chest until they found his heart and proceeded to squeeze. Crayons and Photoshop had been artfully employed to make a 'Have you seen Lady? We miss her. She's so special, and she's lost and we really want her to come home' flyer. The photo was of the girls hugging the small pug, faces lit with the joy only children with a puppy can know.

Herb's hand shook. "Gosh Jerry. That's awful. I... um. I'm sure Lady's just running around the woods. Dogs do that, I suppose. But I'm sure," his voice broke. Clearing his throat, he pushed on. "I'm sure she'll, um. Well, she'll be back in no time."

"I hope so," Jerry sighed. "You haven't seen any coyotes around, have you? Or maybe heard a wolf? I dunno, Pam's got this idea that a wild animal got Lady. Gus lost a goat and a cow a few days back. Can you believe that? I guess there was a lot of blood near the fence on his property line not far from here, but coyotes don't usually go for cows, right?" Jerry's hand fidgeted with the strap on his backpack. "Anyway, like I said, if you see or hear anything, just let me know. It'd mean the world to the girls if we could get that dog back."

"Of course," Herb managed past the pug-sized lump in his throat. "I'll be on the lookout," he trailed off, an uncomfortable silence hanging between the two men.

"Yeah, okay. Thanks Herb. I appreciate it. You have a good day. Sorry again for waking you. Guess you're doing nights at the diner now, huh?"

Herb stared blankly for a moment before picking up on Jerry's assumption. "Oh, yeah. Um. New schedule. Yup. Working nights. It's okay, though." Herb waved as he started to close the door on the blinding sunlight of the outside world. Before the dwindling gap closed for good, Herb stopped and spoke one last time.

"Oh, and Jerry?"

Already a couple of steps toward his parked sedan, Jerry looked back toward the door. "Yeah, Herb?"

"I'm sorry about Lady. Really sorry." And with that, Herb closed and locked the door.

Chapter 22

"AND WHY IN THE hell would you think you have a job here, much less the ability to switch shifts? I don't care if you were abducted by Stanley's aliens and anal-probed with a popsicle. I have people here that need to eat, and I didn't have a cook. Bill and Hector stretched their hours to cover your shift and fortunately, *fortunately,*" Ronnie took a dramatic breath before resuming his rant, "we were able to serve."

The truck stop's owner clenched his fists and forced himself to take a deep breath.

"Do you understand that, Herb? Serving your fellow man? The offering of yourself for the benefit of others? Is that concept so foreign to your pea-sized, beer-soaked brain? When the aliens abducted you and hoovered out your common sense through your fat ass, did they leave a shred of decency or responsibility? One iota of loyalty? Or did they just leave a selfish, self-absorbed, good-for-nothing piece of cud?"

Herb didn't really have answers to any of Ronnie's questions. Stanley had once called them 'rhetorical.' Maybe Stanley was right, whatever rhetorical meant. Herb had called in sick three days in a row, so he supposed Ronnie was entitled to ask a few rhetorical questions or whatever. Fortunately, Ronnie had been laying into him for about twelve minutes already, so another three or four minutes and Herb would be in the clear again. While Ronnie could certainly offer up a good ass-chewing, he favored intensity over duration, and was usually spent after about fifteen minutes.

"I'll bet you haven't even talked to the other cooks or preps about switching shifts, have you? Oh no! Not King Herbert the Third. Not His Royal Herbness. You just decree that you need to work nights instead of days, and the rest of us are just supposed to scurry into line and make it happen. Oh, Your Majesty! Of course, we'll be able to accommodate your request. We exist to make everything work for you. That's all we live for!" Ronnie snorted into the phone, his disdain a palpable thing oozing through the plastic receiver. "Of course you haven't checked. A pea-brain like you wouldn't ever consider that somebody else might be adversely affected by your whims."

Ronnie's silence was a challenge, one that Herb had historically met with meek apologies and placating gestures. This time, though, Herb was ready.

"Actually, I made some calls since I was, um, home sick and all. Anyway, I talked to the guys and the prep cooks, and I think we've got it sorted out pretty good. Bill was getting tired of working the overnights, so he's fine with going to mornings. The guys are plenty happy about having a set schedule instead of rotating hours, too and the preps will hardly have to change a thing."

A threatening silence roared from the other end of the line. Taking a deep breath, Herb forged ahead.

"Bill's also gonna take over stock orders since he's on Wednesdays. He's pretty excited about it, and is having his mom set up a spreadsheet to keep track of everything. I also set up a call-list with a rotating back-up for every shift. That way, if someone ever isn't able to work their shift, there's a go-to guy for coverage. I even put the preps into the rotation in case a head cook can't be in for a full shift, and they were completely cool with it. Actually, the preps like that it gives them a chance to work toward a promotion." Herb took one last deep breath. "So you have standard daily shifts with twenty-four seven coverage, overlapping prep shifts to cover the busy times, a designated backup for every shift so you're never left short-staffed, and a career path for your preps."

After the torrent of words, Herb fell silent and listed to the steady breathing of Ronnie on the other end of the line. Ronnie breathed for what seemed like a very long time while Herb tried not to squirm.

"You re-did the schedule?"

Gulp. "Yes."

"And all the shifts are covered, with everyone's consent?"

"Yes."

"And the preps are on-board with this too?"

"Uh huh. Pretty excited, actually."

"And this magical schedule? Where exactly would I find it?"

"Actually, I was feeling pretty okay early this morning, so I swung by and put a copy in an envelope on your desk. It's manila. The envelope, I mean. It's kind of a dark yellowy color..."

Ronnie cut Herb off with a curt, "I know what color manila is. Hold on."

There was a sharp *clack* as Ronnie slapped the phone down. Herb sank back into his couch, wondering if he had maybe overstepped his bounds a little. When Jerry had assumed Herb was working nights since he'd been asleep during the day, it seemed like the most natural solution for a lot of problems. Being a vamp was cool and getting cooler every day, but he was house-bound from sunup until sundown and still needed to pay the bills.

The night after Jerry had come by looking for Lady, Herb had dug up the crumpled copy of his work schedule and smoothed it out on the kitchen table. Ronnie put it together every month, and it was always a bit of a nightmare. Names were crossed off and added almost at random. Some shifts were two or three hours, others were ten hours plus. As Herb considered the schedule, pieces just started falling into place. Pulling out a bent-up notebook and a pen, Herb set about making some changes. Most importantly, Herb only had night shifts.

"Son of a bitch, Herb. You did this?" Ronnie was back and actually sounded not pissed.

"Ah, well. Yes. I mean, I had to check with the guys, but yeah. I pretty much mapped it out and put it together," Herb offered, a rare spark of pride kindling in his chest.

Ronnie gave a slow whistle. "Herbert, maybe all these years I've underestimated you. Probably not... but *maybe*. Truth be told, this is a fine schedule. A damn fine schedule." Ronnie chuckled. He actually chuckled. "I guess someone that can put together such a well-oiled schedule maybe does have a slight understanding of the importance of our work here. And I think this could work..." Ronnie suddenly and loudly cleared his throat before continuing. "Of course, I'll need to make a few adjustments to make sure we have the coverage we need. The pieces gotta fit, you know..."

"Oh, they fit! Um, I mean. I, well. I think they fit pretty good, but you're right. Um. Sure. Yes, you should definitely tweak it a little. I mean," he stammered, and then inspiration struck. "I learned scheduling from watching you all these years. You always did such a good job. I thought I'd maybe see if I could figure out how you did it. So. Um... Yeah. Do I still have a job?"

Herb fell silent again as Ronnie breathed. Finally, his boss grunted into the phone. "You guarantee, you *swear* that you'll be on time and not miss any shifts anymore, back-ups and call lists be damned?"

"Absolutely! Sir. Um. Ronnie, sir. I definitely guarantee and swear and promise." Herb had launched off the couch to his feet with excitement, vibrating with anticipation.

"Well then, I guess we'll see you on Sunday. And if we don't, you're a dead man." And with that, Ronnie ended the call.

Chapter 23

Herb collapsed on the sofa and dropped the phone beside him. He was ungodly tired, but had forced himself to stay awake until he could talk to Ronnie. After calling in sick all week, Ronnie had been pretty pissed at Herb. This new truce was tenuous at best, but at least Herb still had a job. He had enough problems without having to worry about how to pay his bills.

Since Helen, the cravings for blood had slowly taken over his every waking thought. Tuesday night, the whispers had been a distraction, but one that he could still push aside, like a sore ankle you favor, but still walk on. He had worked on the schedule for Ronnie's, watched some late-night infomercials, and dressed up his dirt bed in the cellar with some green and gold sheets and his favorite pillow. If that was where he was going to be sleeping, he might as well be comfy. When he'd woken Wednesday night, the whispers had clamored like metal pails full of rusty bolts being swung around the inside of his skull, and his intestines curled into knots. Desperation had pushed him outside, where he tried hunting in the woods again. After quickly nabbing a grouse, he bit, sucked in a feathery mouthful, and immediately spat the blood out. Like curdled half and half, a mealy apple, cold cheese curds, it would've been edible, but not pleasant. Apparently, his farmhouse buffet was a dietary exception, not a rule. Having fed on human blood, the thought of drinking an animal was revolting.

The vampire was hungry, but there was no way he'd be able to stomach the same meal that had satiated him just a few nights before. He wanted human blood. After some careful thought, Herb realized that planning a meal was now considerably more challenging than just dialing up a pizza. He wasn't about to start stalking locals into dark corners and drinking their blood. That just seemed rude. No, Herb might be famished and half-crazed with the whispers, but he would have rules. Sure, he was hungry, but he'd learned from Helen that he didn't have to kill anyone. He could just take what he needed and then put the whammy on them. No harm, no foul, no awkward missing person pictures on milk cartons.

A plan started to take shape. It had to be someplace that wasn't too popular. Even if he could whammy his dinner, he didn't think he could whammy a room full of people. It should be someone from out of town, or at the very least someone he didn't know that well from Trappersville. That would be tough, since Trappersville wasn't exactly a megapolis. So, a stranger would be best. But where to find an easy-to-bite stranger? There wasn't really a section in the classifieds for that.

Herb considered places where he could get in and out without drawing too much attention. Someplace that would appeal to a tourist, or folks with actual places to go that had the misfortune of getting stuck in town for a night. He grabbed a notepad and pencil and started jotting down some options, crossing them off the list as soon as they were added. Stein's and Bay City Bowlers were definitely off limits. Too many people knew him, and he couldn't risk bumping into

Dallas or Stanley. If something went awry, he needed to be anonymous and able to make a quick getaway. The grocery store? Closed. Same for pretty much all the places down on Main Street. There were those cabins a ways down the highway on the outskirts of town, but this time of year, folks with cabins were doing daytime stuff. Fishing, tubing, hiking and whatnot. If anyone was out and about at this hour, they'd be sitting by a campfire. Kinda hard to creep up on a group sitting around a campfire, bite someone's neck and make a clean getaway. There was that little roadside bar out past the cabins. What was it called? Weasel's? He'd been there once or twice when Steinknockers was too busy and they couldn't get a stool, but it was a little too far outside of town to be convenient, especially when the usual drive home was under the influence. Weasel's, though, had potential. Small, remote, set back from the highway, and only a handful of yards from the woods that bordered the back.

Herb settled back in his chair, face screwed up in thought. It could work. He could go out Old Route 2 and leave the Pinto in trees a mile or so from the bar. He knew he could easily run that far in a short couple of minutes, especially with a belly full of blood. So he'd park, cut through the woods, find a place to lurk...

Lurk? Really? I have to lurk? Herb was feeling bad enough about planning the whole excursion. Realizing that there was lurking involved just about pushed him back out to look for a rabbit, but the gritty dirt and feather taste of grouse was still fresh in his memory. If getting some honest to goodness human blood meant he had to lurk, so be it.

And so it was that Herb found himself on his first hunt. After creeping to the edge of the tree line near Weasel's, he'd nearly leapt from the bushes ooga-booga style multiple times, only to be driven back into hiding by self-consciousness more than fear. What if he screwed up? What if they laughed? What if he couldn't find a vein and had to bite someone three or four times?

Finally, after a couple of pep talks and whacking his forehead to try and quiet the whispers, Herb made his move. The unsuspecting meal-to-be was a middle-aged man. He looked like a pleasant fellow, not too tough, not too wimpy. As his first real victim, Herb wanted to make a good impression. For whom, exactly, he wasn't sure, but he felt it was important to make a good choice. Herb watched closely from the shadows as the man stepped out the back door of the bar, lit a cigarette, and moved to where the light pushed half-heartedly against the dark. He inhaled, exhaled, sending twin plumes of smoke of out his nostrils. Inhale, exhale.

"Um, hiya."

The man jumped back and coughed out a lungful of smoke, prompting an embarrassed smile from Herb.

"Oh, sorry about that," the vampire offered sincerely. "So, um..."

Shocked by his own speed, Herb struck, grabbed the man's shoulders, stared straight into his eyes, and concentrated.

"Don't scream. Don't panic. Just, um. Relax. Nothing to worry about, okay?"

Face gone slack, the man's head dipped and rose in sluggish assent.

"Good. Well, that's good. Very good. So I'm, ah. Well. I'm gonna bite ya, okay? But not hard. Well, I guess kind of hard, but I'll be careful. And I'm just gonna take a little. Just a sip, really. Then I'll heal your neck right up and whammy you and you'll be A-okay."

The man's brow creased, like he was thinking about something exceptionally complex. Slowly, eyes still trapped by Herb's stare, his head shook minutely from side to side.

"Whadaya mean no? I'm hungry!" Herb implored with a bit of a whine. Glancing around to make sure they were still alone, he pressed on. "Seriously, this is gonna happen. And you got nothing to worry about. Look," Herb opened his mouth to proudly display his fangs. "See? They're really sharp, so you won't even feel a thing. Heck, He len... Oh, you probably don't know Helen. Well, maybe. You been to Steinknockers? Or Nekked's?"

A slack, vacant gaze gave no indication one way or the other, so Herb assumed he probably hadn't.

"Well, she's the first person I. Um. Ate. Drank? Anyway, she actually liked it. Sorta like a really intense hickey. Not like it'd be like that with us. I mean, this isn't. That was... wow. But I'm not. I'm just really hungry is all. But you'll be fine, I promise. I don't kill people. At least, I haven't yet."

The vacant eyes refocused slightly on Herb's, and a thin sheen of sweat broke out on the man's forehead. Herb could feel the man's shoulders tremble in his unyielding grip.

"Oh crap. I'm not doing this right." Herb took a deep, calming breath, and the man inhaled. Herb slowly exhaled and the man did too. "Okay. You just relax, and this'll be over in no time."

Herb looked deep into the man's eyes and willed him to stay calm, stay quiet, and felt the tremors subside. He leaned in, tilted his head. The man didn't move, completely enthralled by Herb's whammy. Herb pulled back, tilted his head to the other side, leaned in. Still not able to get a good angle, he settled back again.

"You aren't gonna make this easy, are you, fella? So, um. Could you like tilt your head to the side a little? Like this?"

Herb demonstrated, tilting his head to the side, ear toward shoulder. Like a marionette, the man's head mirrored Herb's. Satisfied he'd be able to get a good bite in, Herb politely reminded his meal to stay put until he was done. Stretching his mouth wide, Herb leaned in, applied a little pressure, felt his fangs pierce skin and go deeper into the vein. Quickly sealing his lips around the flow of warm blood, he drank, swallowing faster and faster to keep up with the steady pumping of blood. As warmth coursed through him, he realized suddenly and fiercely how cold he'd been, but now fire raged through his veins. Raw power sparked in his throat, burned through to his toenails. He wanted more, wanted it all.

A faint grunt brought him back to the moment. The man was starting to sag, and Herb realized he should probably stop. Should definitely stop. Should pull his fangs out and stop. Right. Now.

And he stopped. As he stood panting, rivulets of delicious blood dripping down his chin, Herb thought stopping a runaway semi with his bare hands and a pair of flip-flops would've been easier, but barely heard over the roar of the whispers clamoring for him to feast, rend, tear, devour was Herb's promise. He'd promised the man that he would be okay. Promised he wouldn't hurt him, and definitely wouldn't kill him. He had promised. Shifting his weight back, he slid his fangs out, pulled his head back. A quiver ran through him from the crown of his scalp to the tips of his toes.

"Whoah, that was good."

Herb suppressed another shiver as he fought to contain the hurricane inside. While he wrestled for self-control, the man's head slowly returned to an upright position. His face was slack, almost peaceful. Almost. Like he was about to fall into a deep, irresistible sleep but desperately wanted to stay awake. Herb quickly bit his finger, the sharp pain helping to bring his whirring mind back under control. Rubbing it over the twin wounds in the man's neck, he then licked his thumb and used it to scrub away the smears of blood until the skin looked mostly clean again. Taking the man by the shoulders, he gave a gentle shake to ensure he had his complete attention.

"Uff dah. That was something. Wow, you're tasty." Herb shook his head, trying to stay on topic. "I guess we should wrap this up, so here's what happened. You wanted to get a little air, right?"

"Air," the man sleepily agreed.

"And uh, that's it. You had a smoke. Cleared your head a bit. You didn't see anyone. Just a quick smoke, and now you're gonna head back in, settle your tab, and call it a night."

"Night," the man offered with a faint smile.

Hoping he'd done it right, Herb gave a quick nod. "Alright, then. Um. Good night. And thanks. So. Right. See ya."

With a last probing look deep into the man's eyes, Herb fought down the impulse to take one more sip, just a little chaser, a nightcap, if you will. Instead, he took his hands off the man's shoulders and slowly backed away, holding the man's gaze as he drifted backward into the shadows, waggling his fingers for good effect.

"I was never here. You never saw me. You won't remember... shit!"

The rock caught the back of his heel, sent him flailing backward, arms windmilling as he dropped onto his rear. He froze like a raccoon in a spotlight, heart thumping as the man looked at the shadows Herb was sitting in, eyes returning from some far-off place. Comprehension following, his eyes widened in fright and a hand flew to the side of his neck.

"You... you bit... who are you? God damned it, you bit me! You bit..."

The crack of a snapped spine split the air like a rifle shot. Herb's hands trembled as they gripped the man's head, holding the body up like a limp puppet.

What the hell just happened?

His eyes refocused as he looked furtively around. Voices from inside the bar were uncomfortably close. Acting more on instinct than with deliberate intent, he slung the lifeless man over his shoulder and ran into the trees. Sighting a fallen oak, he dumped the body to the ground and shoved it half under the trunk. After pushing leaves and dirt up around the body, he crashed through the brush and finally reached his car. Only when he was safely back inside the Pinto did he dare make a sound.

"Oh crap. Oh crap. Oh crap," he repeated, a mantra of horror and disbelief as he drove off into the night. He was completely, totally vamped.

Chapter 24

Herb drove. Manic with fear, he zigged and zagged through the backwoods while watching the rearview for the inevitable red and blue flashing lights. It was hard to stay panicked, though. The guilt of murdering the stranger dwindled, eclipsed by a dark euphoria. He had to keep reminding himself that he'd killed someone, actually killed *a guy*. Then the panic would spark again, he'd drive faster, eyes practically glued to the rearview. Had he been able to cast a reflection, it would've shown the whites of his eyes ringed in bloody, terrified tears. It wasn't sustainable, though. No matter how hard he tried to stay scared or be appalled at himself, it would dwindle. How could he be scared when he felt so powerful, so alive? Soon he was simply driving instead of fleeing while someone else's blood sang in his veins. He had pulled into Nekked's parking lot before he even realized he had a destination.

Helen of Troy was on stage as Herb paid ten bucks at the door and walked in. Electric guitar and heavy bass pumped through giant speakers as strobes cast shifting, multi-colored light across her very naked body. Her eyes instantly locked onto Herb, something he found disorienting given the fact that she was hanging upside down, her long, shapely legs wrapped firmly around a chrome, floor-to-ceiling pole.

With a smile that was one part playful, two parts devious, and entirely for Herb, Helen slid the rest of the way down the pole, rolled gracefully onto her stomach, pushed herself forward, and arched her back as she extended her arms.

Boobs? he asked himself.

Boobs, his eyes confirmed with awe.

Teeth barred in a mock-growl, the stripper started to crawl forward across the stage, oblivious to the truckers, frat boys, business travelers, and other assorted men watching in rapt fascination. They whistled and yelled, most waving ones and fives, the high-rollers waving tens. Spinning around onto her behind and leaning back, she scissored her legs. Pulling them back into her chest, she rolled gracefully into a crouch, stood, and slid her hands from ankles to thighs, up her tummy past the sparkling little gem in her navel. Twisting her arms elbows out, she continued to draw the backs of her hands up past her bare breasts, past her wicked smile. Stretching her arms in a 'Y' above her head, she cat-walked toward the front edge of the stage. Each step was slow and deliberately sensual, knee raised high before lowering her foot to the stage, stiletto heel placed inches in front of fuchsia toenails. Helen plucked bills from outstretched hands, but her eyes never left Herb's as he stood frozen in the middle of the room. Using the convenient shoulders of two front-row fans, she lowered herself to the floor. Stiletto heels still clicking in time to the music, she strode across the room. Pulling up within inches of having her breasts brush his chest, she looked into his eyes and smiled.

"You came."

Herb involuntarily looked down before catching himself. "No! I mean not yet. I mean, yes! I'm here. I came here. And you're... here."

"Yes, I am," she purred, taking his hand.

She led him across the room, past a red velvet rope into a section clearly marked V.I.P., and toward a couch surrounded by thick curtains. Shouts of "Atta boy!" and "Lucky bastard!" followed, but Herb was oblivious to everything except Helen's bare behind and the hand that held his, drawing him further into a Penthouse letter.

The whistles and cheers faded as Helen pushed Herb back on the couch and turned to draw the curtains. Sound still reached them inside the semi-private booth, but it was muffled and indistinct, strands of fuzz wrapped around pounding bass. An amber glass lantern was suspended over the space, casting a warm glow and unusual shadows down on Helen as she moved toward him, all sensuous curves and seductive smiles. Looking up as she crawled on top of him, he couldn't help but think that not only could she launch a thousand ships, but make damn sure that all their sails were at full-mast.

Climbing him like a jungle gym, Helen's body moved in ways Herb wouldn't have believed possible. His attention was torn between gaping with rapt fascination and shoring up his wavering self-control. His fangs kept *snicking* into place. It required a tremendous effort of will to make them go away, only to have them pop right back as the woman doused him with wave after wave of raw sexuality. Fortunately, Helen was so completely engrossed in the lap dance, eyes half closed as she turned, slid, twisted, thrust her way over and around him, that she didn't seem to notice Herb's internal struggle. Herb kept his mouth stubbornly shut, causing his nostrils to flare as he fought to keep from panting with desire. Making things even more difficult was the unshakeable feeling that some strange undercurrents were at work, pulling and shifting below their skins. Why had he come here? The obvious answer was stark naked and doing her best to make sure he had an unobstructed view of every square inch of her skin, but there was something more. Beyond the raw physical chemistry, something deeper, something darker swam in lazy, dangerous circles.

"...so cold. C'mon baby, can't you warm me up? Just a little?"

Herb had been so lost in her body and his own impure thoughts that he hadn't realized Helen was whispering, her breath hot on his ear, his neck, his cheek.

"I'm hungry. C'mon Herby. I knew you were going to come. I knew you'd warm me up, feed me. I need it, baby. I need you..." Helen purred, her sultry voice laced with a brittle edge.

Of their own volition, Herb's hands slid out, gripped her thighs, and traced their shapely form.

Oh gosh, this has gotta be against the rules, a small part of his mind protested.

The old, weak Herb that always had to park in the back row and never got the cheddar puffs, much less the girl. Whether it was the booming bass or something else entirely, that voice was getting harder and harder to hear. In its place, the whispers were growing. As they grew and twined through his mind, his hands moved up and down her thighs, around her back, pulling her in closer and closer.

"What'd you say sweetie? Oooh, yeah. You can tell me. You don't need to whisper. You're here now, I'm here. There's no one else... Tell me you want it, too."

Herb's hands paused. "But I, ah, didn't say anything..."

She kissed him then, hard, pushing her tongue into his mouth. Without thinking, he responded and kissed her back. He heard a faint *snick* and felt a sharp pinch on his tongue, followed by the warm, familiar, enrapturing taste of salt and iron. Blood. His blood. His tongue was bleeding and suddenly the kiss had become something else, something primal. Helen's body ceased its sensual pulsing and pressed hard against him, her hands on his face as she sucked on his tongue, as she drank his blood.

Herb pulled back with a shocked, "Wooahhh!" Eyes wide, he looked up at Helen's face. The amber lamp was behind her, casting her face in shadows, but her eyes held a faint glow, like fool's gold in the moonlight. Her lips were dark red against pale, smooth skin, and her fangs were...

"Holy shit!" Herb tried to scurry back, but was effectively sandwiched between the couch and Helen, her thighs straddling him, her hands now pressed against his shoulders as she arched her back and tilted her head quizzically to the side.

"Oh baby, what's wrong? I just wanted a little taste. I need it, baby. I need you." She pouted as she wiped at a drop of blood in the corner of her mouth and then slowly licked her finger clean. "I'm hungry," she whispered in a petulant tone. "Do you have any meat?"

"You're a.. but you've got... but how'd that..." Herb's earlier arousal thrust into a dunk tank full of ice, he gasped and sputtered as his muddled brain tried to absorb the situation.

"Hush," she purred, leaning back in, heavy breasts against his chest, head nestling into his shoulder. Helen's now-licked-clean finger started tracing lazy patterns through his hair, the back of his neck as she spoke. "Let's get out of here. I'm hungry."

Herb nodded mutely, completely at a loss of what he should do, but firmly convinced Nekked's wasn't the right place for doing it.

"What's that? C'mon Herb. You really need to speak up a little," she cooed playfully. "There's no need to keep whispering."

"But I didn't... Oh. Right. Huh. I just, um. Said that we should. Probably go. Out. Somewhere."

Her smile went from jack-o'-lantern to simply wide as her fangs shrank back to normal incisors. Taking him by the hand, she led him from the couch, out the side of the curtained booth, and along the dark back wall of the club to a small, black door near the stage. Slipping through the door, she pulled Herb into a place he didn't know actually existed, a place where all the women were gorgeous and none wore clothes.

Still being led by the hand, Herb's head swiveled, unable to stop himself from looking. One wall was adorned with feather boas, French Maid costumes, leather bustiers, and sparkly patches of sequins held together with gossamer thin strings, the other lined with vanity mirrors occupied by women in various stages of undress applying make-up and primping their hair. High heels and knee-high boots were scattered haphazardly across the floor. Helen made her way cat-like through the narrow room, Herb following in a stupor.

"How many times do we have to tell you? No boys, Helen!" a brunette called over her shoulder.

"Shove it, Brittany. We're just heading out back."

Helen's voice had switched from purrs and promises to sharp-edged ice. The brunette turned back to the mirror, huffing a comment about double-D's and entitlement issues. Helen's eyes glowed dangerously for a split-second and Herb's breath caught in his throat, but she just kept walking through the dressing room toward a large door marked 'Fire Exit' in the back.

Grabbing a deep red, satiny robe, Helen wrapped it around her shoulders and cinched the front closed, no modest feat given the smallness of the robe and largeness of her breasts. Technically, her nakedness had been concealed, but the result was even more alluring. Herb grunted in surprised annoyance as he felt another *snick*. Helen just smiled a too-wise smile, pushing open the back door and drawing him outside. The warm night air cleared his head a little, and he glanced around at his surroundings. Behind the strip club was a small patio surrounded by a high privacy fence and lit by a single bulb, moths circling the light like tiny versions of the men inside circling the stage. A small picnic table listed to the side, topped with an overflowing ashtray and surrounded by a smattering of mismatched lawn chairs. One of the chairs was occupied by a fiery redhead wearing a black version of Helen's red robe. Long fingers held a cigarette to her lips, cherry glowing.

"New flavor of the week, huh Helen?" she asked with a devilish grin. "Looks yummy."

Helen's sultry smile turned predatory. "Oh hi, Candy. Why yes, I do have a new flavor, but it isn't him. I'm craving something a little sweeter."

Stiletto heels clicked and satin swished as Helen closed the distance to the other girl. Before Herb could register what was happening, the stripper-turned-vampire pounced. Candy spasmed and squealed in shock as fangs pierced deep into her neck. Helen climbed on top, a gruesome parody of the countless lap dances happening inside. As she drank more deeply, Candy ceased her struggles and went limp in the resin chair.

Herb stood frozen in shock, unable to process the scene unfolding before him. After a minute or two, Helen arched her back, robe parting to expose a heavy breast. A thin rivulet of blood was working its way down her chin and neck to her cleavage.

"Holy crap, that's good. So, so good. Herb, you gotta try some," she offered with a bloody smile.

Herb felt stretched to breaking. The whispers roared, his nostrils flared with the scent of fresh blood, and his pulse pounded with desire. He took a tentative step forward before the panic and fear he thought he'd escaped earlier swooped in like a murder of crows, wheeling and clawing around his head.

This isn't right, some small part of him cried. He'd taken hours to plan his hunt and never meant to hurt anyone. For Helen to just attack like that, to just pounce like some wild beast, it just wasn't okay. Was it?

Trembling, he reversed course and stepped back and back again until he thudded against the wall of the strip club. Hands clenching and unclenching, arms trembling, fangs aching, he managed to shake his head from side to side.

Helen leaned in close to Candy, turned the listless girl's face toward him. Her hand slid down Candy's cheek, slid inside her robe, stroked and caressed. Candy moaned softly and closed her eyes. Helen's hand continued to explore while her glowing eyes devoured Herb.

"You sure?" she purred. When Herb remained frozen against the wall, she shrugged. "Suit yourself. Just remember when you grab someone that I offered to share." With a playful wink, she slid back on top of Candy, pressed full lips to the side of her neck, and continued to drink.

It might've been a minute. It could've been an hour. Herb had lost all sense of time as he watched Helen feed. Finally, she pulled back with a long, satisfied sigh. Climbing off the semi-conscious Candy, she stretched her arms above her head and gave a most unladylike burp.

"Oh, that was good. You really should've had some."

Herb's thoughts started to finally coalesce into some semblance of order. Candy was still alive, her chest rising and falling slightly while her eyes roamed aimlessly from Helen to Herb to the moths circling the light bulb over the door.

"She's still. I mean, you gotta. You're gonna whammy her now, right?" Herb asked hopefully, voice cracking.

Helen gathered up a fistful of Candy's red tresses, pulled the girl limply to her feet, and dangled her above the patio for a moment before giving her head a violent shake. The snap of a spine, a sound he'd hoped to never hear again, rapped sharply against his ears.

"What's a whammy?" Helen asked, genuine confusion on her face. As she released the girl's hair, the now lifeless body fell in a tangle to the patio floor. "Be a dear and clean that up. I put the other ones in the dumpster out back. There should still be room." Helen wiped her lips and licked her fingers. "Okay, sweetie, I'm gonna duck inside and get a little color, then we can get outta here. I'll just be a minute."

Sauntering past Herb, she swung open the door to the club, sliding her robe off as she walked inside, giving Herb a parting glimpse of her shapely behind before the door shut completely.

Panic finally thawed his frozen muscles. Not knowing what else to do, Herb crossed to the body on the ground and rolled the dead girl onto her back. Gently, he closed the front of her robe and pushed bright red strands of hair back from her face. Candy looked almost serene, as if the violence of the past few minutes had never happened, and she was simply sleeping peacefully. Choking back a sob, Herb lifted her easily. Even without his vamped up strength, she hardly weighed a thing. Red tears welled up as he shouldered open the door in the privacy fence and spotted the open top dumpster squatting in the shadows. Walking toward it, his keen nose made sense of Helen's earlier comment. Reaching the dumpster, he looked inside and saw two twenty-something guys sprawled across bags of empty bottles and trash. One's shirt had been ripped in half, his chest scored with deep red welts. The other's UW Badgers hoodie was soaked in what Herb already knew was blood. Both necks were bloody ruins.

Anger and fear burned away his shock. His plan of having a quick snack, just a little sip without anyone getting hurt, had devolved into a stack of four dead bodies. By the time he'd settled Candy on top of the college boys and covered them as much as possible with bags of trash, Herb was weeping openly and trembling with rage. He needed to talk to Helen, set her straight, and it had to happen *right now.*

Herb moved purposefully back through the patio gate, only to stop in his tracks as another stripper turned to look past her cigarette at him.

"Hey jackass, go in the front and pay the cover like everybody else, or I'll have your ass tossed out like yesterday's news," the brunette snipped, fixing him with a nasty glare.

Herb recognized the girl that had accosted them inside and quickly scrubbed at the bloody tear tracks on his cheeks. "Oh, it's okay. I'm, um. Here with Helen."

The brunette squinted suspiciously before huffing in reply. "Geezuz. How many guys is she gonna go through tonight?"

Herb swallowed loudly, eyes widening. "I just. Um. I guess I have no idea what you're. Um. Helen and I need to get outta here. Like, now. Did you see her?"

The brunette laughed a smoky laugh. "Put it back in your pants, tiger. She was just stepping in for some color. I'm sure she'll satisfy your every desire," she added with a sneer, "in just a few. So simmer down, hot stuff."

Herb moved for the door, but the brunette stepped in front of him. "Seriously, horn ball. You can wait here for that tramp, but if you wanna get inside, you go in the front, or I have the bouncers beat you bloody.

Not wanting to make things worse than they already were, Herb stepped back and stuffed his hands in his pockets.

The silence stretched as the brunette smoked and Herb fidgeted. "Um. Nice night, huh," he finally offered, unable to bear the silence any more.

"Yup," she replied around a puff of smoke.

"So, uh. You worked here for a while?" he asked politely.

"Umm hmm."

"Oh. That's cool. Really cool. So, um. What's color?" Herb asked.

The brunette frowned. "Huh?"

"Helen was going to get a little color. Before we. Ah. Leave." Herb blushed, suddenly wondering just what he was getting himself into. "I just, ah. Didn't. Don't know. I mean. What's color?"

The brunette smiled, looking at him like he might be a little daft. "Well, you're not one of her sharpest catches, that's a fact." She crushed out her cigarette. "The tanning booth. She doesn't want those stage lights reflecting off a big pale ass. Blinded patrons don't tip as well."

"Oooh, got it," Herb responded. "Color. Sure. I knew that. I mean. Um. Makes total sense."

The stripper shrugged, the silk of her robe sliding up and down slightly with the motion. She fished another cigarette out of a pack and lit up.

Herb tried to relax, but it was tough knowing there were three dead bodies on the other side of the fence. He was also still trying to figure out just what the hell had happened to Helen. She'd obviously been infected or whatever by him. But how? Then it hit him. He looked down at the unblemished skin of his palm, and remembered quite clearly when he'd cut it, remembered Helen licking it, the hungry look in her eyes. She was obviously pretty far gone at that moment, but Herb had no idea she'd get all vampy. Thinking back on the movies he'd watched, he cursed himself as an idiot. Her drinking his blood was exactly how it was done.

Too weird, he thought for the umpteenth time.

Getting vamped by bug bite hadn't really been covered in any of his research, and neither had turning the local waitress/stripper into a vamp while making out in the cooler at a bar. Herb was totally new to this whole vampire thing and felt like he was making quite a mess.

Like Helen, his thoughts reminded him, bringing his worries full circle to the present again. They really needed to go. He wanted to be long gone before someone decided to take out another bag of trash.

A frown darkened Herb's gaze. Something bothered him. He patted his pockets self-consciously, checking to make sure he had his car keys. Keys accounted for, he tried to surreptitiously check his fly to make sure his jeans were zipped. He shifted from foot to foot, wondering if maybe he had left the stove on at home.

I haven't cooked a meal all week, he reminded himself, but he definitely had that I-just-remembered-I-forgot-something feeling.

The lightbulb above the door flashed and flickered like a bug light zapping a moth. Something in Herb's chest pulled taut, snapped violently, and a wave of nausea wracked him. A moment later, Herb's keen ears heard muffled voices and a knocking from inside. Hinges creaked, and there was a sudden, piercing scream. While Herb sat stunned, the brunette reacted. Tossing her half-smoked cigarette to the ground, she ran to the door and pulled it wide. Another dancer stood a short distance inside, facing a smaller door Herb hadn't noticed before, set into the wall just past the vanity mirrors. From his perspective, it looked like it might've been the entrance to a small bathroom or closet. The girl's hands were pressed tight to her mouth and her eyes were wide in terror, her bare chest tinged blue by a strange glow emanating from the room. As Herb looked in puzzlement at the scene, the fluid in his eyeballs started to boil. Gasping in pained shock, he twisted his face to the side while he brought an arm up to shield his eyes. Half-blind and acting on sudden instinct, he leapt up and ran through the door in the privacy fence into the dark lot beyond. Jumping into his car, he revved the engine and pointed his Pinto toward home, shaking hands gripping the wheel.

A little color. She had just wanted a little color, he lamented. *Oh, Helen.*

Chapter 25

IT WASN'T JUST BOWLING night. It was finals night, and Herb was as nervous as a one-armed kid at a paddy-cake contest. Almost two weeks had passed since he'd hung out with Dallas and Stanley, and the past one had been tough. They were supposed to roll last weekend, to stay in what Dallas called 'prime rolling form,' but Herb had begged off, pleading with Dallas over the phone that he still wasn't feeling great and really needed to rest. Herb's excuse was certainly genuine. He just hoped that Dallas and Stanley never learned the details. His visit to see Helen had really messed him up. There was no way he was going to try and bowl with the guys like nothing had gone down. Despite the thermometer stubbornly insisting he was a cool seventy-three degrees, he had felt feverish for days afterward, complete with aches, pains, and nausea like roofing tar boiling deep in his gut.

A suffocating malaise had smothered him like a moldy blanket wrapped with cords of deep paranoia. Every sound, no matter the source, was the police coming for him. Fever-dreams played out the scenes in stark detail. There'd be an investigation. Questions about the collection of twigs, jerky, and cracked leather that used to be Helen curled up inside the tanning booth at Nekked's. They'd find the brunette and ask about Helen's acquaintances. Was she seeing anyone? Did she have any visitors? That brunette, she'd stand there smoking her cigarettes, describing between shaky puffs the awkward man who'd suddenly disappeared into the night. It'd take her a few minutes, the horror of the memory making it hard to concentrate. Then it would come to her in a flash. "Herb," she'd say with conviction. "His name was Herb." Minutes later, they'd find three more bodies in the dumpster, while at the same time some kids would stumble upon a fourth body stuffed under a log in the woods. Then there'd be a meeting, the Trappersville cops gearing up like the Frog Brothers. Stakes and crosses, holy water squirt guns, you name it. Faint sirens would reach his sensitive ears from miles away, growing to a skull-splitting screech as they circled his home. Then the blowtorch. Yes, of course they'd have a blowtorch. And a megaphone. *Come out, you demon, you hell-spawn! Get out here and maybe we'll let you live!* But of course they wouldn't let him live. Not Herb. Then the fire, great gushing geysers of flame. It would be so hot, so damn hot, like Herb was burning from the inside out...

His vivid fantasies had left Herb cowering in his home the remainder of the weekend, vacillating through periods of deep, guilt-wracked depression, manic turns where he'd plot his escape from town and try to work out the details of creating a new life in Nova Scotia, and long stretches during which he just felt too sick to care about anything at all. In his fever dreams, Herb figured his death was a foregone conclusion. It was really just a question of how. Angry mob, fever, or worse?

Time, however, really does heal all wounds. By Sunday afternoon, the aches and pains had become an ache or a pain, then just an ache, then nothing. As the sun headed for the horizon that evening, his temperature was checking in at a much more pleasant seventy-three degrees instead of a fever-wracked seventy-three degrees. He made it to work Sunday night because the only thing that scared him more than the cops was Ronnie firing him again. The Pinto had bounced and jarred over rutted dirt roads that were little more than deer runs through the woods as Herb drove ten miles out of his way to make sure he didn't risk passing any overly curious cops. He'd stayed in the kitchen the entire shift, eyes downcast, avoiding the serve-through window as much as possible. If Dee had thought his behavior strange, she didn't comment, and Herb was too preoccupied to notice that Dee didn't complain about a single order, send a single item back, or scold him for not reading the ticket.

Tuesday was much the same. He took the most round-about way to work, hid in the kitchen, convinced that the next second, the very next second, the authorities would arrive to deliver his comeuppance. But by Wednesday, the cops hadn't burned down his house, the FBI hadn't sent in professional vampire hunters from helicopters, and the Air Force hadn't dropped a tactical nuke on an evacuated and condemned town formerly known as Trappersville. Heading into work Wednesday night, Herb felt the tight coils of fear slowly loosen a bit, and he took his first deep breath in days. Feeling bold, he drove the regular route to work and parked in his usual spot instead of hiding his car behind the dumpster. He'd even managed to shave and comb his hair. While still challenging tasks to manage without a reflection, exploratory patting of his face and head reassured him he'd most likely done a passable job.

Walking into Ronnie's through the back entrance, Herb almost collided with Lois as she stepped outside.

"Oh my gosh! Lois. Hi. Um, sorry," Herb apologized, quickly stepping to the side, realizing that they had almost touched. *Almost,* he thought, warmth spreading in his belly.

"Hey Herb. How are ya?" she asked distractedly as she fished in her purse for a lighter.

Good, he responded easily. Or meant to, except there was no sound. Well, he realized belatedly, there was a sound. A sort-of wheezy release of air through a constricted throat, barely audible over the chorus of crickets chirruping industriously for an inattentive audience. A mouse farting might've made a similar noise, but of course Herb couldn't be sure since he'd never heard mice fart. His mouth might have worked in a vain attempt to give some semblance of shape to the reedy squeak, but honestly, Herb wasn't entirely sure if his face had moved or not. All he knew for certain was that Lois had talked to him, the mouse in his throat farted in return, and she thankfully didn't appear to have noticed. Stepping past Herb, she lit her cigarette and stood staring into the night, oblivious to his inability to move or breathe just a few feet away. Swallowing hard, he finally convinced his lungs to reengage. Bright little flecks of light hovered around the corners of his vision until the night air started to clear his head.

As he tried to remember what he was going to say before his voice left him high and dry, Lois looked back at him.

"Hey, you and Dallas are friends, right?"

Herb felt his head nod up and down of its own accord.

"Is he like, I mean. What's he like?" she asked.

Herb frowned. "Dallas? He's um, well," he trailed off, a stream of images flashing across his mind's eye. "Well, he's Dallas. You know, Big D."

"Hmmm. Okay." She finished her cigarette and studied the night sky through exhaled clouds of smoke.

Herb turned and entered the kitchen, too many thoughts moving through his head at once to allow any particular one much consideration.

They didn't exchange many words after that, outside of her sending through orders and offering the occasional, "Thanks," or, "Huh. That actually looks pretty good, Herb," as she picked up food from the serve-through. A hundred times and more, he almost asked why she wanted to know about Dallas, and a hundred times and more, he choked back the words just as they soured the tip of his tongue and backs of his teeth.

Dallas, he muttered to the dark cloud hanging over his head. *Why was it always Dallas?*

Later, as he finished packing his bowling bag, the dark thoughts still clouded his mind. He and Dallas had been pals for so long, years and years, because their relationship functioned on well-established rules. Herb was Herb, but Dallas was *Dallas.* He was the ringleader, the alpha-dog, the undisputed king, but ever since that night of shooting pool and hustling the Vikings fans, Herb found himself wondering about his natural role in the order of things. He was stronger now, faster. He even kind of knew some Kung Fu, or rather, some instinctive vampirey equivalent that was close enough to count in his book. He could see in the dark and hear the creak of a tendon before a finger pulled the tab on a can of Milwaukee's Best from across a crowded bar. He could put the whammy on people and make them think just about whatever he wanted, and if you cut him, he *healed.* And not just healed healed. He healed like, really, really fast. He even got busy with a stripper that had shot down Dallas.

Before she turned herself into jerky, he reminded himself with a guilty twinge, but the truth of things stubbornly lodged itself in that space where his self-confidence would've resided if he'd had some.

Before last week, Herb would've believed that snowmen would live to retirement age and take up pinochle in Hell before he'd get the sexy stripper instead of Dallas. And that, ultimately, was the issue. In all their years of friendship, Herb had never gotten something instead of Big D. Now, when that was finally starting to change, Lois asks him about none other than Dallas.

As he pulled tickets, pushed an assortment of dead animals around the flat top grill, and pulled fries from the fryer, Herb started to imagine a different world. A world without his best friend. A world without Dallas.

Chapter 26

AS THE SUN WANED on the horizon and shadows moved implacably across the trees, Herb continued getting ready for the big night. Excitement danced a mad jig with his apprehension, the two spinning around and making him burp repeatedly. The Men's Adult League Final Championship was *the* spectator sport in Trappersville. The league was sanctioned and everything, and the winning team walked away with a sweet trophy, a nice cash prize, and their names on the Roll-Masters Hall of Fame board behind the shoe rental counter.

Herb, Dallas, and Stanley had been rolling in the league for years and had only made the finals back in 2003. They'd bowled a hell of a season. It had been down to the wire between them and Fancy Dan's team for a spot in the championships. The weekend before the final night of regular season bowling, when the King Pins were set to square off against Fancy Dan and his compadres, Dan twisted an ankle and broke his wrist at a Prince concert in Milwaukee. Refusing to let a sub take all the glory, Dan had pulled his team out, a move that sent shockwaves through the men's league. Stanley had called their stroke of luck a silver lining. Dallas called it a custom-made miracle and ordered special bowling jerseys for the three of them. Green and gold, each shirt had sharp lapels and shiny buttons, and a cartoon rendition of Dallas's truck Deloris smashing through a bunch of bowling pins. They looked so good that Dallas ordered a fourth and had the guys all sign it. His plan was to frame it and sell it on eBay after they won the championship.

Sadly, Dallas never got a chance to eBay that jersey. They got shut down pretty quick. Dallas had bowled well, he always did, but Stanley and Herb pretty much sucked from the start. Stanley complained that it was the restrictive nature of the jersey and said it didn't lie properly across his shoulders. Had it been one-hundred percent cotton, it might've performed better, but cotton-poly blends didn't have the same elasticity as good old cotton, according to Stanley. Herb was more direct in his search for a scapegoat, blaming his performance on the ridiculous amount of beer they'd consumed the night before, the day of, and during their first game. Dallas took the loss pretty hard and didn't come round much for a week or so after that night.

What Dallas had dubbed The Letdown was buzzing at the front of Herb's brain as he readied himself for the big night. His favorite jeans slid up his legs, and comfortable socks stretched over his feet. A clean undershirt slipped over his head and down his torso like a second skin, and then it was time. With a nervous sigh, Herb prepared to put on his new, one-hundred percent cotton bowling jersey.

Like back in '03, Dallas had ordered them special for the big tourney, and they were top-of-the-line. Custom made by a specialty tee-shirt shop in Oconomowoc, they were black with dark red trim on the lapels, red piping on the sleeves, and matching, blood red buttons. Nice, sure, but it wasn't the piping or buttons that made them magical. The trio had sent a photo with their order form. Dallas then called the shop to provide further art direction while Herb and

Stanley offered helpful suggestions over his shoulder. The resulting airbrushed caricature of the trio on the back of the jersey was more than they could've ever hoped for.

Herb opened the plastic bag containing his jersey and drew the smooth fabric out with the care and attention paleontologists reserve for the most precious of fossils. He sighed, stunned by the beauty of the airbrushed artistry on the black fabric. As the team captain, Dallas was in the center, with Herb to one side and Stanley to the other. Rather than typical caricatures accentuating flaws in comic fashion, the airbrush artist had latched onto their best features and brought them out in sophisticated detail. Dallas's strong chin and sharp jaw looked stronger and sharper, his head tilted slightly forward over a broad chest. Herb's stubble-clad cheeks looked rugged rather than frumpy, and his rebellious hair, captured perfectly by the artist, conveyed *edgy and hip* instead of *disheveled hedgehog*. Even Stanley looked tough. Their expressions were serious, focused, committed. Arced above them in pearly white, the words 'King and the Pins' virtually glowed with divine radiance. Each of them held a bowling ball in front of their chest, each ball depicting a word from the phrase 'You're. Going. Down.' It was a professional jersey, a powerful jersey, a winning jersey.

Herb slid his arms into the sleeves and buttoned the front. He rolled his shoulders, grunting in satisfaction and smiling a wicked smile when he felt the fabric slide and heard it whisper *awesome*.

The pillow he'd worn to replace his former paunch sat questioningly on the bed. Herb picked it up and patted his stomach as he considered his options. Not wearing it meant they were definitely going to notice he'd lost some weight, but he didn't want to bowl with a pillow under his shirt. Quickly reaching a decision, he decided to face the world as skinny-Herb and tossed the pillow back onto the bed. It struck the ragged blankets at the same moment that the sun dipped below the horizon. Finally free to leave his home and clad in his bowling finery, Herb strode to the Pinto, fired up its four manly cylinders, and set out to make history.

Chapter 27

B AY CITY BOWLERS WAS packed. Herb checked in with Slow Johnson for his lane assignment and hurried to join his teammates. Dallas and Stanley were already laced up—or Velcro'd up in Stanley's case—when Herb walked over and deposited his bowling bag.

"Hey, guys. How's it going?" he greeted them with a nervous grin.

"How's it going? How's it going? I'll tell ya how it's going!" Dallas yelled before jumping up and jigging around in circles.

His enthusiasm was infectious. Soon, Herb and Stanley were clapping in time to his ridiculous jig. Heels kicking higher, arms waving, and fingers snapping like a backwoods flamenco dancer, Dallas chanted in a sing-song voice, "King Pins! King Pins! How we gonna roll?"

Still clapping, Herb and Stanley hollered in unison, "Like kings! Like kings! *That's* how we roll!"

The three gave a whoop, instantly dispelling the tension Herb had been feeling all evening. Finishing their customary pre-game chant with a flourish, Dallas gave a hoot and smacked Herb on the back. Old Herb would've been knocked off balance by the affectionate whack, but new Herb barely swayed. Instead, he returned the gesture, thumping Dallas on the back and giving a hoot of his own. Dallas went reeling, tripping over himself and landing in a pile near the molded plastic seats facing the lane.

"Holy shitballs, Herb! Guess I've had a few more than I thought. That, or you've been working out."

"Yuh-you do look good, Herb," added Stanley. "Buh-buh-Billy Blanks Tae Bo? I got them DVDs too, but I nuh-never really used 'em none."

Herb latched onto Stanley's suggestion faster than a drowning man catching a life preserver. "Oh, yeah! Um. Billy Blanks. Saw the infomercial. Awesome workout. And the. Um. Atkins diet. You know. High protein, and uh," inspiration struck, "no beer." He laughed self-consciously as he turned profile and patted his slimmed-down midsection. "Works wonders. But that means I'll be staying sober for this one."

Dallas had picked himself up and threw an arm around each of the guys. "Thank Elvis. Last time we was here, you drunken monkeys made a mockery of the sport. Now, I'm not going to bring up The Letdown or make anyone feel bad or ratchet up the pressure. No, I love you guys too much to do something shitty like that. I'm just saying, keep your game faces on, and stay frosty. Herb, you not drinking beer gonna mess with your game?" He flexed his bicep and pulled Herb's face closer to his own, staring intently.

"Um. No? No sir. My game is good. Great. Um, super great!" Herb stood a little straighter and found that he and Dallas were actually of a height. Maybe he'd always known that, but he usually felt short next to Dallas. "Big D, you got nothing to worry about here. We're going to rock this night Billy Ocean style."

Dallas beamed. "I have no idea what the hell that means, but it sounds good. Stanley, you and me are drinking for three. But I swear on my old scout instructor's necktie, if you get drunk and roll like you did in The Letdown, they're gonna find your body at the bottom of Green Bay. Now, go get some beers."

Dallas clapped Stanley's back and sent him scurrying for the bar while Herb settled into the rhythms of the bowling alley. It had only been a couple of weeks, but everything felt so different. The noise of the crowd was a layered tapestry. Cocking his head from side to side, he could identify voices, actually hear individual words from people in the farthest corners. As he concentrated on the myriad of voices, he realized a startling similarity to the whispers he'd been hearing. It was like he could faintly hear the conversations of the entire world, voices from the present and ghosts from the past, all adding their voices to the collective. Breathing deep, he opened himself up to the surrounding night. The smells of wood oil and shoe disinfectant, sweat and smoke, beer and fried grease wrapped around him and through him, at once slightly nauseating and softly comforting. It was a feeling of belonging, of being in his element, his natural habitat. Always the outsider, Herb suddenly felt at home.

Turning his head, Herb took in the crowd. There was Fancy Dan and his teammates, Dylan and Two-Shirt Bert. A large and sweaty man, Bert usually had to change shirts about halfway through an average game. Looking beyond that trio, Herb saw Moe, Gerry, Wyatt, Joe, Ted One and Ted Two, Rick, Alan, Dozer, Tiny Tony, Jimmy, Steve-O, and a host of other regulars from Trappersville. Wives and girlfriends mingled with the menfolk while cagey-looking cougars prowled the edges. All those faces that he'd seen over the years. How many of them had eaten the food he prepared at Ronnie's and never looked twice at him? How many had passed him at the Get'n'Gobble, a quick meeting of eyes sparking an awkward, "Oh, hey. Yeah, you're uh... Um. Well. Good to see you," before hurrying down the aisle? How many of them bullied him in junior high, or passed him on the right at four-way stops? And even in a town as small as Trappersville, how many remembered his name? But tonight, none of that mattered. That was the former Herbert Knudsen. Little did they know that the Herb sitting in their midst was something else entirely. Settling comfortably into the lime green molded plastic chair, Herb breathed in again, pulling all the threads of the night deep into his lungs, and exhaled slowly. Tonight, he was going to introduce Trappersville to the new and improved Herbert Knudsen.

They're going to know me, he thought. Unbidden, a darker thought followed. *Even if it kills them. Every last one of them.*

Chapter 28

S TANLEY HAD RETURNED WITH the beers while Herb and Dallas were taking a few warm-up rolls. They were slotted to start their first match in twenty minutes, and Dallas was immersed in his 'lube and limber' routine. According to him, you had to prime the engine by slamming the first beer and rolling five balls exactly fifteen minutes before the first game. Not four, not six. Four wouldn't warm you up nearly enough, and six ran the risk of tweaking your back or chaffing a thumb before the game officially began. Once the game commenced, the perfect ratio was half a can of Milwaukee's Best every three frames, or two beers a game since you'd slam the second half of beer number two before rolling the third ball of the tenth frame.

Despite also being a firm believer in lubing and limbering, Stanley was still terrified of Dallas's warning about The Letdown of '03. Instead of slamming it, he was nervously nursing his beer. Watching them drink was making Herb thirsty. He'd made it a point to grab a quick snack before heading over. Not wanting to draw any attention or get involved in a complicated game of stalk, suck and whammy, his new favorite pastime, Herb had settled for a rabbit. While animal blood could quench his thirst and perk him up a little, it was gross and nothing compared to the real deal. The more he dwelled on it, the more he realized he had probably made a big mistake. Tonight was the finals, the winner of which would take home all the glory. Herb couldn't roll his best after a mere bunny. No, he needed some real blood.

The vampire-disguised-as-a-bowler scanned the crowd, looking for someone he could single out of the herd. Everyone was clumped into twos and threes, no stragglers to be seen. Deciding he would be more successful on the move, he gave the guys a quick wave.

"Gonna swing by the bar and hit the little boy's room. Put me third on the rotation and I'll be back in a minute."

"Whatever, douchebag. But if you're late for the match, I'll tie you to the front of Deloris and drive through a cow field," Dallas responded with a smile.

Stanley just took another timid sip of his beer and gave a friendly thumbs up.

Cover story firmly in place, Herb made his way toward the bar. Heads turned to follow his movement, unknowing sunflowers tracking the brightest object in the room, before returning to their conversations. No more did he have to be content with tapping shoulders, politely excusing himself, zigging and zagging through a resisting crowd of unawares and unconcerneds. Bodies moved out of his way, subconsciously shifted by his presence, and then pulled back into his wake as Herb subtly parted the crowd like Moses practicing on a local pond before the big show. He couldn't help but smile as he reached the bar's saloon-style doors and stepped through.

Chapter 29

RHONDA WAS WORKING FURIOUSLY while the bar back struggled to keep a steady supply of mostly-clean glassware on the ledge and fresh ice in the bins. People were lined up at the bar two and three-deep waiting to order. Herb calmly walked up behind a younger couple, and placed a hand on each of their shoulders. Both turned their heads and were caught in Herb's dark gaze. They shifted, allowing Herb to slide in between them and belly-up to the bar. Rhonda flew past him once, twice without even looking up as she grabbed cheap beers, poured cheap whiskey, and faked a variety of fancier drinks. Knowing his time was short, Herb quietly said her name.

"Rhonda."

Sound receded and time slowed to a molasses-crawl as the bartender looked up midway through scooping ice into a rocks glass. Her eyes met Herb's, widened slightly, and then her face went lax.

"Oh. Hi, Herb. Nice to see you. What would you like?" she asked in a pleasant, slightly vacant monotone.

"Hello, Rhonda. You look lovely tonight." Herb thought for a brief moment. He could order a beer and not drink it, but try to keep up appearances with the guys. Or he could try something different.

Something... new. "Could I trouble you for a Bloody Mary, please? Oh, and no ice." Herb smiled, his eyes fixed on hers.

"Of course, Herb." Rhonda's eyes stayed melded to his, waiting for his approval to look away. Still smiling, Herb nodded and glanced to the side. Awareness snapped back into Rhonda's eyes, and her smile widened, became genuine. "Herbert! Holy hell, you guys made the finals. Let me get that drink for you. On the house, buddy. On the house."

As Rhonda whipped up the bowling alley equivalent of a Bloody Mary, topped off with a strip of day-old bacon and a pickle spear, Herb's eyes moved around the bar.

There. Her.

His eyes settled on a youngish woman he didn't recognize standing by herself on the far side of the bar. Brown hair feathered back, puffy bangs, a slight pout. She glanced at her watch and looked around the bar. She pulled out a flip-phone, closed it, returned it to her purse, and looked around the bar again. Perfect. He didn't recognize her as a local, which meant she was probably in from some nearby town to watch the finals. Whoever she was supposed to meet was obviously a no-show, and she was alone. Just perfect.

As the young brunette looked around the bar again, her eyes met Herb's. Like a hare in a snare, Herb felt her heart rate jump before Herb's whammy wrapped her up like a wool blanket. Still looking deep into her eyes, he accepted the Bloody Mary from Rhonda, oblivious to her words, and worked his way around the bar. Arriving on the far side, he took the girl's hand and drew her toward a dark corner in the back. Sure that his hold on her was solid, he risked breaking eye contact to quickly scan the crowded room. No one was paying them any attention, as most people were either thoroughly engrossed in their current drink or focused on getting their next one. Turning back to the brunette, Herb tilted his head toward a utility closet door. She reached out and turned the handle. Still holding her with one hand and carrying his drink in the other, Herb drew her quickly into the closet and closed the door behind them.

The darkness was absolute, but Herb could see easily and kept his gaze fixed on her now sightless eyes. He could feel the butterfly wings of her pulse as her deep, subconscious panic warred against his enforced calm. He slowed his breathing, and hers slowed in time, synching with his. He drew her arm up, felt his fangs snick into place, and gently bit down on the inside of her bare wrist. The girl moaned softly as Herb began to gently suck on the wound he'd inflicted. Each drop was electric, burning his throat and chest as the girl's life became his own. Still focusing on her eyes, he moved his drink up under her wrist and pulled his head back. Blood ran in thin rivulets down her wrist and dripped into his drink. Squeezing her wrist caused more blood to well out, but the girl gasped in pain. Holding her wrist more gently, Herb pressed his bloody lips to hers. Instantly, her body sagged as her knees went weak. She leaned in toward him, pushing herself into the kiss. Herb massaged her wrist again. This time, the girl didn't react at all, she was so completely absorbed in Herb's kiss. After a few more moments, Herb disengaged and drew back, her mouth searching in the dark for his. He bit his lip and brought her wrist back to his mouth, kissing it gently and rubbing his lips across her skin. The puncture wounds closed as Herb licked the remaining blood away. He lowered her arm and took an experimental sip of his drink. The vodka burned, and the V-8 and Worcestershire tasted... like blood. Like yummy, spicy blood. Another sip and his stomach held its ground.

Aaahhh, that's nice, he thought.

"What's your name?" he softly asked, returning his attention to the girl.

"Mary," she sighed, voice heavy with longing.

Okay. That's funny, thought Herb with a sardonic grin.

"Nice to meet you, Mary. You were waiting for someone, weren't you?"

"You," she sighed in reply, leaning toward him.

"Oh, um. No, not me. Your friend. You were supposed to meet a friend here, right?"

"Friend," she agreed.

"Okay. So, you wanted to call your friend, but the bar was too noisy. So you came into this closet by yourself to make a phone call. You'll try to call your friend two times and then come back into the bar. You will have no memory of me. Do you understand?"

"Yes," she whispered in a forlorn voice.

"Okay, Mary. Um. Thanks for the drink. Now, take out your phone and dial your friend..."

The illuminated keypad of her phone was like a small sun in the pitch-black closet. As her attention turned toward the phone, Herb reached behind him to grasp the doorknob and slowly open the door. Backing out of the closet, his rear end ran right into Rhonda's son Jasper, causing his Cosmopolitan to slosh.

"Ope! Sorry about that," Herb offered, placing a hand on Jasper's shoulder and looking into his eyes. "You're not mad, are you?" The same eyes that moments before had seduced a complete stranger now bored like shards of black ice into Jasper's.

"Uh. Um. No. I'm not upset. Not at all. Sorry I got in your way. Sir. Ah, Herb. Sir." Jasper's voice quavered as he cowered.

"No harm, no foul," Herb offered magnanimously as he slid back through the crowded bar. "I was just getting a drink."

Chapter 30

Herb rejoined Dallas and Stanley a few minutes before their first game was scheduled to start. Dallas pulled them in close for a huddle and glared at the opposing team. The Finkley twins, Ted One and Ted Two, and their third Roy, glared back from their side of the ball return. The twins weren't both named Ted. Ted One was Theodore, and Ted Two was Edward, but that barely lasted past grade school. Both preferred Ted, and since Theodore was born 6 minutes earlier, he got to be number one.

Sometimes things just work out, Herb thought with a smile before Dallas brought him back to the moment.

"Bring it in, guys. Bring it in. Now, this is normally where the coach would make a long and impassioned speech about the Davids and the Goliaths and the underdogs and Rudy's and whatnot, but I ain't your coach. Tonight, I ain't even your friend. Tonight, I'm the guy that's gonna kick your ass around the block with steel-toed boots if we lose. You got me?"

Herb and Stanley's heads bobbed in unison.

"I said, 'You got me?'" Dallas repeated more loudly.

"You betcha!" Stanley burst out at the same time Herb whooped, "Hell yeah!"

The three broke their huddle and turned to Roy and the Finkley's, Dallas wearing a hunter's smile, Stanley fist-pumping the air, and Herb clapping Stanley on the shoulder. The two teams shook hands, exchanged empty pleasantries, and quickly got down to business.

Since Herb had Dallas finagle a later slot, the first four teams had already bowled and the bracket board was slimming down. Fancy Dan's team had moved past round one and was about to start their second game. Out of the twenty-four teams in the bowling league, only eight were in the finals, so it was going to be a fast and furious evening. Each match-up rolled one game, and the winner advanced to the next round. After three rounds, the final two teams would compete in a winner-take-all smack down. There was no room for error. No make-ups or take-backs. Herb fought to quell the butterflies in his stomach with another sip of his Mary Bloody Mary and readied himself for the game.

Ted One stepped up and rolled a strike. Dallas took the next roll. Strike. Roy grabbed his fourteen-pounder and clipped seven, picking up the spare on the next roll. Stanley rolled a six and a gutter, causing the vein in Dallas's forehead to swell and his neck to turn red. Ted Two nonchalantly rolled an eight-spare, nodding in cool acceptance of his teammates' praise. The moment had finally arrived. It was Herb's turn to roll.

Taking a long swig from his grisly concoction, Herb rose from the molded plastic seat facing the lane. He felt each woven fiber of his undershirt slide a fraction of an inch across the skin of his shoulders, heard the soft hiss as the bowling jersey realigned itself across his back, catching and sliding on the tee-shirt beneath. Herb felt the muscles and tendons in his ankles and knees stretch and pull as he glided over pine planks scoured smooth as glass by decades of leather-soled shoes. His pupils made minute adjustments, dilating and contracting as his eyes scanned the lane, reacting to the varied quality of fluorescent and neon lights reflecting off of well-oiled maple boards in the heads. Further down, the triangles delineated the heads from the mid-lane like a line of stealth bombers waiting to guide his projectile to its intended target. And there, at the end, the pins waited in the pin deck. When Herb softly inhaled through his nose, he swore he could smell their fear mingled with the scent of oil, maple and pine. Moving to the ball return, he floated his palm over the vent blowing a gentle, continuous stream of cool air. The sensation—like electricity coursing through his nerves to his shoulders and down his spine—was almost more than he could bear. He could hear the quiet whoosh change in tone and tenor as he rocked his palm first to, then fro. With some effort, Herb refocused his attention and continued his advance. Fingers slid across the slightly marred surface of his bowling ball, each tiny scratch and divot a moment with its own unique story that he could almost recall. Again, he found himself dwelling in the mystery of sensation as each fingertip sought more understanding from the polished surface. Finally, his fingers and thumb settled into the holes. Muscles contracted, and the ball became a natural extension of Herb's hand, wrist, arm. Like Steve Austin or Luke Skywalker, Herb and the bowling ball were a perfect union of man and the man-made.

Mary's blood still singing in his ears like an aria, Herb glided forward, arm swinging back and forward like the pendulum of the clock at the center of the universe. As leather soles slid across smoothly oiled pine, a slight relaxing of the muscles in his fingers gave physics permission to reenter the equation. Circular velocity became linear velocity, mass held in sway suddenly cut loose to carve its own path through reality, and the path the ball chose was straight and true. It met the lane with a slight backspin, catching for the slightest moment as it reoriented into a furious roll. About halfway down the mid-lanes, the ball shifted minutely. The forward roll had become a rotation working slightly against the line of travel, as if the ball were only now starting to realize the impending collision and was taking hesitant steps to avoid the impact to come. Destiny had other plans for the unfortunate ball, and it connected solidly with the headpin at the perfect, slightly off-center angle. Molecules collided, springing away from one other in commensurate angles, their violent reaction playing out across millions of other molecules as they reacted to the same event, creating on a much grander scale a scene of deliberate chaos as ten pins flew, spun, ricocheted, slid, and finally came to rest in the pit.

Strike.

"Hell yeah!" whooped Dallas, followed by a pelvic thrust toward Roy and the Teds. "How da'ya'like them apples?"

Stanley grinned, head bobbing like a balloon on a rising breeze while Herb sauntered back to his seat, an enigmatic grin playing across his stubbled cheeks as he reached for his drink.

"Uh oh," he said to no one in particular. "Looks like someone's gotten a little better at bowling."

Chapter 31

IT WAS A DREAM come true. *Champions*. Funny how such a simple word could have such world-changing implications. Dallas wore the title like a familiar coat, but to Herb, it still felt funny. He could remember the evening clearly, but thinking back on the individual moments: Mary in the utility closet, rolling three perfect games, the cat fight, the punch, and now being *the* center of all the revelry... Herb just shook his head in bemusement. Life certainly was different as a vampire and getting better all the time.

The players milled around the bar while Jasper sound-checked the karaoke system, swapping stories of heartbreak and heroics, more than a few recounting Herb's amazing run or rehashing the cat fight or the punch. Such banter after a tourney wasn't unusual. There was griping and back-slapping and high-fives and stink-eyes after every night of bowling, but the championship tourney always upped the ante. Winners got the royal treatment all over town. A free round at Steinknockers, a free milkshake or upgrade from French fries to cheese curds at Ronnie's, a free VHS or DVD (non-new release) rental at Petro Patt's, and so on. It usually took a week or so for the glow of victory to finally fade. That week was always an interesting one, though. Alliances shifted like sands in the Sahara as people watched the champs live large around town, evaluating their current bowling mates and sizing up the other players. And then there was the infidelity. You'd think that in a town like Trappersville, folks would be pretty stable. So-and-so married such-and-such and they had a couple of critters and that was the end of it, but somehow the bowling tourneys always turned up scandal. One such patch of drama had occurred a couple three years ago. Ted Two had celebrated their team's win with Ted One's then-girlfriend of almost two years. The ensuing fist fight was the stuff of legends. The town paramedic still spoke of it on occasion, always with the same awed tone.

In years past, Herb had been the bystander watching everyone else share in the post-championship happenings, looking from the outside in at the people he'd known for years but had never really been close to. Dallas, though, was a fish in water after every bowling tourney and had even made a tradition of leading the Big Toast. Herb couldn't recall when that had started. It just seemed like ever since he, Stan, and Dallas had been rolling in the league, Dallas always led the championship toast. He'd mount a table, a chair, a couple bar stools, or if the crowd was especially unruly, the bar itself, towering over the revelers like the incarnation of old Paul Bunyan. No sir, it wasn't officially the Championship After-Party until Dallas had kicked off the celebration.

Last year's after-party was still fresh in Herb's mind. He, Stan, and Dallas had gotten bumped out early on, but you'd never have known it watching Dallas. You'd think the guy had invented revelry and drinking, so adept was he at revving up the crowd while imbibing enough alcohol to stun a grizzly bear. With a full mug of beer, a lopsided grin, and a wink for the barmaid, he'd let out an ear-splitting whistle and called out in a loud, clear voice.

"Enough, you rascals! Enough! It's time to grab a drink. Yours, the guy next to you's, whoever's! I mean, as long as you got a drink in your hand, right?"

His question was answered with cheers of agreement and a few shoving matches as people grabbed drinks that weren't rightfully theirs to begin with. Once the bedlam had subsided a bit, Dallas plowed ahead.

"To the victors... a toast!"

The crowd had chanted, *Toast! Toast! Toast!* until Dallas quieted them with a gesture.

"Here's to doing and drinking, not sitting and thinking! We admire your skill, envy your strikes, hate your victory, and love your trophy!"

Raucous cheers had followed, along with more drinking and friendly back-slapping. A maestro conducting a symphony, Dallas had let the cheering build to a crescendo and then deftly took control again before the fervor waned.

"And to the losers, you sorry dogs. To strive and toil only to end up drowning your sorrows in your watery beer... No offense, Rhonda. We know you didn't water it down."

"Nah, I just spit in yours, Dal," Rhonda had shot back, spurring more laughter and a few jibes about getting his comeuppance.

Dallas had just smiled his million-dollar smile and pressed on.

"But to the rest of us... Me too, me too, so calm the hell down, ya unruly bastards. Well, here's to trying! A toast to the fallen! While we didn't win the tourney, may we still have a life both long and merry, a death quick and easy, a girl pretty and true, and time for one more brew!"

Like a cannon at the start of a marathon, Dallas's final toast had unleashed a celebration that lasted well past bar close. No one really minded, though. The town sheriff was a better bowler than drinker, and had passed out in the bathroom long ago.

That night from one short year ago, Herb had watched Dallas with envy as he sat off to the side with Stanley. The two men had knocked back their beers in solitude while the crowd celebrated around them. Drunk, a bit depressed, and feeling contemplative, Herb had wondered why someone who was so charismatic and beloved by everyone in town remained his friend, and how the friend of one so charismatic and beloved could still remain such a non-thing in the eyes of everyone else. Sensing his mood, Stanley had raised a mug and offered a commiserating belch before laying his face down on the tabletop and passing out.

This year, this time, things were different. Herb had bowled a three-hundred, his first ever, and one of just a handful of perfect games that had graced the lanes of the Bay City Bowlers over the decades. As if to show it wasn't a fluke, he'd done it two more times. Even if they hadn't won the championship, Herb would've still been an overnight legend. Easily half of the town turned out to watch the bowling championship. Most of the bowlers were accompanied by a mix of family and friends, neither of which Herb had in spades, so he wasn't used to rolling for a crowd. In years past, folks would watch Dallas, cheer him on and buy him drinks. Even Stanley had a few devotees, anxiously hoping to *be there* if he got abducted again.

Herb merely got bits and pieces of spilled-over camaraderie, like a dog catching scraps around the picnic table. But after rolling a couple of back-to-back turkeys, it was like Herb had appeared out of thin air. By the end of the night, he'd become a god.

After the first turkey, people had shrugged and asked one another who that guy was that just rolled a turkey. By his fifth strike, Herb's keen ears heard his name mentioned across the breadth and depth of the lanes. In two's and three's, more people had drifted over to take a peek at 'that guy Herb or something' who'd just rolled five strikes. After yet another turkey, so many people were watching Herb bowl that Stanley had to push through a sea of mullet-draped shoulders to go to the bathroom. By Herb's seventh frame, every strike was followed by loud cheers and applause. Even Roy and the Teds had cheered, despite their rapidly fading odds of winning. When the tenth frame closed out, they'd put up a respectable six sixty-five, but to no avail. Stanley had pulled off a one-eighty and Dallas finished with two-hundred and ten. Herb, though, had been flawless. His perfect game had carried King and the Pins past the first round of the tourney while the crowd chanted his name.

The second round had whipped by in a blur as Herb contin-ued to shock and amaze everyone, including himself. Strike followed strike, the crowd growing larger and more boisterous by the frame. Fancy Dan, Dylan, and sweaty Two-Shirt all bowled well, but they just couldn't keep up. Herb was incapable of not rolling strikes, and the few frames Dallas didn't strike, he spared. Despite their amazing games, Dallas hadn't had much to say. Herb had figured he was just 'in the zone,' and didn't want to risk jinxing things by talking.

The final match-up pitted them against Stu, Wyatt, and Dozer. Herb always thought of them as Bluto and the Goons, but not without fondness. In truth, he'd been a little scared of them back in school. The trio were star wrestlers in high school, due in part to an aptitude for the sport and in part to the fact that there weren't any other kids in a six-county area even close to their size. They were *big* and could've easily used their oversized muscles to shove Herb into any manner of uncomfortable spaces. Fortunately, they were a pretty mild-mannered bunch and paid little attention to Herb. Apparently, body slamming and choking out other kids as a legitimate recreational activity didn't leave much appetite for pummeling the weirdo after class.

After growing up together, the three now worked at the lumber mill. For fun, they had made their own bowling lane at work with two long logs for bumpers and firewood as pins. Dozer had an old, nicked-up sixteen-pounder that they would hurl down the packed dirt toward the stumps. Dubbed 'extreme bowling,' it was a pastime Herb remembered them starting back in high school. It began with late-night trips to the Get'n'Gobble, where they would set up two-liter bottles of soda in the aisle and use a frozen turkey for the ball. Their pinnacle achievement was taking over a whole block on Main Street. Wyatt had scored a bunch of old pins from Bay City's dumpster. They'd set up the pins at one end of the block and whipped the ball from the other. A decent crowd was enjoying the spectacle, and there was even some talk of it becoming an annual event for charity. Sadly, local authorities had to put the kibosh on the fun after a local storefront window was cracked by a careening gutter ball.

Solid bowlers all, they were a staple in the league finals just about every year. What they lacked in finesse the three men made up for in brute, devastating strength. League rules required men to roll with a least a ten-pound ball, but there were always a few cry-babies saying Dozer and his gang should be required to roll fourteen-pounders. None cried as loud as Bay City's owner, Slow Johnson, since Dozer in particular had a knack for breaking pins. Johnson had finally taken to charging the oversized trio extra when they bowled to offset the cost of replacing so many pins. With that kind of fire power at their disposal, Herb wasn't surprised to see them race through the brackets to the final match. What was surprising was the fact that this year, it was King and the Pins that had gone toe-to-toe with the bowling leviathans... and won.

While the post-tourney crowd milled around him, the vampire took a sip of his recently refilled Bloody Mary and let himself relive the final game of the tournament. It had barely been an hour ago, but the memory already felt timeless.

Chapter 32

A S HE WATCHED THE three giants prepare for the final game of the tournament, Herb didn't feel the bowel-freezing intimidation he'd felt in the past. Usually, he wanted to grab a helmet and stand about twenty or thirty feet back from the lane when the monstrous trio bowled. This night, though, he felt different. Riding the cloud of rolling back to back perfect games, Herb found himself coolly evaluating the seven hundred-plus-pounds of combined bowling monstrosity standing across the return from him.

After the customary pre-game hand-shakes, Stu rolled first, the ball hitting the pins with a thunderclap and sending them screaming in every direction. When the calamity receded, the ten-pin wobbled and came to rest, standing perfectly straight, albeit right at the lip of the pit. Stu grunted at the blowout and waited impatiently for his ball to roll up the return. It had barely cleared the hood when Stu picked it up and launched it back down the lane. His impatience was his downfall. The ball sped past the pin and smacked loudly against the back of the pit. The wind of its passage actually rocked the pin a fraction of an inch closer to the pit's edge, but it didn't go down.

Herb was first on the roster to roll since he'd had the best game prior. Dallas glared, but Herb was too caught up in the moment to give it much thought. He walked over to the return, picked up his ball, and turned to face the alley. What happened next was almost too fast for the naked eye to see. Three steps carried him down the approach with unnatural speed. In a blur of motion, his right arm swung back and sped forward in a perfect arc. The ball was released with so much velocity that it didn't even touch the maple at the top of the lane. It cruised a fraction of an inch above the boards and finally touched down well past the arrows. The ball hardly even seemed to roll and instead traveled like a missile toward the one-two pocket. It hit the pins so hard that the head-pin ricocheted across the lane, bounced in the gutter, flipped over the next lane, and finally landed two lanes down. A stunned crowd watched the screen above Herb's head. The digital display lit up with dancing bowling pins marching a picket line, each carrying a sign reading 'Strike!' The scorecard reappeared, with Herb's frame marked with an X. In the lower right-hand corner, the speed of the ball read thirty-two miles per hour.

Herb turned with a pirouette and offered a half-bow toward the beefy trio next to him. Stu's mouth worked like a guppy. Dozer stared down the lane as if a great mystery was about to unfurl and he didn't want to miss it by blinking. Wyatt finally cleared his throat and offered a gruff, "Holy hell. That was quite the roll, Herb."

Dallas and Stanley sat stunned on the chairs behind the score desk. Stanley spoke first as Herb calmly walked back to his seat.

"I g-g-gotta start doing me some Billy Blanks Tae Bo."

Dallas was less inclined to look for an innocent explanation.

"What the hell's going on, Herbert? A perfect game, that can happen. Folks get lucky sometimes. But a second perfect game? You? Not goddamned likely. And now you're rolling like Arnold effin'

Schwarzenegger?" Dallas moved in close, turning his back to the crowd. Bringing his face close to Herb's, he snapped in a hushed whisper, "Spill it, Herb. I know this finals thing is a big deal, but juicing? Are you on the 'roids? Deer antler spray? What is it? Where'd you even find the stuff, anyway? Shit, Herb, you get caught, we're barred from the league. From the league!"

With a final finger-wag and pointed nod, Dallas walked to the lane, picked up his ball, rolled an angry strike, and returned to where Stanley and Herbert were still standing. Neither had moved in the ninety seconds or so since Dallas had said his piece. Stanley was mumbling something about not getting how "hemorrhoids could make someone bowl so good." Herb was simply shocked to his core by the accusation. Drugs? Him? Who the hell did Dallas think he was, accusing him of using drugs? The one time, *one time* that Herb was actually doing something better than Dallas, and he gets accused of using steroids. Herb's mind reeled as the other bowlers rolled, Dozer and Wyatt both trying to show up Herb's thirty-two miles per hour roll, Stanley just trying to stay between the gutters. Inevitably, Herb's turn came around again. He looked long and hard at Dallas, who returned his stare without flinching. Eyes never leaving Dallas, Herb addressed the crowd.

"Who thinks I can roll thirty-three miles per hour? Thirty-four? Who wants to see this sucker hit thirty-five *miles per hour*?"

A surprised cheer went up from the crowd, and one clear, sultry voice carried above the rest.

"I'll bet you can do it faster and harder than anyone here!"

Herb watched the voice's owner work her way to the front of the crowd. Hungry eyes peered out from beneath bleached and feathered bangs. A skin-tight, low cut tee-shirt showcased an impressive set of curves, and long, fishnet clad legs stretched from beneath a swath of black sequins fabric that almost had the thread count to qualify as a skirt. Herb's eyes reached a jaunty pair of bright red pumps before reversing course and sliding all the way back up to those eyes.

Hands on her hips, lips crooked up in a seductive smile, the woman continued, "Now get over here and lemme give you some sugar for good luck."

The laughter and cheers reached a fever pitch, and Herb groaned.

Geez, can we just get through a single night without Dallas taking a chick-break?

He turned with every intention of telling Dallas to play grab-ass on his own time, but instead found his teammate looking for his fallen jaw, incomprehension plain on the man's face. Turning back, Herb yelped when he realized the woman had moved to stand directly in front of him, looking up from beneath press-on lashes and blue eyeliner.

"Hi. I'm Jenni. And I just love a guy who's good with his balls." Breasts suddenly pressed full against his chest, Jenni took a playful nip at his ear and whispered, "You really know how to roll. How about a little time in the gutter once you're done?"

Jenni. Jenni Colton. Memories started to click. Rumors had it she was a trophy hunter, dumping a guy the second she thought she could upgrade with the next one. Herb wasn't the brightest light above Roswell when it came to women, but having a girl pressed against you was a pretty clear signal, so it didn't take long for the pieces to fit into place. Jenni was obviously on the prowl, and he was solidly in her cross-hairs. Him. Herbert Knudsen.

Not some other guy with a bigger motorcycle or better paycheck, he realized. *And not Dallas. Me!*

Tossing a cavalier wink to a shell-shocked Dallas, Herb wrapped an arm around Jenni and dipped her down and back until her hair almost swept the floor. The tee-shirt that had been showing her to best advantage while standing up now found itself struggling mightily to contain her ample bosom as Herb kissed her long and hard.

Smoothly pulling her back to her feet, he waited until her knees were working again, then walked to the return, picked up his ball, and nonchalantly launched it toward the pins like the trapped soul of Hermes. Turning his back on the lane as the ball impacted the pins, he blew a kiss toward Jenni. The crowd's sudden outburst confirmed what he already knew to be true. He'd rolled another strike, and the ball had gone a record thirty-five miles per hour.

A cagey look crossed Dallas's face, and his eyes took on a dangerous glint. When it was his turn to roll, he pulled another strike. Herb's turn came. Another strike. Dallas was up. Strike. Herb. Strike. Dallas, another strike. Frame after frame, the two men sent the pins flying and their scores racing toward three-hundred. Dallas matching Herb frame for frame was tilting the universe back toward its previous alignment. While people still cheered for Herb and Jenni looked like she was about to rip his clothes off, more and more cries of, "Atta boy, Big D!" and, "Hell yeah, Dallas!" were coming from the crowd. He even had his own buxom cheerleader. Colette, another serial man-killer and frequent booty call of Dallas's, pushed her way to the front. As the men bowled strike after strike, she started competing with Jenni to see who could bounce up and down better and show more cleavage. By the seventh frame, their antics had gone from PG-13 to a solid R and were quickly heading for NC-17. The handful of kids in the crowd suddenly had their parents' hands across their eyes and were shuttled away from the lane.

At this point, Stu, Wyatt, and Dozer were irrelevant. Even with Stanley as a built-in handicap, they had no chance of winning. Despite being on the losing end of the match, they were just as excited about the unfolding Clash of the Bowling Titans.

Eighth frame. Strike, strike. Ninth. Strikes again. Tenth frame. The final frame of the final game of the championship tournament. Climbers reaching Everest's peak might have understood in some small way the elation Herb felt at that moment. He rolled. Strike. Two balls left. Strike. One more roll. Herb picked up his ball, turned to the crowd, and gave a deep bow. He glided toward the lane and at the last possible second sent the ball *between* his legs. The ball hooked just a smidge, catching the pins at the perfect angle and pulling them all down into the pit. Another perfect three-hundred.

Dallas looked up from where he sat, Colette massaging his neck and mouthing some threatening profanities at Jenni. He stood, rolling his broad shoulders as the crowd bounced and cheered. He approached the ball return and held his hand out over the stream of cool air from the vent. After a moment, he picked up his ball and stood looking at the lane. He took three long, steady strides, arm arcing back and forward, and released the ball as his toe stopped millimeters from the foul line. Frozen in a forward lunge, arm outstretched, palm tilted slightly upward as if in supplication, Dallas watched his final ball roll, hook slightly, and clear all ten pins.

The crowd erupted as Dallas slapped his hands together and let out a, "Hell yeah!" Herb watched with Jenni molded to his side as

Dallas rooster-strutted back to the ball return. Lifting his chin in unspoken challenge, he grabbed Colette and planted one on her lips while goosing her denim-clad behind. Colette leaned in and threw a leg up around Dallas's hip. Finally breaking the kiss, Dallas gave a nod to the laughing, cheering crowd. The pins had reset and stood waiting for their next punishment. Dallas held his ball in front of his chest, took a deep breath and released it through pursed lips. Three strides, lunge, release, and the ball glided down the lane. A few infinitely long seconds later, all ten pins fell a-clatter into the pit.

Colette tackled him, both legs wrapping around his midsection, and kissed him hard. Pulling back like a cowboy on a mechanical bull, she whooped, "Take that, you scrawny scamp-tramp! I got me the real man here. You got nothing!"

Dallas was turning a slow circle with Colette attached to the top of his belt buckle when Jenni grabbed her by the collar and wrenched her backward. The tee-shirt tore, Dallas stumbled forward, and Colette collapsed in a heap.

"Bitch! I'm gonna kick your little hussy ass," she screamed, coming to her feet.

"That's right," Jenni agreed. "Little ass. That you wish you had, you budonk-adonk skeeze!"

Jenni and Colette attacked one another with total gusto and no regard for the gathered spectators. Herb and Dallas and the final moments of their epic battle were momentarily forgotten. As the already large crowd swelled even further, money started to change hands. The betting was happening fast, but Herb thought odds were long on Colette. However, despite the wicked fake nails and feral snarls, neither girl had suffered more than some pulled hair and a few scratches.

Their respective wardrobes, however, were being torn to shreds, and the betting had shifted from which girl would win to which girl's bra would fail first. Dozer and Wyatt finally intervened, each taking a girl over a shoulder and carrying them through the whistling and clapping crowd before depositing them outside.

Intermission over, the crowd returned all of its attention to the bowlers. Dallas had one ball left to roll. Herb knew they had already won. Hell, the game had basically been over two or three frames back. Still, everything hung on this moment. Dallas looked over his shoulder at his teammates. Stanley was about to burst, but Herb kept his face stoic and still. Despite having just rolled three back to back perfect games, this was the moment that truly mattered. Suddenly all he wanted in the world was to beat Dallas. Not tie, but win. Definitively. Decisively. No room for excuses or fluke explanations. Just this once, Herb wanted to be undeniably, absolutely, one-hundred percent the best. Sitting there, everything started to fall away. The crowd, the lights, the smells, even Stanley's erratic gulping and excited hiccups withdrew. Only Herb and Dallas remained, holding each other's stare. Dallas gave a self-satisfied huff, Herb raised an eyebrow in his best Cool Hand Luke, and the moment collapsed, letting the rest of the world back in. Dallas turned back toward the lane, self-assurance incarnate. One, two, three strides, lunge, arc and release, watch the ball head toward the pins. Collide, spin, crash, twirl and roll. The game was over.

Dallas stood rigid at the foul line, fists clenched, shoulders tight, spine ramrod straight. He started at the eight-pin extending from the alley, a bone-white middle finger wearing a blood-red ring. The only sounds were the whirring of the central air, the muted notes of Jasper's karaoke machine as he sound-checked the system, and, finally, the collective sigh from the onlookers. The game was over. Herb had rolled a three-hundred. Dallas, a two ninety-nine.

The choreography of the next few moments would live forever in Herb's mind. Dallas turned, his body coiling. Herb stepped forward, extending a hand. Dallas matched his step while swinging a fist. Like dancers in a twisted ballet, Herb continued his advance, wanting to congratulate his friend and accept congratulations in return on a game well played. Seeing Dallas's fist part the air and arc toward his face, the new, deadly part of Herb's brain clicked off facts. He could easily avoid the punch, or catch the fist and crush Dallas's fingers, do any number of things in the split second it would take the fist to complete its journey toward his jaw. But the other part of Herb's brain, the part that was still deeply rooted in his fading humanity, was stunned to the core. His friend, his best and oldest friend, was about to punch him in the face.

Fist met jaw with a wet smacking sound, followed immediately by Herb's yelp and Dallas's grunt as both men reacted to the mutual pain of the experience. Herb had instantly covered his mouth with his hand, hiding a split lip and sudden fangs from Dallas and the others. The split healed almost instantly, but retracting the fangs took an extra moment or two, so Herb simply stood there, mouth covered, staring with wide, uncomprehending eyes at what had once been his friend. Dallas managed to look Herb in the eye for a moment, shaking his hand to take the sting out of bruised knuckles. Herb saw anger give way to guilt a split second before Dallas grabbed his ball and stomped from the lane. Stopping just long enough to yank off his bowling shoes and shove his feet into his boots, he continued toward the exit and out into the night.

Stunned, Herb watched Dallas storm off while Stanley rushed up to his side.

"Don't you s-sweat it Herby. He's j-just-mad he lost. Even though we won. Hey! We won. We won!" Stanley realized, stutter disappearing in his astonishment.

His proclamation broke the crowd from their stunned trance, and they all began to cheer. Dozer, Stu and Wyatt took turns clapping first Herb, then Stanley on the shoulder, pumping their fists in meaty handshakes. Even Fancy Dan, Dylan, and Bert, clad in a mostly dry shirt now that their games were over, had come over to offer their grudging congratulations.

"But where's Dallas?" Dan asked, craning his neck. "What good is winning if you ain't gonna hang around to enjoy it?"

"It ain't any good, god damned it. No good at all!" Dallas's voice boomed over the crowd. "Holy shit, Herb. I don't think I've ever done something so rotten or stupid," he said after pushing back through the crowd to face Herb. "Well, there was that girl I picked up outside the free clinic in Milwaukee..." Dallas's old grin returned, lopsided and devil-may-care as always. "But shit," he continued, the grin replaced by a rare look of consternation, "I had no business cold-cocking you like that. Never mind that you're my friend, or even that we're on the same team for chrissake. You rolled a helluva good game. Shit, *all* your games were good. Not good, great! No one outta take a swing at their buddy for rolling a damn fine game of bowling, especially when we won. I don't know what the hell got into me. I'm sorry, Herb. Drinks are on me."

Herb just shook his head, smiled, and punched Dallas lightly on the shoulder. "Lucky for both of us, you hit like a little girl."

The look on Dallas's face made the whole ordeal worthwhile. Herb threw one arm around Dallas's neck and the other around Stanley's, pulling them toward the bar. The night had been one hell of a night, and it was time to celebrate.

Chapter 33

Herb was trotting back from the restroom, having just refreshed what had been a Bloody Mary and was now a Bloody Mark. It was about time for Dallas to raise the traditional championship toast, and Herb didn't want to miss it. Dallas took his toastmaster responsibilities very seriously when he wasn't the big winner. This year, with him, Herb and Stanley being *the champions*, Herb knew that if he missed the toast, Dallas would do a lot worse than just punch him. Herb walked back into the bar as Dallas made his way through the crowd and climbed up onto the bar itself. It took a few piercing whistles and a few more cries of, "Shut the hell up!" before the volume in the room fell to a level low enough for his booming voice to carry.

"Alright, you chuckleheads! Here we are again, and it's time for the god damned toast!"

The bowlers and their respective entourages all started to clap and cheer, chanting *Toast! Toast! Toast!* It was easy to see that Dallas was more excited about making the toast than ever before, but right as his mouth opened to make way for the first syllable in what was sure to be his best toast yet, another voice jostled its way forward, amplified by a set of speakers mounted on either side of a make-shift stage in the back of the bar.

"Herb! Herby! What's this year's toast gonna be?"

The sea of intoxicated smiles swiveled toward the sound of Jenni's voice. As comprehension filtered through the booze, most of the heads swung back to face Herb. A few blurry stares stayed glued on Jenni, as her earlier tiff with Colette had left her shirt torn in some suggestive places, but suddenly Herb found himself the focus of most of the bar's patrons. Dallas had literally stopped breathing, rictus grin stretched thin as his eyes moved from Jenni to Herb. A choked, "Urgh," escaped his lips, causing the sea of confused faces to swivel toward him once again.

Dallas quickly regained his aplomb, raising his mug along with his voice. "Lovely Jenni has the right of it! I'm sick of making toasts. This year, the real winner needs to lead the toast. Three perfect games? Are you kidding me? C'mon Herbert. Get your pasty ass up here and lead these fine folks in the victory toast!"

He extended a bear paw hand toward Herb. Suddenly self-conscious, ears burning red, Herb tried to wave him off, but the crowd wouldn't have it. Chanting again, but this time *Herb-ert! Herb-ert! Herb-ert!,* he felt a myriad of hands pushing him toward the bar and then Dallas was pulling him up.

Turning slowly, Herb surveyed the room full of familiar, drunken faces, people he'd known for years, decades even. Over all those years, these people had paid him no attention at all. Until now. Only now that he could bowl, now that he was the *best bowler in Trappersville,* was he finally worthy of their attention, their affection. His eyes settled on Jenni, all vixen curves, pouty lips, and rip-my-clothes-off eyes, wobbling in broken heels on the karaoke stage. Yesterday, she didn't know who he even was. Today, she was coming on like an X-rated freight train.

That's right. Look at me now, he thought as the words of a toast started to form in his mind. *Just look at me now.*

"I'll give you a toast." Herb took in the room with eyes that gleamed like moonlight on fresh-spilled blood. "Here's looking at you, though it's a hell of a tough thing to do!"

Laughter from the crowd followed, with a few, "Here, here's!"

"No, seriously," Herb continued, a mean glint in his eyes. "Here's to good friends, and you guys, too."

More laughter, but a few frowns appeared, too. Herb took a long pull from his drink.

If they only knew what was in this cup, he thought, the metallic tang of blood swirling with the alcohol as it coursed along his tongue and down his throat.

Throwing his arms wide, he offered another. "In fact, in honest-to-goodness truth, I'd rather be drinking with you all tonight than with the finest people in the world!"

Grunts and confused scowls were outpacing the laughter and cheers, but every scowling face quickly averted their eyes as Herb looked across the room. A pall was slowly creeping across the celebratory mood that had prevailed just moments before. Herb could feel the slow change and knew that he was the cause. Whispers in the cracks and corners started to slouch and crawl their inevitable way through him, scratching and skittering like leaves in the autumn wind, wheeling and swirling like a murder of crows. Herb's pulse quickened, senses heightened. A wolf pacing the herd, he could smell the weakness, nostrils flaring as he identified his victims. He wanted nothing more than to rip the smiles and scowls alike from all the greasy, insincere faces. Fingers clawed, he'd sink his nails into their flesh and tear skin and muscle from bone. His fangs would rend their necks until the geysers of blood soaked the room from ceiling to floor and the walls dripped red. He could feel his fangs start to cut the inside of his lip as his breaths came faster and faster.

A heavy hand landed on his shoulder. Whipping around with every intent of literally biting off the fingers of the audacious fool that dared to touch him, Herb locked eyes with Dallas.

"Whoah! Hey, buddy. Play nice, huh?" his friend advised. "You got one more shot to give us a toast worth drinking to!"

Herb looked at Dallas, smiling and laughing, oblivious to the fact that he and every other person in the room was a hair's breadth from becoming a smorgasbord of gristle and blood. Dallas, his first and oldest friend. His friend.

Like a kettle taken off the burner, Herb's rage subsided. Whispers sulked their way back into the dark spaces of the room. Fangs receded down to normal incisors. Exhaling a shaky breath and nodding to Dallas, Herb turned back to his almost-victims and newfound admirers.

"Well, okay then. Here's a toast. May we all come to peaceful ends, and leave the bar tab with our friends."

Dallas clapped Herb on the back, Jenni whooped into the karaoke mic, and the crowd nodded and cheered with approval. Herb had given them their toast, and the biggest party Bay City Bowlers had ever seen commenced.

Chapter 34

T HE BAR HAD LONG since closed, and Herb and Jenni were back at her trailer. Herb had never had a one-night stand before. Despite his still-deep pining for Lois, the rush of victory, a few sips of Jenni's blood in a dark corner, and the chance to show Dallas that yes, chicks did dig him, was too much for him to resist. They'd taken his car back to her place, and only his supernatural reflexes had allowed him to keep his car on the road as Jenni took to him like a monkey to a tree. After they had arrived, an energetic evening ensued. They had done things that near defied physics, leaving her in an exhausted, satiated sleep.

Her soft snores reached Herb's sensitive ears where he sat on a chair across her small bedroom. He looked out the window at the moonlit night, seeing shapes and colors he would've never noticed in the light of day. The vampire turned bowling champion had been pondering that for the last hour or so as Jenni slept. The light of day. Only a few short weeks as a vamp, yet he could barely remember the sun. He tried to remember his last sunrise, his last sunset. How it looked on a hazy summer day, or the crisp, brittle quality of its light on a clear January morning after a deep freeze. He tried to remember how the sun looked dancing on the waters of the Wolf River, but had trouble forming the picture in his mind.

Turning his head slightly, he looked at the profile of Jenni's cheek, the side of her neck, the way her hair fell carelessly across a bare shoulder. In the moonglow's half-light, all he could see was Lois. The knowledge that it wasn't her filled him with a dark melancholy. He'd experienced a wide range of emotions since *the change*, the peak of elation, the abyss of anger, hungry rage and even gut-wrenching fear. This melancholy, though, cut deeper than any other.

Backlit by a lonely night sky dissected into crisp lines by Venetian mini-blinds and framed by the trailer window, Herb contemplated his sleeping fling. Shifting his eyes and turning his head, he took in the utter destruction of their earlier lovemaking. The contents of the tiny kitchen table had been strewn across the floor. Pictures had been knocked off their nails in the wall, and a low shelf had been ripped free with such force that the paneling had pulled back to reveal the studs beneath. Despite his melancholy, a grin tweaked the corner of Herb's mouth.

A bit more than just a fling, he thought with a measure of pride.

His own body bore no marks from the night's amorous activities. The deep scratches Jenni had clawed into his shoulder, the bruise from where his arm had slammed into the nightstand when they hit the mattress like twin meteors streaking toward the planet's surface, they had healed almost as soon as they were made. While Jenni's own mementos wouldn't heal like Herb's, the sheer volume of alcohol she'd consumed in the after-tourney party had made her similarly immune to the side-effects of their violent coupling. She'd feel it tomorrow, though, of that Herb had no doubt. Grin fading, he realized he could've really hurt her if he'd gone even a little further.

He crossed the carpet like a ghost, coarse fibers bending and scratching against the soles of his bare feet. Coming to a stop at the side of the bed, he dropped lightly to the floor, crossing his legs and leaning in toward Jenni's sleeping face. Guided by instinct more than rational thought, he began to lightly stroke her cheek with the backs of his fingers. Slowing his breathing, he fixed his gaze and all of his will on her and softly called her name.

"Jenni. Wake up, Jenni."

A soft whimper, the mewling of a kitten safe in its mother's embrace. Her lips worked and her back arched as she stretched and let out a long sigh. Herb waited for her eyes to open. Instead, her lips parted with a soft snore.

"Jenni. Wake up," he repeated. This time, her brow furrowed, turning her expression from peaceful sleep to waking confusion. Her eyes opened, saw him, and twinkled, a mischievous smile curving her luscious lips.

"Hmmmmm. Morning already?" She yawned prettily, covering her mouth as she did. "Sorry, where's the cat?"

Confused, Herb looked around the room. "Cat?"

"Yeah," she continued. "The one that shit in my mouth while I was sleeping." She pushed herself up to a sitting position, the bed sheet pooling around her waist, and batted her eyes. "What's up? You feelin' frisky again?"

Herb's eyes did not want to look up. They were perfectly happy to take in the moonlit curves of Jenni's nude torso as she sat expectantly on the bed.

No, he reminded himself. *Maybe just once more?* he asked himself hopefully. *NO.*

Shaking his head, taking a deep breath, and convincing his eyes that yes, they really should look up at hers, yes, now, no, they couldn't look back down again, and yes, they really, really needed to look at her eyes, he leaned in and took her hands in his own.

After he finished, Herb dressed silently, but quickly. It had taken longer than he expected to put the whammy on Jenni, and he was quickly running out of night. But he'd wanted to make sure that this really was a onetime thing. He'd already made a mistake with Helen, and diner-talk had it that the insurance company was still investigating the 'malfunction' in the tanning booth. According to the gossipers, the cops had found three dead bodies in the dumpster covered with her fingerprints and saliva, linking her to a triple-murder of two out-of-town college kids and a co-stripper. The most widely accepted theory was that she somehow rigged the booth to fry herself up in a fit of guilt after the murders.

Herb knew he'd dodged the proverbial bullet. He definitely didn't want something like that happening again, no matter how strong the allure of having a very flexible, very enthusiastic, and very naked girl totally digging on him. So he'd used the whammy to strongly recommend that she stop liking him and fall for another guy, maybe someone taller. It felt like telling Ed McMahon that no, he didn't really want that sweepstakes check, and he could maybe just drop it in the neighbor's mailbox, but Herb managed to stay the course. Stepping out the door of her trailer and quietly closing it behind him, he could feel just how close morning was. The sky had taken on that crystalline quality, causing the backs of Herb's eyes to ache in response. Moving quickly to his Pinto, he backed out of Jenni's drive, turned onto the main road, and raced down the highway toward the safety of his root cellar. A short time later, snuggled up in a blanket at the bottom of a man-sized hole in his cellar floor with a large, gleaming trophy in the crook of his elbow, Herb fell asleep as the first hint of sun touched the pre-dawn sky.

Chapter 35

THE DINER WAS BUSY, even for a Saturday night. Herb and the prep cooks were a flurry of activity as Lois and Dee tried to keep up with the rush. The yearly classic car show had taken over the town, filling the two small local motels with a melting pot of humanity unified solely by a passion for fins and white sidewalls and chrome grills. Herb had gotten his schedule down to three nights a week, leaving plenty of time for bowling, hustling pool, and other general hang-outty things on the weekends, but with the car show, he'd decided to help Ronnie out since he knew they'd be busy. The extra cash wouldn't hurt, either.

It had been two weeks since the bowling tourney. Gone were the strings of nights when Herb would sit alone on the couch watching infomercials. Now he had a social life. People knew him and were actually excited to see him. Nights out with the guys became nights out with the crowd, forcing Herb to banter and turn down free drinks and give impromptu bowling lessons. He'd pretty much wiped out his meager checking account to update his wardrobe. What good was being the best bowler in town if you looked like a schlub? New Wranglers, a new Packers jersey, some snappy new flannels, and sweet Nike cross-trainers replaced the Goodwill rejects that had previously filled his closet. Oh yeah, Herb was looking good, but dressing sharp wasn't cheap. Plus, with his newfound celebrity in the greater-Trappersville bowling circles, he wanted to get his bowling ball polished, pick up some new shoes, and grab a couple of new towels.

There was also a really slick bowling bag Slow Johnson had put up on display in the alley's pro shop. Black leather, deep purple lining, and the face of Bela Lugosi as Dracula in sharp black and white on the side. To Herb, it was like someone climbed into his skull, drew out his deepest fantasy, and stuck it on the side of a super sweet bowling bag. In the weeks following the change, Herb had become quite the vamp film enthusiast and was a huge fan of the 1931 classic. Dracula was cool, classy, and Bela Lugosi reminded Herb of his Maker. Alluring, dangerous, mysterious, but also refined. While Herb was still pretty rough around the edges, he'd been making a deliberate attempt at polishing up and pouring a little extra water on that growing self-confidence he'd found. He couldn't really explain why, but if he ever bumped into his Maker again, he wanted to make a good impression. So he'd happily signed up for the extra shifts at work, eagerly hoping that if his Maker saw him again, he'd be looking his best and carrying a damn fine bowling bag.

There was another perk to the extra shifts, specifically Lois. In the two weeks since the finals, she'd been different toward him. She wouldn't just say hi when they passed. Now she'd linger. Not long, no, and usually not much was said, but with each encounter, a little more ice would thaw, and a little more warmth would show through.

Like that moment at the serve-through window at Ronnie's, when she'd reached for an order of toast right as he was putting it up. Their fingers met for the briefest moment, the sensation nearly buckling his knees and dropping him to the tiles.

"Good timing, Herby," she'd said, and actually smiled at him.

Good timing. Not, "Dangit Herb, watch where you put the toast!" or, "Is that butter? On the order for dry toast?" leaving him to frantically toss more bread in the toaster and curse his stupidity. He gave her toast. Their fingers touched—actually touched—and she'd smiled and said, "Good timing!" Herb's glow could've lit up Lambeau Field for a night game. And it wasn't just the smiley toast, as he'd come to think of the incident. There were other moments, bright little spots in his otherwise sunless nights. It was almost like she was maybe, just maybe, starting to like him. But of course, right when Herb was starting to think that maybe, just maybe, he and Lois might have something, someone had to get in the way.

Just thinking about the previous Sunday still tied his guts in knots. Ronnie's had been busy as people started to filter into town ahead of the upcoming auto show, and Herb was looking forward to a good day's sleep on Monday. Tossing his apron in the hamper, he walked out the diner's back door and there she was, standing outside, finishing her cigarette. Thoughts of the impending sunrise vanished like the curls of smoke rising into the night.

Bela Lugosi. Bela Lugosi. I'm smooth, I'm classy. I'm Bela Lugosi, running through his mind, Herb's mouth made words.

"Good morning, Lois. How are you?"

Frantically twisting the valve on his brain, he managed to stop his mouth before it poured out anything else. Despite the hoard of angry butterflies rampaging through his stomach, he didn't fidget or stutter. He stood straight, almost casual-like, with what he hoped was an easy-looking smile on his lips. Like a fourth grader convincing himself that getting kicked by a girl meant true love, he waited in nervous anticipation, but the most wonderful thing happened. Lois actually smiled back in return. Like the smiley toast smile, but longer and with no toast. A real 'it's nice to see you' smile.

Cushing out her smoke on the side of the garbage can and tossing the butt inside, she replied, "Hi Herby. Doing good, can't complain. I forget sometimes how pretty it is right before dawn, and wasn't quite ready to head inside. Keep me company for a minute, would you? Was it busy tonight?"

So unexpected was her reply, so normal and friendly, that Herb was at a loss. He glanced over his shoulder to confirm that his wildest dream had come true and she was, in fact, talking to him. Clearing his throat to cover his momentary distraction, he frantically thought of what to say next. Despite endless conversations with Lois in his head, he had never expected to suddenly have his fantasies become reality. Should he be funny, suave, flirtatious? Maybe brag about his pool hustling or whipping the kitchen at Ronnie's into better shape than it had ever been in before?

As these thoughts whirled through his head, his mouth took over and casually replied, "Not bad. Busy, but we had it covered pretty well. Ronnie was in for a bit, and was actually, well, pretty cool. How 'bout you? Do anything fun last night?"

Herb's brain skidded to a halt, awed at how totally awesome his mouth had just been. After a few moments of consideration, Herb's brain decided it had better just take a back seat and let the mouth run the show.

Lois smiled again, but this time it held a slightly nervous quality as her eyes glanced to the side.

"Not bad. I was, ah. Well, your friend Dallas and I, um. We had a, I guess you could call it a date. Last night." She fumbled in her purse for a moment, pulled out another smoke.

Herb's mouth lost its previous poise, and his brain ran in circles. Lois had been on a date with Dallas? Herb remembered Dallas saying something about a hot date on his calendar, but he hadn't really given it much thought. Dallas always had a 'hot date' lined up. He had a sort of rotation going with the eligibles and mostly eligibles in town, and even the occasional tryst with a not-eligible-due-to-marriage-but-what-the-hubby-didn't- know-couldn't-hurt-him swinger. For variety, he was usually pretty successful at picking up a tourist passing through, referring to those flings afterward as "playing tour guide." Stories regaling such conquests usually included a few of his choice lines, like, "Then I said to her, 'And if you'll look to the right, you'll see old D's bedroom, probably the happening-ist spot in Trappersville,' or 'Keep your hands inside the vehicle, it's going to get a little bumpy!'" So frequent were Dallas's escapades with the opposite sex that Herb usually paid more attention to Canadian weather reports than Dallas's stories. So Herb found himself trying frantically to recall what Dallas had said the other day about his upcoming date. Had he actually said he had a date with Lois?

"Oh. Um. That's, well. Sounds cool. So, um, what'd you guys do?" Herb could feel heat rising up his usually cool skin, and those whispers that had been relegated to white noise in the recesses of his mind started to squirm to the surface.

"Oh, you know. We went for dinner and grabbed a drink. I stayed out a little later than I probably should of. You know how Dallas is. But I finally convinced him I should get some sleep since I had to work today." She shifted her weight slightly from one foot to the other, brought an arm across her midsection, and propped her elbow up on a wrist. Perfect fingers brought the cigarette to full lips

Herb's imagination exploded, the words, 'How Dallas is, How Dallas is,' echoing like a klaxon in his ears. Too often had he been forced to listen to the sordid details as Dallas recapped his conquests. Herb knew *exactly* how Dallas was. Unbidden memories of Jenni's ransacked trailer danced across his vision, but instead of seeing himself and Jenni in a whirlwind of lustful devastation, he was picturing Dallas and Lois. He forcefully pushed that image aside, only to have it replaced by an image of Lois and Dallas in the back of his truck, a million stars slathered across the night sky, their cries of passion echoing across the countryside. A sudden *snick* caused Herb to quickly close his gaping mouth, the tips of his fangs pricking the skin inside his lower lip. Ducking his head and turning toward the parking lot, he forced a laugh that he hoped sounded sincere and said, "Oh. That sounds nice. Yeah, that Dallas. He'll stay up 'til sunrise if you give him the chance. So."

An awkward silence settled in. Lois smoked. Herb sort-of stared at something of sudden interest on the ground. "Well, glad you had fun. Have a good day at work. Lois. Um. Bye."

He was halfway to his car before Lois called after him. "Um, you too, Herb. I'll see you later, right?"

The question had lingered unanswered in the pre-dawn sky, eventually mixing with the Pinto's exhaust and dissipating into nothingness.

To Herb's knowledge, they hadn't been on another date since, but he couldn't be certain, because he'd studiously avoided Dallas that week, a task made easier by his regular work schedule on top of his extra shifts. He overlapped with Lois a few times, and while she was friendly enough, neither one brought up their earlier conversation. Dallas also didn't stop by the diner, a fact Herb clung to with a desperate hope.

Coming back to the moment, Herb pulled another ticket off the wheel and threw another chicken breast on the grill. Ronnie's was busy, but Herb was in a flow, the steady rush of orders almost keeping his thoughts away from Dallas and Lois. In addition to the many other changes brought about by being a vampire, Herb had mysteriously gone from cook to frickin' awesome cook. It didn't matter how many orders were coming across the ticket wheel, or how random the orders were. Herb rolled through them like a well-oiled machine, each item cooked to perfection and timed so entire tickets went out fresh and hot. The patrons were noticing, too. Ronnie's had always been blessed by geography. It was a convenient stop for both truckers and tourists, and an easy-to-get-to spot for the locals. Staying busy had never been a big issue for Ronnie's, and Herb and the other cooks had always been proficient, steadily delivering mostly eatable food day in and night out. Now, though, with his heightened sense of smell, preternatural reflexes, and improved situational awareness, Herb found he could easily tell if something needed an extra sprinkle of sauce, or pull food off the grill when it had reached the perfect temperature.

In addition to making the standards, Herb had even taken to making special dishes. Lots of truck stop diners had a chef's special on the menu, but it was usually a cheap cop-out. Corned beef hash with Thousand Island dressing in the hollandaise or a bacon cheeseburger with potato chips on top, that sort of thing, but Herb had decided it was time to bring Ronnie's a touch of class. Walleye with a red wine reduction and fresh asparagus, or a gourmet Angus burger with blue cheese and cranberry compote. Since he couldn't eat the food himself, he tested the dishes on Ronnie first before asking to put them on the menu, an arrangement that worked well. Ronnie had a surprisingly good palate, allowing Herb to tweak his recipes while also strengthening the growing rapport between the two men. Ever since Herb had set the new schedule in motion and taken over the midweek night shifts, he hadn't missed a single night of work. Ronnie had taken note and, as was typical of Ronnie, taken credit for Herb's 'growth as an individual.'

The patrons loved the new specials, too. A few of the items had been so popular that Ronnie made brand new menus for the restaurant. Gone were the ten-year-old laminated menus that were so coated with grime it was hard to read the food descriptions, with prices crossed out and raised every few years in the margins to keep up with the ever-rising costs of ingredients. The new menus were pleather-bound with "Ronnie's" written in gold, flowing script across the front at a jaunty angle against a background of deep red, and had three whole pages inside. The Chef's Special section had a blank space where special-made cards could be inserted to proudly display that day's culinary concoction. Herb's creation of the specials had even sparked some new life for the other cooks. Coming up with something new for the menu had become a running contest. Even Bill had whipped up a couple of winners, like his Mama's Boy PB&J: white bread with the crusts cut off and crushed up cheddar puffs sprinkled across the top of the chunky peanut butter and Concord grape jam, served with half a banana and a side of string cheese. It was all paying off. Even without the classic car show in town, Ronnie's was doing more business than ever before. Everyone was happy. Ronnie obviously was on cloud nine, but the wait staff were bringing in more tips, the cooks were having fun, and Ronnie had even given everyone a generous raise. All in all, thought Herb, things were going pretty well.

"Order up Herby! It's my last table, and I'd love to end on a high note. They've got a lot of add-ons and subs, but if you can swing it, I'll split the tip with you," Lois called through the window.

Herb turned to see her face framed in the window, an easy smile on her cherry-red lips. Willfully banishing thoughts of her and Dallas from his mind, he smiled back.

"You bet, Lois. I'll jump on it right now." Snapping the ticket off the wheel, he gave it a quick glance, dropped it in the 'order up' pile, and started grabbing ingredients. "They do know we have a menu, right?" he asked Lois with a laugh.

To his delight, she laughed in return. "I know, I know, but like I said, it's my last table and I'm outta here for the night. Thanks for being a sweetie."

Herb responded with a good-natured wave as he turned back to the grill. The entire exchange had only lasted a few seconds, but the whole night had been that way. Fun, pleasant banter, Lois complimenting him on her happy tables, even a bit of good-natured ribbing. It had been one of the best nights of Herb's life. A quick glance at the clock on the wall told him it was quarter to one in the morning. He was scheduled until five, but there were two of them in the kitchen since they were so busy. Lois usually stayed after her shift to have a light meal. Maybe tonight, Herb could cook her up something special, and then wash up quick, throw on a clean shirt, and join her for a meal.

It wouldn't be a date, he thought. *Just two coworkers enjoying a meal before she went home for the night.* They'd share a meal, he'd tell jokes, she'd laugh. Just the two of them, together.

Order finished, Herb grabbed the hot plates and turned to put them up in the window, calling out, "Order up!" and scanning the diner, waiting anxiously to meet Lois's eyes as she wove her way back through the tables toward the kitchen. But as he laid the plates down on the stainless steel and looked out, it wasn't Lois he saw. Instead, at a stool directly across the counter from him, sat Dallas.

Chapter 36

"HERBY! HOW ARE YA?"

Herb's heart thudded, and his smile froze. Pure habit had just forced a, "Oh, hey there Big D," through his clenched jaws when Lois swooshed by, grabbing the plates he'd just set in the window.

"Oh my god, Herb. These look amazing! You're the best, and you're definitely getting half the tip," Lois said with a wink as she turned, plates in hand. "Hey Dal, let me drop these off and I'll be right over," she continued, flashing Dallas the smile Herb had coveted for himself.

"No worries, babe. Just thought I'd surprise you. I'll jaw with Herby for a bit. Take your time." Turning back to face Herb, he continued. "What's up buddy? You missed a helluva good show. Me and Stanley actually got to put a '54 Chevy up on a lift and get underneath her skirts. Sexy sexy! Oh, she was a beaut. Looks like you guys are jumping here, though. Guess it's good you got a good day's sleep!" Dallas gave a guffaw. "Day's sleep. So weird. I mean, I get you like working nights and all, but it's still funny. Have you even seen the sun in the past month?"

Herb's brain clicked like the stuck gears of a broken ten-speed. What was Dallas doing here? Why tonight? Did he and Lois have another date? Why didn't Lois say anything?

"Oh, um. You know. Guess I've turned into kind of a night owl these days. Nights. I guess," he answered. Frozen in place, he simply stared at Dallas as Lois, returning from delivering her order, took a seat at the counter next to Dallas.

"What a surprise, you stopping in. Causing trouble, as always?" she jibed, propping an elbow on the table and resting her chin on her fist.

Herb's blood boiled as Dallas grinned an oily grin.

"You know me! Always up for some trouble. I was at the car show all day, worked up a thirst, and thought you might want to, you know, grab a little night cap after your shift. We could swing over to Stein's. Maybe pick up on our last conversation," he offered, wiggling his eyebrows.

Lois laughed in return. "If Dee is fine with wrapping up my last table, I'll take you up on that drink. Gimme one sec, okay hon?"

As she stood to find Dee, Lois reached out a hand and placed it on Dallas's arm. It was only there for a second, but the sight of it filled Herb's insides with vipers and scorpions. Woodenly, he waved at Dallas, mumbled, "Well, better get back to cookin'," and shuffled back to the grill. When Lois called to him a few minutes later to say goodbye and to make sure Dee gave him half that table's tip, he couldn't even turn to face her. Head down, he focused on the food on the grill, hiding the bloody tears streaking down his cheeks.

Chapter 37

WHEREAS BEFORE THE STEADY stream of orders had kept Herb in a zone of perfection, thoughts of Lois and Dallas now made each order seem like an arduous ordeal, a strain his taxed psyche could barely manage. Every time he dropped a plate on the serve-through, he'd hope for Lois's smile and instead see Dee's frown. Every laugh he heard from the people in the diner made him think of Dallas saying something funny and Lois lighting up in response. He could picture every detail of her laugh, from the way her eyes would crinkle and her perfect teeth would shine out from those cherry red lips, to the way her hair would ripple and sway across her shoulders as she turned her head.

Yes, Herb could imagine every detail, but it was Dallas who was getting the actual experience. He was the one that got to bask in the glow of her smile, reap the fruits of making her laugh. Thinking of it made Herb want to punch him in the throat, shove his eyeballs back into his head, and set his hair on fire. That'd be a sight, no doubt. Dallas with his rugged mane aflame, eyes bleeding, mouth opened in a scream of pain and terror. Herb could smell the singed hair, could taste the acrid smoke, could feel the heat on the skin of his own face, pulled tight against his cheekbones in a rictus grin. The fantasy drew him in, wrapped him in rage, and fanned the flames that seemed so real now that his eyes were starting to water.

"Sonofabitch Herb! Put that out. Put it out!" Dee screamed from the serve-through.

Herb looked down to see the steak that he'd been cooking had become a shriveled, blackened lump spewing smoke and a few threatening flames as the fat and gristle started to ignite. Yelping in surprise, Herb grabbed a pot cover, slapped it over the incinerated steak, and slid it to the far side of the grill. Grumbling about having to remake the steak, he waved off Dee's complaints and stalked back to the walk-in cooler for a fresh piece of dead flesh. Standing in the cooler, his fists clenched and unclenched as he fought to control his breathing and will his fangs back to normal size. Dallas. It was Dallas. He was ruining everything.

Herb couldn't take it. He had to get out of Ronnie's, out of the kitchen, away from everyone. The rush had tapered off, so they really only needed one cook, anyway. With the blackened steak in the food scraps bin as evidence of his foul mood, Herb told Dee and Hector he needed to leave early and stomped across the pavement to the side of Ronnie's parking lot, where his Pinto waited patiently. Sliding behind the wheel, Herb cranked the starter, gunned the engine, and whipped a tight circle toward the road, the little car's wheels *brong brong bronging* as he turned. Hands clenched on the wheel, he decided it was time to feed.

A few miles toward town, Herb was cruising down a dark stretch of the highway, wondering who he would eat tonight. Maybe he'd swing by Stein's, see if any left-over classic car aficionados were talking mufflers and running boards, eight-ball gear shift knobs and fuzzy dice before calling it a night. Or he could linger in the shadows outside of Nekked's, and nab some unsuspecting trucker or frat boy with his drunken friends. While appealing, he quickly discarded the idea. His last visit to Nekked's had not gone well. Herb toyed with the idea of popping into the local jail, putting the whammy on the overnight deputy, and munching on one of the drunks sleeping off a bender. Drink-a-drunk had become a sort of weird indulgence. Ever since his first Bloody Mary, Herb had developed a bit of a taste for mixing alcohol and blood. Through experimentation, he had recently discovered he could get a little tipsy if he drank from a thoroughly inebriated sot.

Yeah, he thought, *a little nightcap would be just the thing. Take the edge off.* And sneaking a drunk from right under the nose of the local authorities was exactly the kind of rebellion Herb's bruised soul needed.

Destination set, he continued down the darkened highway, wondering which of Trappersville's finest would be passed out in the drunk pen tonight. Dark, heavy clouds matched Herb's mood as they rumbled with deep-voiced threats high above and began dumping rain on the world below, but Herb didn't bother slowing down. His preternatural eyesight and inhuman reflexes more than made up for the car's balding tires as they occasionally skidded on the slick pavement. A reckless drive through the building summer storm was a welcome distraction from his thoughts.

Despite the sluicing rain, Herb saw the tail lights far down the road. Besides the solidly burning red, he discerned a rhythmic amber blinking. It wasn't long before he realized he wasn't just catching up to a vehicle. Rather, the lights were off to the side of the road and immobile. Squinting a bit allowed him to make out the shape of the vehicle, a pickup truck. Mostly upside down, it listed in the roadside ditch. Pushing the struggling Pinto past its limits, Herb raced down the final stretch toward the scene of the accident. Despite the rain and his dangerous speed, his keen eyesight picked out the swerve marks in the highway, first left into oncoming traffic, then right toward the ditch, left again, and once more to the right where the truck crossed the dirt shoulder into the taller grass alongside the road. Deep ruts in the rain-softened soil showed two more tight swerves. Slamming on the brakes as he neared the tumbled truck, he saw a sizeable chunk of rock half buried in the dirt, a remnant of old glaciers that had carved out the landscape thousands of years before. The unfortunate truck's front tire must've struck the small boulder mid-swerve, bucking the truck into the flip and tumble that had left it testicles-up in the night-shrouded ditch.

Testicles up? thought Herb, realizing that the strange blinking he'd noticed a couple mile earlier was a turn signal reflecting off of a giant pair of chrome testicles attached to the truck's trailer hitch. *Who would put testicles on a truck for Chrissake? That's just trashy...*

As the Pinto finished its squealing stop alongside the truck, Herb's eyes opened wide in shock.

Deloris. Dallas's truck Deloris. The pieces fell like tumblers in the gummy lock of Herb's brain. If that was Dallas's truck, and Lois was with Dallas...

Not allowing himself to think anymore, Herb climbed out of the Pinto and leapt into the air, landing on the far side of Deloris. Bending over, his worst nightmare took focus before his eyes, only to go all fuzzy again as his eyes welled up with bloody tears. Just inside the mud spattered glass was Lois. She dangled upside down and unconscious in the passenger seat, trapped by the seatbelt that had kept her from smashing through the windshield. Herb could see Dallas just past her, stuck in the same gravity-defying pose, a hell-bound roller-coaster passenger frozen at the top of the loop de loop. Airbags hung toward the inverted truck's ceiling, looking like the sloughed off skins of bloated, molting lizards. Lois's arms hung at awkward angles above her head. One bare shoulder and a bra strap showed through her tee-shirt's stretched and torn neckline. Her golden locks were streaked with blood that flowed slowly but steadily from a nasty gash above her temple. Dizzy with the scent of so much fresh blood, Herb shook his head to clear the fog of indecision. He'd been through more than a few fender-benders over the years and was fairly adept at trading insurance information, but nothing had prepared him for how to handle an upside down pickup trapping the unconscious girl of his dreams inside. Herb knew he had to do something, and he had to do it fast, but had no idea what specifically to do.

He didn't want to smash the door's window for fear of hurting Lois more than she already was. The windshield was a web of cracks and would probably be easy to kick in, but again he worried about shoving more broken glass toward her. The back window was an option. If he punched it in, most of the glass would fall behind the front seats, but dragging her across the broken glass and pulling her out the much smaller rear window seemed like a rotten option. Focusing instead on the door and grasping the handle, he pulled, but couldn't get it to budge. Bracing his feet in the slippery grass, he planted one palm on the side of the doorframe and wrapped the other around the door's handle. Taking a deep breath, he pulled with his more-than-human strength, groaning with the strain as tendons creaked in his shoulders and veins on his neck stood out like cables. After a few tense moments, all he was rewarded with was a sudden snap as the handle wrenched free from the door, tumbling Herb into the ditch. Scrambling to his feet, he clawed his way back up to the side of the truck and placed his hands against the glass. Panic boiled up as he watched droplets of blood run down strands of blond hair like grains of liquid sand flowing inexorably through the hourglass.

Herb had to get in there, had to save her, but the door wouldn't budge. The frame must've bent when the truck rolled, jamming the door. Herb roared in frustration. What good was being super strong if he couldn't even open a pickup truck door? She'd be dead soon if he didn't do something. All that blood...

Blood.

Herb whipped around and crawled under the bed of the truck. Curling his fingers, his fist shot out and shattered the rear window. He rolled onto his side and reached toward the back of Lois's chair. Glass gouged his armpit and scalp as he stretched his arm and grasped the headrest. Pulling and sliding and wriggling forward, his groping fingers finally found their destination and traced along her temple, above her ear. Drawing his bloodied fingers back, he stuck them in his mouth and sucked. The cuts and scratches he'd suffered closed of their own accord. Reaching forward again, he covered his fingers in red, moving more aggressively as the blood keened in his veins. Bringing wet fingers back to his mouth, he sucked hungrily again. Herb had to calm his frantic nerves to avoid biting off his own digits with his spear-sharp fangs.

Whispers rumbled in his head as the now-familiar quickening consumed Herb. Pushing himself out of the window, he cleared the truck bed and rose to his full height. Veins thrumming, he returned to Lois's door. Herb's clawed fingers grabbed, his shoulders flexed and pulled, and the door wrenched open with a vicious screech. Another yank and the door snapped from its hinges. Twisting to the side, Herb flung the door across the ditch and into the woods. He was distantly aware of a sharp clang and muffled thud as the door struck a tree trunk and rebounded into the dirt, but Herb was too focused on Lois to give it much thought. Reaching in, he used one hand to free the seatbelt clasp while the other arm caught her falling body. Careful not to move her too much, he rolled her into his arms and hunched over to back out of the truck.

Herb set Lois gently on the rain-soaked grass. Her beautiful face was drawn and pale, dark circles rimmed her eyes, and her hair clung in blood-soaked tendrils. He leaned in close, pressed his ear against her chest, and was rewarded with the faint but regular *tha-thump* of her heartbeat. A shuddering exhale wracked Herb's body. The wound near her temple still oozed sticky red. As he set a finger gently to the cut, Lois moaned in pain. The sound went through Herb, twisting his insides into knots of fury. To see her in pain was more than he could bear. Without another thought, he raked his hand across his incisors and opened a gash across his palm. Reaching forward before the gash could heal, he pressed his bloodied palm to her forehead and ran his hand gently along the cut. When he first made contact, Lois groaned again, her still-unconscious features contorting in pain, but suddenly, the pained grimace was gone, almost as if the steady rain had washed her face clear of emotion. As Herb's hand passed, the wound on Lois's skull mended and closed, leaving behind unbroken skin and smears of blood which the rain was steadily erasing with each new drop.

Lois's blue eyes flickered open and focused through the rain on Herb's face. Herb returned her gaze, his smile incapable of showing the full magnitude of his relief.

"Herb," she whispered, her throat rough and dry. She coughed weakly and spoke his name again. "Herb, what happened? What are you doing?" Reaching up, she pressed her hand to his cheek, left it there as she continued. "You're all wet. Are you crying? What happened?"

Herb made a noise somewhere between a choke, laugh, and sob. Grabbing her hand with his own, he impulsively kissed her palm, still unable to speak.

She turned her head, taking in the night rain. As she stretched her neck, she noticed the upside down truck and the silhouette of Dallas trapped behind the wheel.

"Oh. Oh god. Is that Dallas? Herb, what happened? Was there an accident? Oh Herb, we have to help Dallas! We have to do something!" Turning onto her side, the hand that had been holding Herb's face moved instead to grab a handful of grass and mud, pulling as Lois weakly started to crawl back toward the hell Herb had just rescued her from.

Herb had completely forgotten about Dallas, so lost was he in saving Lois, so elated was he to see her draw breath, open her eyes. The rest of the world had simply vanished, but now crashed back in with the weight of a V8 pickup flipping over in the night.

Dallas, who'd been driving while obviously hammered. Despite the rain, mud, and diesel smells all around, Herb could easily detect the reek of bourbon and beer. Dallas, who must've made a drunken grab at Lois while driving, all stupid and horny. Her torn shirt was proof of that. Dallas, losing control of the truck in the process and flipping it ass over teakettle into the ditch, damn near killing the both of them.

Herb snarled like a feral beast. In one fluid motion, he'd gone from kneeling in the soaking grass to leaping up and over the truck. Landing on the far side, he pivoted to face the driver's side. Without even checking to see if it was stuck like the previous door, he punched out the glass and wrapped his freshly bloodied hands around the panel. With a sharp pull, the door wrenched free of its hinges. Herb continued the pulling motion into a two-handed discus throw, sending the door careening over the highway and far into the night-soaked trees. Crouching down with his arms splayed, mouth stretched unnaturally wide and wicked-sharp fangs glinting in the blue glow of the dashboard lights, Herb roared at Dallas. A lifetime of pent-up resentment and rage came pouring out like vitriol, brought to a volcanic head by the fact that Dallas had nearly killed Lois. The vampire's vision reddened, and the whispers turned into a multitude of demons roaring in his skull, demanding blood, demanding vengeance. Herb's arm shot out. Fingers like steel claws gripped Dallas's skull, nails dug deep into his scalp. Violently pushing his head back and to the side, Herb leaned in, already stretched-wide jaws creaking as the tendons pulled even wider. Breath hot on the side of Dallas's neck, he clamped his jaws shut, fangs piercing skin, muscle, vein, unleashing a torrent of blood into his waiting mouth.

All the emotions roiling inside him spun to a new frenzy with each hungry gulp. Like a drunkard trying to drown all his pain at the bottom of a whiskey ocean, Herb squeezed his eyes shut and guzzled

Dallas's lifeblood, trying with each swallow to drown all the anger, the angst, the insecurity that had built up shovelful by shovelful over the years of their friendship. For so long, Dallas had gotten everything, *everything*, while Herb had been content with the scraps. After all the long years, Herb finally realized it was all a lie. Their friendship, every moment they'd shared, all of it was just a way for Dallas to take and to leave Herb the beggar.

No more, thought Herb, his thoughts soaked in bloodlust and revenge. *Now it's my time to take. And I will. I will take it all. The glory you crave, the girl you want, the life you so callously take for granted. All mine.*

Shifting his grip to ensure the maximum flow of blood from the gash in Dallas's jugular, Herb opened his eyes. With his mouth sealed against the side of Dallas's neck like a lamprey, he looked through the truck to the darkness beyond and found himself staring directly into fear-widened eyes. Lois stared at Herb's murderous feeding, horror plain on her face.

Releasing Dallas's torn and bloody neck, Herb fell backward, shocked and revolted by what he was doing. His eyes shifted from Lois's terror-stricken visage to the nasty tear in the side of Dallas's neck where blood flowed like a macabre faucet.

"Oh shit. No no no no! No way. Oh crap," Herb panted as he scurried back into the truck. Dallas was sheet-white, comatose. Biting hard into his own hand once again, Herb slapped his bloody palm against the wound and pressed hard.

"Come on! C'mon c'mon c'mon Dallas. You're gonna be okay. You've gotta be okay." Pulling his hand back, he looked and saw the torn and jagged holes his fangs had made were starting to close. The gush of blood slowed until it wept like tree sap. Grabbing the seatbelt release, Herb freed Dallas and caught him as he fell, pulled him from the truck, and stretched him out on the grass. Dallas's chest rose and fell with shaky breaths, and Herb heard him groan in pain. He was still unconscious, but Herb knew he would live, assuming he got to a doctor soon. Looking again at Lois, fear warring with incomprehension on her face, Herb made the only decision he could. Looking straight into her eyes, he said, "I'm sorry Lois, I'm so sorry, but you have to forget. You have to forget this happened. I wasn't here, okay? I wasn't here and you gotta sleep now. Just sleep and everything will be okay. I promise Lois. I promise."

Palm out like a benediction, Herb reached toward Lois as he worked his whammy. Her eyes misted over, face went slack. Lying down in the soaking mud and grass, she cradled her head in her arms and fell into a deep sleep. Not wasting any time, Herb raced back around the truck to her side. Finding her purse in the disheveled wreck of the truck's interior, he pulled out her cell phone and dialed 911. After two rings, the operator picked up, and Herb screamed with a high-pitched voice.

"Help! Oh, please help! We flipped over, Dallas is hurt. Please hurry! We're on Highway Nineteen." Herb stood quickly and looked around the nightscape before returning to the call. "Um, we're maybe ten miles from the Lafayette turnoff, heading west on Nineteen. Please, hurry!"

Ignoring the operator's response, he left the phone connected and set it in the mud next to Lois's head. Backing away, he returned to his car and drove up the highway. After about a half-mile, he pulled off and headed into the trees. After almost getting stuck twice, he finished a three-point turn and reversed into the cover of the tree line, killed the engine and headlights, and waited.

Herb anxiously looked first to his left toward where Dallas and Lois lay unconscious in the mud, then to his right, hoping to see the telltale red and blue of help on the way. A sob of relief shook him when he saw the lights and heard the sirens as the ambulance and sheriff's car raced down the highway. Only after they'd reached the accident, moved both Dallas and Lois into the ambulance, and raced down the highway did Herb crank the engine and pull back onto the road. Since he didn't need his headlights to drive in the dark, Herb left them off until he neared town. Following the blue H's on the side of the road, he made his nerve-wracked way to the hospital.

Chapter 38

ERB SAT FIDGETING IN his car. He'd parked in a corner of the hospital parking lot that the lights couldn't quite reach. While he desperately wanted to go inside and see Lois, he knew there would be questions. Lots of questions. Maybe not from Lois or Dallas, but from the cops or paramedics. He also knew he couldn't stay much longer. Every minute he fretted in the Pinto's front seat, he could feel the sun drawing inexorably closer. He had just decided to leave when Trappersville's only cab arrived. Herb watched from the shadows as first Lois and then Dallas exited the building. Seeing that Lois was okay loosened the vice in his chest a couple of twists, but the relief was short-lived. All it took was one look at Dallas and that vice cranked right back up again.

As Herb glared from deep in the shadows, he noticed Dallas wasn't walking naturally. He seemed unsteady on his feet and raised his hands up to catch his balance. Herb's sharp eyes caught the glint of chrome on Dallas's wrists. A moment later and the deputy sheriff walked out of the hospital as well, whistling at Dallas like calling a recalcitrant puppy. Herb squinted to better see the scene unfold. When Dallas pulled up short, Lois kept walking determinedly toward the waiting cab. Dallas called out something to Lois. She ignored him and opened the cab's door. Stopping suddenly, Herb watched her shake her head, turn on her heel, and walk straight back toward Dallas. Once she was within arm's reach, Lois slapped him across the face, hard. Dallas's head snapped to the side and sprung back, his visage a study in pained confusion. Even from where he was parked across the lot, Herb could read his lips as he said, "It was an accident! An accident!" over and over.

Herb settled back into his seat, arms crossed and index finger lightly tapping his chin, and watched the deputy put Dallas in the back of a squad car. As soon as they had pulled away and turned out of the hospital's parking lot, Herb put the Pinto into drive and headed home, a look of grim resolve hardening on his face.

Chapter 39

Lois was back at work three nights later. Herb was mid-breakfast platter when he heard her car. He made a quick excuse—something about needing to empty the trash—and let the prep cook take over the grill. On his way around the building, he met Lois as she'd finished one cigarette and was lighting another one.

"Hi there, Lois. How's it going? You, uh. You doing okay?" Herb offered a tentative smile and a half-wave, instantly elated when Lois returned his gesture with a smile and wave of her own.

"Oh hi, Herb. I'm okay." Suddenly nervous, she ducked her head and pushed her bangs back. "I suppose you heard about me and Dallas the other night, huh? News travels fast in a town like this." Taking a long drag on her cigarette, she met his eyes for a moment, and looked down again, her attention suddenly focused on a divot in the concrete.

Herb nodded. "Sorry. Yeah. The mechanic from Patt's was in yesterday talking about how bad Delor- ah, Dallas's truck is banged up. But I'm really, really glad that you're okay."

Lois's laugh was empty of all humor. "Deloris. I swear that damn truck means more to him than anything else." Lois pierced him with a sharp gaze and asked in a low voice, "But Dallas, he hasn't come 'round? Hasn't seen you or told you what happened?"

Herb shook his head, doing his best to play dumb. In truth, Dallas hadn't been around. In the days since the accident, Dallas had barely left Deloris's side. Or so he'd told Stanley. Herb didn't doubt it, though. Lois had the right of it. Dallas loved that truck.

The waitress crushed out her cigarette and went to get a third from her purse. As she pulled it out, her hand shook so badly that she dropped it on the cement. Cursing under her breath, she bent down to retrieve it and flicked her lighter once, twice, trying to light it. Hands still shaking, the flame kept extinguishing before she could light the smoke. Herb stepped forward, guided by sudden instinct. He reached out and plucked the plastic lighter from her fingers and held it forward. Leaning in, Lois lit the cigarette, inhaled deeply, and pulled it away from her lips. Herb watched the glowing tip jitter and grow steadier as Lois exhaled through her nose.

"That son of a bitch." Lois gave him a searching look. "I know he's your friend, Herb, and I don't want to start shit between you two. But that jackass damn near killed me."

When Herb said nothing, she continued. "Okay. So you know how Dallas has been, well. Kinda chasing me for a while now, right? He's nothing if not persistent. Anyway, I dunno. He's never really been. I mean, it's not that he's not. Um." She shook her head, continued on. "Well, I guess let's just say that I've dated my share of self-involved, egotistical a-holes, and apparently haven't learned my lesson yet." Third cigarette only half-finished, Lois checked her watch, glanced inside.

"They're fine," Herb offered. "There's only like three tables, and they've all got their food. We've got a little time." Sitting on the slatted bench next to the ashtray, Herb patted the flaking paint of the boards next to him. "Have a seat. Tell me the rest."

Sitting beside him, she pushed a still trembling hand through her hair. "Well, anyway. So Dallas kept saying just give him one date, right? One date. If we had a terrible time, or even a kind of whatever time, he'd leave me alone. Never ask me out again. But if we had even just a tiny bit of fun, well then..." Her mood made her smile look sad. "Such a talker. Anyway, so we had a date. One date. And he was nice. Funny. Attentive. Even sweet. I found myself thinking, maybe I'd misjudged this one. I mean, I know he has a reputation around town, but people change, right?"

Not Dallas, Herb thought as he nodded, waiting quietly for her to continue.

"So anyway, when he popped in the other night, it was a nice surprise. You were there. You saw how he was. He didn't seem like he'd been drinking or anything. But over at Stein's, he must've put down five or six beers and a few shots of whiskey and was really getting revved up. There were a couple of guys playing pool. Dallas kept trying to get me to play, to help him 'hustle the little bitches,' as he put it. I suck at pool, but what the hell right? So we played. I had a few drinks, Dallas had more than a few. But even then." Lois stopped, shook her head angrily. "God, I'm so stupid. I still thought he would be, like. You know. Okay to drive. And my car was here, and it was so late."

Lois paused in her narrative, her eyes focusing on some indeterminate point in the darkness.

"Geezuz, Herb. We were driving, and he... I mean, I can't believe he. Dallas was, well. He was trying.," Lois's voice broke a little, and she cleared her throat before continuing. "Dallas was doing something when he lost control and we swerved off the road." Herb didn't miss the look of disgust that crossed her face like a dark cloud across the sun. "Christ. Forget it. He lost control of *Deloris* and we flipped over in the ditch and that jackass cares more about the damn truck than me." She ground her teeth in frustration while Herb shrugged woodenly, not trusting himself to speak.

Lois turned her head and looked at him strangely for a moment. "But I guess what is there to worry about? By whatever miracle, I'm fine, even though the truck is damn near totaled. It was upside down, for Chrissake." Lois paused again, struggling with the memory of the accident. Her voice dropped a little as she continued, causing Herb to lean in closer. "But how the hell could I have been okay? The doors. Both doors were completely ripped from the truck."

Herb felt the back of his neck flush, and his palms started to get clammy. "Oh. Um. So, like the doors broke off or something. That doesn't sound so weird. I mean, since the truck flipped and all, right?" he offered.

"They didn't just get knocked off when we flipped. The Sheriff found one on our side of the highway, but we were in the ditch and it was all the way over in the trees. The other, Dallas's door, they finally found it *across* the highway. In the trees on the other side of the road. Herb, that's like thirty or forty yards away. Straight across the highway from the truck. It's like. Oh, I don't know. I feel stupid even saying this, but it's like something threw it across the highway."

Ice cold beads of sweat trickled down Herb's spine, causing him to squirm uncomfortably. He really wanted to change the subject, but Lois continued before he could speak.

"The crazy thing is that I was fine, Herb. When I came to in the ambulance, there was nothing wrong with me. I was muddy and dirty and soaked from the rain, so I must've been tossed from the truck when it flipped. Which I guess means the door had been ripped away first. But I was wearing my seat belt. I know I was! The police were grilling me on that, giving me the whole "seat belts save lives" spiel. I told them that maybe when the door got ripped off, my seat belt was torn, but the seat belt was fine. So I don't know, Herb. I have no idea what happened. I just know that the truck flipped, the doors came off, my seat belt somehow magically unbuckled itself, and I was tossed into the ditch."

Lois's eyes widened in remembered fear. So intense was her inward stare that Herb worried she'd gone comatose, but then she spoke.

"My shirt, my hair were covered with blood. *Covered.*" She paused again before continuing in a near whisper. "But I was fine. There was barely a scrape on me. So where did all that blood come from?" Her head shook in confused frustration. "I can't remember, Herb. I can't remember! I know Dallas tried to grab... um. Dallas swerved, we flipped, and I woke up in the ambulance like nothing worse than a quick tumble in the mud had happened. What the hell, right?"

By this point, Lois was shaking and on the verge of sobs. Herb shifted on the bench, arms open, and watched dream-like as Lois leaned into his arms. Pulling her in close, he stroked her perfect hair, held her tight to his chest. Herb and Lois sat in the fluorescent light outside of Ronnie's as she fought to control the tears that wanted to spill out. Finally, she took a deep breath and released it. Herb felt the muscles shift in her back, felt her chin rise as she brought herself back under control. She returned Herb's embrace fiercely before pulling back. Suddenly, she leaned back in and kissed him on the cheek, lips lingering for a moment before she pulled away.

"Thanks, Herb. I mean it. I haven't really talked to anyone the past few days. Thanks for listening. Sorry, it sounds all crazy, but still. Thank you."

Herb looked deep into Lois's eyes, all his nervousness and insecurities blown away, dandelion fluff in a summer breeze. Reaching out to trace her cheek with his thumb, he replied, "I'll always be here for you, Lois. No matter what happens, no matter how weird. Just know that I'll be here."

The grateful smile she gave him before turning to walk into Ronnie's was the closest thing to the sun Herb had seen in weeks, and it lit up his world for the rest of the night.

Chapter 40

Herb hadn't seen Dallas and had carefully dodged his phone calls. It must've been rough for Dallas, waiting for Deloris to go through major surgery. The voicemails alone were pretty telling.

"Holy crapballs, Herb. Where the hell you been? Do you do anything besides work nights anymore? Shit. I'm going crazy here. Patt took back the loaner, said he needed it for another customer. Can you believe that shit? So anyway. I'm, ah. Well, old D is kinda stuck here, and he's kinda going crazy. So c'mon. Pick up. Pickuppickuppickup. Get me outta here. Let's go to Steins. Or better yet, we should get some pizza. I need me some pizza. Hello? Okay, you hose bag. I'm calling Stanley."

Force of nature that Dallas was, he didn't handle inaction well. Better luck telling the Tasmanian Devil to sit still and watch paint dry. Old habits die hard, and Herb had been hard pressed not to jump into his car and head straight over to his friend's place. But then he remembered Deloris upside down in the ditch, Lois's torn shirt, blood flowing freely from that gash by her temple. Each image was burned into his brain, tinting all of his other thoughts red. Dallas could stew in his own shit for all he cared. If he was bored, he could build a card house, or watch infomercials, or hang himself from the rafters and save Herb the trouble. He knew he couldn't avoid Dallas forever, but still wasn't ready to face his best friend.

Sooner than Herb would've liked, Deloris was patched up, and Dallas was on the loose again. Their unavoidable confrontation came around eleven p.m. when Dallas pulled into Ronnie's. It was a slow night. Dee had only had a handful of tables and had spent much of her shift alternating between catching up on recorded soaps and reading the 'missed-connections' section of one of Madison's trashier papers. Herb was in the kitchen when he heard Dallas blow into the diner with his usual gusto. Herb's first reaction was fear for Lois, followed by instant relief when he remembered she wasn't working that night. Shifting to better see out the serve-through, he watched Dallas stride into the diner.

"Damn. This place is a ghost town. Where the hell is everyone? Oh, hey George! How's it hanging? Over the belt, as usual, eh Georgie-porgy?"

Herb heard George, a long-haul trucker that regularly passed through Ronnie's, growl back, "Up yours, Dallas. Them mamby-pamby pretty boys in Madison can have their six-packs. I prefer the party ball." Rubbing his ample belly appreciatively, he added, "Plus, it helps me steer the rig when I'm eating. You should get one. Might help you keep your wheels on the ground."

Dallas barked out a brittle laugh. "Good one George! Too true. A little extra weight on the cab probably does help keep her steady. Thanks for the tip." Looking around, he asked to no one in particular, "Who's on tonight?"

"Not Lois," Dee snapped, appearing from the back with George's check. "Need anything else, George?" When he shook his head, Dee dropped his check on the table, scooped up his empty plate, and finally spared a glance for Dallas.

"Herb will take care of you, Dallas," she said, her usually warm voice suddenly and significantly cooled. "Herb," she called into the kitchen, "I'll be in the break room watching my soaps. Let me know if a table comes in, 'kay?" Without another word, Dee whipped her head around and vanished, her disappearance followed by the slam of the break room door.

Dallas swung around and mounted a stool at the Formica counter. Tall as he was, he could easily see over the serve-through window into the kitchen while seated. After settling on the stool, he looked up, eyes suddenly staring directly into Herb's. Both men registered mild surprise at the hostility they saw reflected at themselves.

With a smile that stopped at his mouth, Dallas said, "Well, it's my old buddy Herby! Haven't seen you in the longest. How're things?"

Herb wiped his hands off on his apron, eyes never leaving Dallas's. "Oh, you know. Same shit, different day. You need some food? I imagine flipping trucks works up quite an appetite."

"It was an accident. No one got hurt. Lois knows that, and she knows I'm sorry. So let's not make it a thing, okay?" Dallas growled. "Like I said, an accident. From the beating Deloris took, I know it was pretty bad. Guess it's a miracle that Lois came out okay and me with just a few bumps and bruises. Damn, I love that truck. Whatever the hell ripped her apart like that, she still looked out for Lois and me." Dallas shifted on the stool, striking a thinker's pose on the counter. "Now that's the thing, though. What ripped her apart like that? It's like some crazy monster went all Hulk-smash on my poor Deloris. Flipped her over, smashed a window, and ripped the doors right off."

Dallas paused as Herb walked around the window through the swing door and came to stand across from Dallas behind the counter. He leaned back, arms crossed over his chest. Keeping his face blank, Herb replied, "Yeah. Real shame about your truck."

. Her name is Deloris, Herb. Show some respect. You never hear me say, "That piece of shit hatchback," or, "that crappy hamster trap." Dallas still wore the painted-on smile, and the paint was starting to chip.

"Okay. Geez. I heard *De-Lor-Is* got roughed up. Must've been a helluva flip. I'm," Herb's throat worked for a moment to choke up the words, "just glad you're okay. And Deloris too," he added, with a quick glance toward where the truck's freshly repaired grill was visible through the diner's window.

"Yup. Everyone's fine, Herby. Thanks for that. Sucks, though. Me and Lois, we were having a good time that night before it all went to hell. Now she seems all pissed at me. Blaming me for what happened. Like it's my fault Deloris flipped like that. But we both know that's not true," he added in a conspiratorial tone.

"Well, actually, Dallas, Lois does think that's true. She thinks you were drunk, you lost control, and you flipped the truck. I was surprised to hear that, 'cause I know you can handle your booze and all, but it sounds like you…"

Tried to molest her and your stupid drunk ass lost control of the truck in the process, Herb thought.

"… must've been drunker than you thought, huh?" he snarled instead.

Dallas leveled an even stare at Herb. "I didn't mean me and Lois. I meant me and you. Me. And. You. We know that's not true, right?"

Herb returned Dallas's accusatory look with his own confused scowl. He didn't want to deal with Dallas right now. He was having enough trouble keeping his cool already without Dallas making vague allegations of... what exactly, Herb wasn't sure. The whispers were circling again like a distant swarm of wasps. With a forced shrug, Herb turned back toward the kitchen door.

"Not sure what you're getting at Dallas."

"No? Huh. Oh well. Hey, did you hear about that dead guy they found in the woods?" Dallas asked.

Herb's shoulders tensed, their muscles corded like tree roots. "Oh, uh, yeah. I guess I might've heard some guys talking about that. Some tourist drank too much, tripped in the trees and broke his neck, right?

"Oh, is that what happened?" Dallas asked after letting the silence stretch thin.

Herb huffed. "Look Dallas, I gotta work. You need something to eat, or a Coke or something?"

The smile-that-wasn't-a-smile pulled Dallas's lips back even tighter across his teeth. "Sure, Herby. I'd love something to eat. You guys still serve that turkey dinner with the garlic mashed potatoes?"

"Yup. I'll get it going for ya. Gimme a few and it'll be right up," Herb called over his shoulder without looking back.

"That'd be great Herby. Just fine indeed! Oh, and lots of garlic in those potatoes, okay? I heard garlic is a cure-all for all kinds of problems. Like bloodsuckers."

Herb stopped in mid-stride, understanding crawling over him like cockroaches. Speaking through a suddenly dry throat, he asked, "Bloodsuckers? What, you mean, like skeeters or tics or something?"

Dallas had pulled his ever-present pocket knife out and was studiously cleaning his fingernails. Without looking up, he drawled, "Why yes. I think it must've been Stanley that told me that one. You know how Stanley is, all that crazy stuff that sticks in his bird-brain like sweater fuzz to a five-o'clock shadow. I guess garlic is good for keeping away nasty little bloodsuckers. Seems to be the case that they just can't stand the stuff. So yep, lots of garlic in those taters, Herb. Oh, and a Coke would be fine."

Herb moved automaton-like as he grabbed a glass, filled it with ice and pop, and set it on the counter. Heading back into the kitchen to cook up a turkey dinner, his mind whirled. Was that true? He saw in those movies that vamps hated garlic. Well, in some of the movies. Which ones, though? He'd made a lot of garlicky food since his change, but had never thought to eat any. Herb tried to think back to the last time he'd handled a bulb of garlic. Did his eyes water more than normal? Did he get a rash or loose bowels? He couldn't seem to remember, which made him think he was probably in the clear. But then again... A lot of other things he'd learned about vamps in the movies were true. He was crazy strong, could see in the dark, and sunlight left him crispy as the unlucky pig at the luau, but he couldn't fly, his face didn't get all weird when he turned, and despite being stronger and faster, he never really mastered Kung Fu. He could whammy folks into thinking just about anything, and mirrors for the most part just ignored him...

Whammy. Herb's mind did a double-take. *That's it*, he thought. Make the potatoes garlic-free, do a quick whammy, and Dallas would think they were the best garlic mashed taters outside of Eden.

Better safe than sorry, right? Smiling a devious smile, Herb set himself to the task of making Dallas's dinner.

Less than ten minutes later, Herb brought out the promised meal and set it on the counter. Dallas looked up as he approached. If Herb could still cast a reflection, he'd have seen two of himself reflected in Dallas's mirrored aviator shades. As it was, he saw two of his shirt and apron and a floating plate piled high with steaming slices of turkey breast, peas and carrots, and a healthy mound of mashed potatoes.

"Bright in here, ain't it?" Dallas asked with a smile. "Hope you don't mind." Grabbing his fork, Dallas scooped up a helping of potatoes, held them to his nose and inhaled deeply. Frowning, he put the fork in his mouth and chewed slowly. "Herby, you disappoint me. You call these garlic potatoes? Christ on a stick. I'm gonna have to fill out one of them comment cards Ronnie's got over there. Tell him his *best chef* can't find the garlic. Nope, not a happy customer. At. All."

Herb leveled his *look* at Dallas. Staring into where he assumed his eyeballs were behind the shades, Herb quietly said, "But Dallas. Those are garlic mashed potatoes. In fact, they're probably the best garlic mashed potatoes you've ever had. Isn't that right?"

Smiling, Herb waited for Dallas's face to go slack and for him to agree that yes, they were good potatoes, the garlic was great, and they were the best he'd ever had. Instead, Dallas drew his mouth into a tight line. Standing suddenly, he grabbed his plate and walked over to where George was finishing his coffee and counting out nickels onto the table.

"George! How are ya, big fella? Sorry to intrude. Take a taste of these here potatoes. No, it's okay. Herb's just trying to mess with me, but he should know by now that no one messes with old Dallas." Dropping the plate on the table, Dallas prodded George with a smile. "C'mon George. Take a forkful and tell me if there is or is no garlic. I say is no. Herby says is so. So which is it?"

"C'mon guys. I gotta get back on the road. I don't have time to get dragged into your horseplay again. Maybe next time." Sliding the plate back toward Dallas, George called out to Dee as she was coming out of the ladies' room. "Much thanks, sweetheart. Cash is on the table." With a dismissive wave, George ambled past them, belly swaying in rhythm to his steps.

"G'night George. Thanks for the nickels! My kid's gonna love 'em. Piggy bank's halfway full!" Dee called after him as she walked around to collect the tab. Her wave to George turned into a quick flip of the bird at Dallas before she walked back to the break room.

"Well shit. Everyone really thinks I'm the asshole, huh?" Dallas lamented as he picked up his plate and carried it back to the counter. "So. Back to these potatoes. There's no garlic. God's own truth."

Herb leaned closer, staring at the shiny curved glass perched on Dallas's nose. "They are garlic potatoes."

"Are not."

"Yes, and they're the best damn garlic taters you've ever had!"

"Nope. Why you being so weird about it? I'm not trying to hurt your feelings. Here, try some. You'll see."

As Dallas pushed the plate toward Herb, Herb took a clumsy swipe at his sunglasses. Dallas leaned back, causing Herb's hand to just brush the tip of his nose instead of connecting with the shades.

"Whoah ho ho! What's this now? Getting feisty? What's the matter, Herb? If even you won't eat your cookin', how d'you expect someone else to?" Dallas stepped off the stool and reached around behind his back, causing Herb to tense suddenly.

"Easy buddy. Wow, you're tense. Just getting a little cashola for the din-din here. Though why I should pay when I didn't get what I ordered beats me." Flashing his wallet, brown leather with an eagle in bright colors on the face, Dallas dropped a ten on the counter. "But hey, I'm not hungry. Just thought I'd drop by, see what I'd see, and I guess I've seen enough. Catch you later Herb."

Sliding his mirrored shades down the bridge of his nose, Dallas's steely eyes peered out over the frame and drilled into Herb's. With a mean smile, the kind of smile you give the cow right before the bolt hits it square between the eyes, Dallas asked, "Maybe you want to come round to my place tomorrow? I'm gonna be, uh, fixin' a few things round the yard. Be nice to have an extra set of hands, catch up a bit, get some *sun*." Dallas used his extended middle finger to slide his glasses back up his nose. "Whaddaya say?"

Still stewing over his stymied whammy, Herb grunted and said, "Uh. Sorry. Maybe next time. Gonna be here all night, and I probably won't wake up 'til it's time to head back to work."

Dallas tipped an imaginary hat on his head and turned toward the door. "Thought not. Guess I'll manage. But you really should get out more Herby. You're lookin' a little pale. A little sunshine would probably do you, or at least me and Lois, a world of good."

The clomp of Dallas's cowboy boots on the diner floor had the sound of nails being driven into a coffin. Long after Deloris had roared to life and raced out of Ronnie's lot, Herb still stood by the counter.

Many thoughts chased their tails, piling onto each other, cawing for his attention, and then scurrying back into the dark corner of his mind, but one thought, one dark thought kept crawling back into the light: Herb should've ripped Dallas's throat out when he had the chance.

Chapter 41

"Karaoke? I, um. R-really? Like, with me? And you? You mean like together?"

All of Herb's affected cool had fallen like ice from a warming roof, leaving him a hot mess. Lois's proposal was something he'd never expected—not in a million years—even considering how things had been better lately. Herb didn't know what to think. The previous week, she'd really opened up to him, and then last night, Dallas had basically spelled out in crayon that he knew Herb was a vamp. And now tonight, here was Lois asking him—him!—on a karaoke date.

What a difference a day makes, he thought with an inward grin. However weird his life had been recently, if a date with Lois was the end result, then every single moment was worth it.

"Of course with you! I just thought you seem to know Bay City Bowlers pretty well, what with being this year's big bowling champ and all, and figured you might want to head over there tomorrow, since we both have the night off and all."

Lois smiled, but there was an unexpected nervousness beneath it. It took him a moment, but Herb realized she was worried he'd say no. The thought almost made him laugh out loud. Him? Say no to a date with her? Not frickin' likely.

Sweeping one arm behind his back and the other across his waist, Herb bowed. "I would be honored to escort you on an evening of karaoke and merriment. In fact," he continued, straightening, "there's actually nothing in the entire world that I would enjoy more."

Lois blushed prettily, smiling in her special way. With a sideways glance and a mischievous tone, she asked, "You're sure Jenni won't mind? You two made quite the pair at the finals, after all..."

"You were at the finals?" Herb gasped in shock. "I mean, like, really there? You saw me bowl?"

"Toward the end. I didn't really see the game, but I heard all about it later. I mean, c'mon. It was all anyone talked about for a week! You and Dallas rolling like a couple of bowling gods. The tramp twins cat fight, Dallas taking a swing at you. I guess I wish I had seen all that. I wouldn't have made the mistake of going on a date with him." She smiled away the bad memories. "But I did see you guys riding the crowd to the bar after, all home town heroes and what-not. Seems like Jenni was quite enamored with you," she added with a sly grin. "So, like I said. She's not going to mind if I steal you for an evening, is she?"

Herb's head shook vigorously. "Nope. No, um. We, well, I kinda. I mean, we weren't ever, you know. It was just. We were just. Huh." Squirming under Lois's knowing look, he skipped all attempts to explain what exactly he and Jenni were that night. "Well, anyway, I called that off, and I'm pretty sure she's seeing some other guy now. Which is good."

Lois let him off the hook with another knowing smile and a wink. "Well, that's settled then. You're going to pick me up at nine o'clock sharp. We'll grab a couple of drinks and go sing our hearts out, and it'll be great." Lois stuck out a hand, the other planted on her hip. "Do we have a deal?"

Herb reached out and took Lois's hand in his own, glad to have something to anchor him for fear that he'd float off into the ether. With a firm shake and a nod of his head, he agreed. "Deal. Now, I hope you don't mind, but I have to go learn how to sing, so I don't make a complete ass out of myself."

Lois laughed. "But of course. You do that Herb. I'll see you tomorrow. And remember: nine o'clock sharp."

And with that, she was gone.

Herb wasn't kidding. He hadn't sung a note since fifth grade choir. Any other day he would've been terrified of the prospect of joining Jasper on the little stage in the corner of the bar at Bay City Bowlers, but Lois had just asked him on a date! Every other concern that had ever weighed on his mind suddenly and completely dissolved. Humming a jaunty tune, he headed back into the kitchen.

Chapter 42

*T*HUNK THUNK THUNK!

Herb ran, and the nightmare followed. His legs and arms pumped madly, but no matter how fast he ran—and he could run very, very fast—the monster closed the distance between them. Belching steam from wide nostrils, spittle and slobber spewing out from a wide mouth ringed with jagged, steel teeth that made a mockery of his own little fangs, electric blue sparks arcing from its eyes, curled chrome horns dripping black venom, and an absolutely gigantic pair of chrome balls, it cut a mile-wide swath of destruction. A burning, smoking trail of ruin and blight stretched behind it to a grim horizon. Herb gathered his secrets to his chest, tried to keep a grip, but like greased ball bearings, bits of secrets slipped from his sweating palms and fell to the concrete beneath his hard-pounding feet. He tried once, twice to stop and pick them up, but there was no time, no time left. A steampunk dragon, it came after him, angry, seething. Perched high on its back, wearing a cowboy hat and a bloodied bowling jersey, sat Dallas. One hand was curled in the metallic blue mane of the beast named Deloris, the other carried a giant Magnum forty-five, each shot a deafening crack of thunder.

Thunk thunk thunk!

Eyes opening, Herb climbed awkwardly out of a deep sleep. It wasn't time to be awake yet, and the headache started behind his left eyeball almost immediately. He hated being up during the day. It was annoying and made him feel like his world was slowly being pulled inside out. Adding to his annoyance, someone was pounding on the front door, hitting it so hard it was rattling pictures on the adjacent walls. Herb figured some insurance salesman had finally tracked down his backwoods-bungalow, or an over-eager Boy Scout was hawkin' over-priced candy bars. Whoever it was, they were going to get a piece of his mind, the really nasty piece that was full of curse words, colorful visuals, and clear warnings to never set foot on his property again.

He dragged leaden feet up the root cellar stairs, angry mutterings building toward the tongue-lashing he was about to unleash, and made his way through the spotless kitchen. It was cleaner now that he didn't eat regular food, except for a thin layer of dust that covered the counter, stove, and his unused alarm clock. Having tripped over that thought, he succumbed to a slew of others. It seemed like ages ago that he'd stood in the front lawn in his old terrycloth robe, sipping coffee and watching the sunrise. Remembering made him miss his simple routines. Things were definitely different now, but maybe he could find comfort in some new routines. Like saving some blood in the fridge and having a glass at moonrise. He could still wear Scary Terry, stand outside, and breathe in the scents. Still enjoy the woods that had always felt like home to him.

Habit raised his eyes to the kitchen window so he could look out upon the trees. Instead, he saw the crumpled scraps of newspaper and grocery bags held in place with a conglomeration of tape. His eyebrows crept toward one another, pulled down by a growing frown. Sure, things were different now. He was a night person, well, night *vampire* if you wanted to get technical, but still. Lots of people worked nights, slept days, and had normal lives. The stuff over his windows didn't convey 'normal.' It made him feel like a crazy hoarder trying to avoid peering eyes, rather than a respectable citizen that just happened to be sort of allergic to the sun. No, he had to be more presentable, more respectable. He was *somebody* now. A champion bowler, respected chef. Hell, even Lois had noticed the difference, and it seemed like she was really starting to not just like him, but 'like him' like him. And if they had fun tonight, they might even end up back here...

Thunk thunk. Thunkthunkthunkthunk! THUNK!

The knocking had grown more insistent, as if the knocker knew that Herb was standing a short distance away but not moving as expected toward the door. With a fresh volley of curses and threats locked and loaded and ready for release, Herb stomped through the living room to the front door. His keen sense of smell registered a mixed bouquet of beer, whiskey, sweat, and mild halitosis. Leaning in, he squinted through the peephole to identify the smelly visitor and saw two small, intersecting lengths of silver.

The language center of his brain had just dredged up the name Dallas and the word 'crucifix' when a super heated bolt of plasma pierced his cornea, incinerated his iris, boiled the jelly inside his eyeball, and ignited his optic nerve like a fuse to the bundle of dynamite in his cranium that subsequently exploded like a thousand suns going supernova.

At least, that's how it felt to Herb as he lurched back, hissing and covering his offended eyeball with his hand. As quickly as the pain lanced through his head, it subsided, leaving a cold rage in its place.

With a quick twist, he unlocked the deadbolt and pulled on the door. The safety chain gave a sharp snap and strained the screws securing it to the doorjamb. Glaring out through the resulting gap, his right eye's field of vision filled with a smug-looking Dallas.

"What in the hell do you want, you stupid son of a turkey baster?" Herb snapped before fully processing that Dallas was standing at his front door with a silver crucifix. Once his brain caught up to the situation at hand, Herb carefully kept his good eye locked on Dallas's mirrored shades and continued his tirade. "I was working until five o'clock this morning and was sound asleep. Did you really find it absolutely necessary to drive all the way over here to show me your new jewelry? Son of a Viking fan's mother! You'd better have a damn good reason for being here."

For a moment, the tiniest moment—a span of time so small that only well-qualified scientists with long strings of letters following their names could measure it with highly calibrated equipment—Dallas looked unsure of himself. But before that very natural and healthy self-preservation instinct could take control, his ego grabbed the wheel once again.

"Good afternoon to you too, Herb. Sounds like you've been borrowing from Ronnie's book of rants. That was good, though. What was it again? 'Son of a Viking fan's mother?' Very creative. I'm gonna use that one, that's for damn sure. But, hey. What happened to your eye?"

"Nuthin'," Herb growled in response.

"Really? Looks like you're bleeding..." Dallas offered helpfully.

Herb pulled his hand away from his face, and sure enough, a trickle of blood had smeared his palm. The good news was that he could see his bloody palm, so he wasn't blind after all. Pressing it back to his eye again, he grumbled, "Cut myself shaving. What do you want, Dallas? Mashed potatoes again? Wait until I'm back at work. Right now, I really need to get some sleep."

"Well, Herb. I just thought I'd stop by, say hey. You want a beer? Gotta couple cold ones in Deloris. When I was patching her back together, I added a little travel fridge in the storage under the back seat. Neat, right? Road brews, always cold. Thought we could sit out in the sun, have a beer, talk about a few things. Been awhile since we've done that, huh? You and me. Just sat, tossed the shit, had a beer or two. So, whadaya say? Come have a beer with your old buddy. We can talk about, oh. I dunno. Movies, bowling, strippers, that dead guy in the woods, whatever. Lots to talk about, Herb."

Herb looked with his one good eye at the man that had been his friend for most of his life. A loneliness opened up somewhere in his chest. Him and Dallas and all the wonderful ways they could waste time. Simple pleasures. Drinking, bowling, occasional farting contests that Dallas sometimes let Herb win.

But things were different now. Herb couldn't look at Dallas and not see the man that punched him when he'd had the best night of bowling in his life. The man that was convinced Herb could only bowl well if he used deer antler spray or steroids. Dallas, who in one fell swoop had tried to molest and then almost killed Lois.

Pulling on a smug smile of his own to match Dallas's, Herb replied in a honey-toned voice, "Gosh. That sounds real nice Dallas, but I have a date tonight with Lois and will probably be out pretty late. So I really need to get some sleep."

Taking his left hand away from his eye, he glowered at Dallas's mirror-clad gaze. Grabbing the door with his bloody left palm, he moved to slam it shut. Dallas shot out a hand, pushing the door back open and causing the security chain to once again snap and groan. Dropping the fake smile, palming the little crucifix and extending his index finger, he pointed straight at Herb.

"I know your little... secret. You hear me Herb? I know what you are, you freakin' monster."

Herb froze, watching Dallas with unblinking eyes, one clear, one rimmed in drying blood. Time stretched, grew brittle as the two men stood like rams before locking horns.

"That's right. Got your attention? Not so sleepy now, huh? See, I was starting to wonder, what with you and that game of pool you shot. You have never, ever, run the table on nobody. Then the bowling finals. Three perfect games in a row? Not possible. Not for you. I figured you had to be on something. I just didn't realize what you were on."

Dallas took a deep breath before continuing. "Then Helen nukes herself and the cops find the dead folks in the dumpster and a body turns up on the outskirts of town. Too weird, but nothing to do with you, right? Of course not. But I couldn't shake the feeling."

He shook his mane, puffed his cheeks, and exhaled slowly.

"Shit Herb. When was the last time you covered a day-shift at Ronnie's? Haven't seen you around town at all. Not the grocery store, not the bank. Nope. Always at night. Ronnie's, Stein's, Bay City's, the usual haunts. And you," Dallas barked a harsh laugh, "Hell, you haven't been you in quite a while. So I made some calls. Did you know all them bodies, every single one, had suffered from unexplained *blood loss*? Well, once I found out that juicy tidbit, I did a little investigating. A little piecing the puzzle together. A little sleuthing. See, you're not the only one in town with a video rental card at old Petro Patterson's. I went to pick up a flick and must've just missed you. Molly, she made a joke, see? 'Hope you're not looking for a vampire movie,' she said. 'Cuz the last guy just took the last ones we had on the shelf.' I laughed, made a quick remark about people loving Halloween all year round, and you know what she said?"

Dallas was taking obvious delight in warming up to his big reveal. He let the silence stretch for a long moment before finishing.

"That you must be the pumpkin king. The pumpkin king! Ha!" This time, the bark of laughter had no mirth in it at all. "With a little of the old Dallas charm, why that Molly was more than happy to talk about your taste in video rentals. And boom! Like a bolt of lightning, I knew. It all made sense."

Herb slowly exhaled through his nose, eyes still boring into the mirrored shades less than a foot away. The whispers were crawling out of the moldy cracks and crevices deep in his brain. This time, though, he swore he could understand the multitude of raspy voices.

Kill Dallas. Kill him. Drink him. End him.

Oblivious to the mounting danger, Dallas leaned in even closer. "I. Know. I know what you are, I know what you did, and I won't—I will not—let you do anything to Lois, or anyone else. You and me, we're gonna have a reckoning. And let me tell you, old D's gonna come down like a hailstorm, and you, you're gonna be like the shitty, thin sheet metal on a Japanese import's hood. And I'm gonna start by denting the crap outta you, a million little pea-sized divots all over your face. Then that little hail storm, it's gonna kick it up a notch. And

that hail, now it's starting to look golf ball sized. That's right, you...
whatever the hell you are. Golf balls. Then baseballs. Baseballs the size
of fists. Fist-sized hailstones raining down, smashing your face. You get
me Herb? There's gonna be a hailstorm, and it's gonna be righteous.
People won't be looking at me like I'm the asshole. Oh, no! No damn
way. They're gonna see. They're gonna learn. And that'll be it for you,
old buddy!"

By the end of Dallas's tirade, Herb was shaking. A nasty concoction
of fear and rage had just been forced down his throat. His bloodied
palm still gripped the door, and his fingers were leaving impressions
in the dense wood. The whispers had mounted to a roar so loud Herb
wanted to grab his skull and rip the voices out of his head. Inside, Herb
was raging. Outside, a gossamer of self-control held him motionless in
the face of Dallas's threats.

"What the hell are you talking about, Dallas? I'm a cook, a damned
cook at a truck stop, and I haven't done anything to you or Lois."

Dropping his voice to a conspiratorial whisper, Dallas said, "She
says I was drunk. She says I don't remember. But I do. I remember
Herb. Sure, I'd had some drinks. I mean, c'mon! We were having fun.
A damn good night. And we were on the way back to my place when
you flipped my truck. I don't know how the hell you did it, but I know
it was you."

Interpreting Herb's sudden, shocked look as vindication for his
theory, Dallas plowed on, voice rising in volume with each sentence.

"That's right, you son of a bitch. I should've just driven right over
you. Let Deloris chew you up and spit you out like a raccoon pancake.
Let's just say you're lucky you're alive, you damned vampire!" Dallas's
booze-lubed rant poured like pus from an infected wound. "You tried

to eat me, you no good sonofabitch. I'm your best god damned friend, and you tried to eat me! What stopped you? Figured out you couldn't kill Dallas that easy-like, huh? Even upside down and banged around, I was still too much for you, wasn't I, you little pansy!"

It was too much for Herb to take. Ripping the chain plate from the wall, Herb swung the door wide, risking the midday sun to rage back at Dallas and his booze-twisted recollection of that horrible night.

"You stupid bastard! You were blind drunk, and you tried to rip Lois's shirt off and cop a cheap feel while you were driving. That's why you lost control of the truck, and that's when you flipped into the ditch. You want to know what happened? I was going home after work. I saw your flipped truck, and I saved Lois's life. And yours. I saved you, too."

Herb felt his fangs, knew whatever chance he had of hiding his secret was lost, but indignant rage kept him from caring. "I could've killed you. I should've killed you. But I didn't. I *saved* your drunk ass."

"Oh really? Is that how it happened, you Satan-spawned blood-sucker?" Dallas turned his head and raised his chin, a demented giggle slipping out. The midday sun brought the two pink puncture scars into sharp relief against the canvas of tanned skin. "Doctors said this must've been little pieces of flying glass. Glass! When auto glass breaks, it breaks into small, dull pieces. Not perfect little spears conveniently spaced the same width apart as a pair of vamp fangs. Okay, yeah, I was drunk, but I remember the important shit. And I remember you biting me! That was your plan. Scare me into flipping Deloris, and right when me and Lois were starting to get romantic. Then kill me as an appetizer and get Lois for the main course. But the cops showed up, and you had to skedaddle. That's what happened. I don't know how you tricked Lois and the cops, but no one tricks old Dallas, no one! So now what? What's your plan? Get Lois all to yourself? Turn her against me so I won't be there to protect her?"

Herb remembered watching an old Looney Toons cartoon a long time ago. Bugs Bunny was playing Dr. Jekyll and Mr. Hyde. The switch between the two was comical back then, but watching Dallas now, Herb found the recollection terrifying. Dallas had driven himself nuts, pure and simple. Gone was the fun-loving megalomaniac he'd called his friend for all these years. In his place was a paranoid delusional that knew Herb's secret. Dallas had whammied himself, stitching together booze-soaked recollections of a handful of details and filling in the blanks with a coarse brush dipped in half-truths, haphazard discoveries, and pure conjecture. The conclusions he'd drawn weren't just skewed, they were dangerous.

Taking deep breaths, Herb fought to bring his bloodlust and blood pressure down to reasonable levels, and almost swooned as exhaustion swept over him. He felt and heard his fangs *snick* back to their more normal size, and sagged, now using his hand to support his weight.

"I don't care what you want to believe. But understand one thing. I would never, *ever*, do anything to hurt Lois. You don't need to protect Lois, because nothing bad is going to happen to her. I swear on the friendship we used to have, and maybe we'll have again someday: I will not hurt Lois. Now go home, Dallas. This conversation is over."

Herb closed the door in Dallas's face and snapped the deadbolt back into place. Seconds later, a rock shattered the front window, followed by angry yelling.

"You're damn right nothing's gonna happen to her, you bastard! This ain't over! There's a storm coming, Herb, or whatever the hell you are now! And it's gonna send you straight back to hell."

Herb's sensitive ears heard Dallas stomp to his truck, fire up the engine, and roar down the dirt driveway. Shoving and pulling a number of heavy thoughts around, the vampire made his way back toward his earthen bed. Frustrated, exhausted, and saddened at the realization that his oldest and best friend wanted to kill him, Herb curled up in his hole. Eventually, he passed into a troubled, fitful sleep.

Chapter 43

THE SUN HAD SET, and Herb was awake. He'd showered and dressed, and was doing his best to tame his unruly hair with an uncooperative mirror. It was already close to nine, and he knew he'd have to push the Pinto to its four-cylinder limit if he was going to be on time for his date. Thoughts of the evening ahead were anxious things, cart-wheeling with excitement one second and the next cowering with dread the next. His earlier encounter with Dallas had left him badly shaken. Now that Dallas knew, truly knew, what Herb was, it was only a matter of time before he convinced more people. Despite Herb's newfound celebrity in Trappersville, Dallas was still the big man on campus for a lot of the townsfolk. While they might not believe him if he just walked up and said, 'Hey! Remember Herb Knudsen? That nobody who turned rock star bowler extraordinaire? He's a vampire,' he could certainly start to raise some uncomfortable questions. The more Herb thought about it, the more he felt that going to Bay City Bowlers might not be the best idea. Maybe Lois would rather rent a movie, stay at her place. With a final hopeful swipe of the comb across his scalp, he nodded to his non-existent reflection. That was the perfect idea. Something romantic, like *Sleepless in Seattle* or *You've Got Mail*, would be perfect.

Herb checked his watch, fervently wishing he'd left enough time to pick up a video. Instead, he rummaged through his own collection to see if there was an acceptable substitute for Meg Ryan and Tom Hanks. Tossing aside a video recap of the best Super Bowls in history and rifling through his complete collection of Ernest P. Worrell movies, Herb was made painfully aware of his lack of romantical cinema. Settling on *Slam Dunk Ernest,* he grabbed the wildflowers he'd quickly picked from his backyard, jumped in his car, and headed out for his date.

The walk up to Lois's home reminded Herb of the moonwalk from Stevie Jackowski's eighth birthday party. Herb was not the most welcome addition to the score of romping second-graders. The kids at school hadn't liked him much in general, and Stevie had hated his guts. His mom had forced him to invite Herb, but when the adults weren't listening, Stevie told him he could only have a half-piece of cake. In an act of sullen rebellion, Herb waited until the other kids ran off to bounce in the moonwalk Stevie's parents had rented. Herb slipped over to where the rest of the birthday cake sat, sugary frosting melting slow in the afternoon sun. Pushing first one, then another, then a third and fourth slice of cake into his mouth, Herb preceded to eat most of what was left on the platter, gulping down huge chunks of frosted batter as quickly as he could. Satisfied that he'd taken the appropriate revenge for Stevie's earlier slight, Herb headed for the moonwalk. Climbing inside the hot, sticky enclosure, smothered by the smell of sunbaked rubber and the dirty feet of eight or ten other boys, sugary cake distending his belly, Herb bounced across the undulating surface. The sudden explosion of vomit caught everyone by unpleasant surprise, Herb, most of all. Needless to say, he didn't get any invites to other birthday parties that year.

Now, moving determinedly toward Lois's door, he felt much like he did then. The ground seemed to warp and roil under his feet, and a large and unruly population of butterflies had taken up residence in his stomach. If Herb had been able to eat solid food, he was certain he would've lost it all well before reaching her steps. Instead, a low belch escaped right as Lois opened her front door.

"Huh. You sure have a way with words, don't you, Herb?"

Face flushed, he held out the bundle of weeds that had been wildflowers when he'd left his house. To his surprise, Lois's face lit up immediately.

"Oh, my god! You are so sweet!" She exclaimed. Noticing his self-conscious grimace, she added, "Seriously, Herb. It's been, well, like, forever since someone's brought me flowers. They're beautiful. Let's get them in some water. There's a pitcher in the kitchen. Could you grab the scissors? I think they're on the coffee table."

Lois turned and headed toward the kitchen. Still speechless and reeling from his ill-timed belch, Herb moved to follow her instructions. At least he tried to. His feet managed to get him up the two shallow steps of the front stoop. He caught the screen door before it swung shut, but when he tried to take a third step forward, he couldn't. Looking down in confusion, he lifted his right foot again and moved it forward, only that didn't happen. His foot remained exactly where it was. Glancing up quickly to see if Lois had noticed his predicament, he looked back down, grabbed his pant leg with his free hand, and gave it a tug. The fabric of his jeans moved willingly enough, but pulled taut against the back of his completely immobile leg. Panting with exertion, Herb willed his body forward, willed his leg to move like a normal, well-behaved leg should, and remained exactly where he was.

"Hey slowpoke! I need those scissors. What's the hold-up?" Lois asked, poking her head back into the entryway from the kitchen.

"Oh. Ah. Sorry. Shoes on? Shoes off?" Herb asked.

"Such a gentleman. On's fine," she added with a smile and headed back to the sink. Herb heard a running faucet and the splash of water as she filled a pitcher. He took a step back and almost fell over when his legs responded so easily. Before the screen door could close, he leapt forward again, catching the door and hoping his momentum would carry him across the threshold. As before, once he reached the top step, he simply stopped, feet awkwardly planted on the concrete, hand holding the screen door. Try as he might, he simply couldn't walk through the door.

Cursing himself for an idiot, he suddenly remembered one of the many rules he'd learned in his vampire research. Panic setting in, he started to twist to and fro, an animal suddenly discovering its cage.

"Geez, Herb, would you get in here? You'll be covered in mosquitoes if you stay out there any longer!"

Mid-twist, whatever force had been preventing Herb from just walking through the door evaporated. His ears popped, and the momentum of his frantic twist pulled his feet from the ground and launched him into a mid-air sideways somersault. Lois had just returned from the kitchen, her admonition about uninvited mosquitoes replaced with a surprised smile as Herb acrobatically flipped into her living room and landed in a deep lunge with his knees crossed and arms splayed gracefully out to either side. Standing slowly, Herb felt his cheeks flush again as Lois started to clap.

"Wow! Where'd you learn to do that?" Lois exclaimed with delight. "I guess there's a lot I don't know about you. So you can flip around like a circus acrobat, but getting the scissors was a little too much of a stretch?"

With a good-natured punch to his shoulder, Lois grabbed the scissors from the coffee table and sauntered back toward the kitchen.

"Well, not to ruin any surprises," she said over her shoulder, "but I'm pretty agile, too."

With a wink, she disappeared around the corner. While Herb's libido tried to sensibly sort through all the possible implications of her comment, Lois returned with a decorative pitcher full of blooming wildflowers. Setting them on the coffee table and giving them a quick sprucing, she said, "Wow. These really are lovely. So. Are we ready for some karaoke?"

"Um. Well, sure. I mean, no. I mean. Well, I was kinda thinking, you know. It's gonna be busy. And. Um. There's singing and stuff. So I was thinking, maybe we'd like, you know. We could just watch something here."

"…I suppose. Did you have something in mind? To watch, I mean?" Lois asked.

Herb could tell she was disappointed about not going out. He felt rotten for trying to cancel her plans, but was still unsure if a public appearance was the best thing for him right now. He ran to his Pinto, grabbed *Slam Dunk Ernest* and raced back to her door, holding it up with a proud grin.

Lois laughed, shaking her head. "Oh my god, Herb. Chef extraordinaire, professional bowler, acrobat, and comedian! What else have you been hiding all this time?"

Hooking her arm through his, she drew him outside and closed her front door behind them. Out of options, Herb helped her into the Pinto and set out for Bay City Bowlers.

Chapter 44

B AY CITY WAS BUSY. Herb supposed there was something strange about so many people wanting to be inside a dark space without windows on what was a beautiful late summer evening. After more thought, though, he couldn't pin down just what was so strange about the notion. After all, you couldn't bowl outside, or sing karaoke outside, and there certainly wasn't a bar outside.

Yep, he thought. *Inside has way more going on than outside.*

As he and Lois walked through the bowling alley toward the bar, he was pleasantly aware of the nearness of her. She hadn't taken his hand, not yet at any rate. But she was walking close enough that her shoulder sometimes brushed his, sending schools of electric minnows through his skin. They talked about little things as they walked, pleasant things that made her smile. It was perfect. He was on a date with Lois, a real date in the real world, and it was absolutely perfect.

Walking past the alleys, he saw the faces he'd seen for so much of his life. Slow Johnson lorded over his domain from the lane and shoe rental counter. Fancy Dan, in a riotous blend of colors as usual, was a puffed up polyester peacock patrolling his territory. Two-Shirt Bert and Dozer were in the middle of an arm-wrestling match while Dylan collected dollars from a group of onlookers. Cheryl and Jimmy, apparently still an item, were mid-game on lane four. As Herb and Lois passed various groups of locals, they all paused for a second to smile, wave, and offer a friendly, "Hey there, Herby!" It was surreal, but he knew it must've actually been happening because Lois commented on it, too.

"Gosh, I guess I didn't know that you knew everyone in town." As they neared the bowling counter, she paused, eyes wide with excitement.

"There's your name! On the winner's board! Herb, that's so cool! It's like I'm walking with a celebrity!" Fingers intertwining with his, she smiled and swung their arms. "C'mon, you big superstar, and buy me a drink."

Moving through the swinging doors to the bar, Herb felt the usual sense of traveling through universes. The music in the bar was never the same as the music in the bowling alley, the lighting was different, even the carpet and walls were different. The result always made for an odd transition. Distracted, he bounced along behind Lois like a balloon on a string. When they reached the bar, Rhonda dropped the dishrag she'd been using to dry some pints and headed their way.

"Herb! And it's Lois, ain't it? Yeah, sure it is! Seen you in here before once or twice." Watery ice cubes clinked as she cleared a few empty glasses out of the way and tossed down a pair of cocktail napkins. "Herb, you want a bloody? I'll whip that right up. And how 'bout you, sweetheart? Oh, you know what? Pretty thing like you, you should try a Cosmopolitan, like my Jasper drinks. It's fancy." As Lois nodded her consent, Rhonda waved at her full-grown son up on the little stage, disco light fully engaged and karaoke screens ready to go. "She's drinkin' a Cosmo too, sweetie! Ain't that something?" Rhonda yelled up.

Eyes wide at the newly discovered kindred spirit, Jasper gave an enthusiastic two-thumbs up, panicked for a moment when he couldn't find his own drink, and quickly recovered his aplomb when he lifted a pink-filled martini glass. Lois laughed and returned the double-thumbs up as Jasper busied himself with final touches. Tea light candles, song books in two stacks, the first sorted by artist, the other sorted by song title, a little plastic basket full of golf pencils and sign-up slips.

While the bar still had about half of its tables open at present, Herb knew they would fill up quick enough. People loved their karaoke. He'd always been a bowler, just a bowler, not a singer or performer. It wasn't from a lack of appreciation of music. Herb had a ton of cassettes and often sang in the shower, but karaoke... The thought of him, Dallas, even Stanley taking turns singing at one another was so absurd he almost started to laugh, but then Dallas stuck in his brain like gum in a lock of hair, and the humor was gone.

Don't think about him. Don't worry about him. You're here, he's not. You're with Lois, he's not. So just don't think about him and have a good time.

Herb's self-admonition helped squeeze the whispers back into their dark corners, helped tighten the chains holding himself together. Carrying his red-filled pint and Lois's pink martini, they made their way through the bar toward an open table near the stage.

Chapter 45

"I CAN'T BELIEVE YOU'RE not going to sing," Lois chided. "I've already been up there twice. You owe me," she threatened.

She wasn't kidding, either. Lois had sung twice, and both times Herb just about fell off his stool in shock. The girl could sing. She stunned the slowly growing crowd with a sultry rendition of "Black Velvet." A lot of people in the room knew Lois, either from Ronnie's or from around town. When she took the stage, she got plenty of claps and whistles, which made Herb immensely proud to be her date. Then she started to sing. Herb watched in rapt fascination as her hips swayed and her lips almost touched the microphone. A sudden *snick* caught him completely off guard, and he quickly shut his mouth. Unsure of what to do, he fished an ice cube out of his mostly untouched Bloody Mary, popped it in his mouth, and studiously watched a spot on the wall just over Lois's left shoulder until his fangs returned to normal. Lois was crooning out the last verse of the song by the time Herb felt he had himself under control.

Lois's first song definitely set the hook, but it was her next number that completely reeled him in. When the opening guitar riff for Heart's "Magic Man" came through the speakers, the whole crowd started to cheer. Before Lois had even sung a note, Herb's fangs had *snicked* back into place, but he was too enthralled to care. By the end of the song, Herb felt like he'd been whammied. There was nothing that he wouldn't do if Lois asked. He was hers completely.

So when she insisted he sing, he really had no choice. After leafing through the book a few times, he finally settled on something he thought he could pull off. Scribbling on the white slip with a tiny pencil, he coyly avoided sharing his choice with Lois, despite her appeals.

"Nope," he replied to her entreaties. "I'm scared enough already. So you're just gonna have to live with the suspense, 'cause if I tell you the song, I'm gonna lose my nerve."

That had been about fifteen minutes ago. Desperately needing some liquid courage, Herb had followed a patron into the men's room, whammied him in a stall, and quickly spiked his Bloody Mary. Back at their table, he and Lois watched familiar faces from around town get up on stage. The old saying was apparently true. You may not be able to carry a tune, but you can always karaoke. Despite the liberal interpretation of keys and melodies, there was a lot of love in the room. People clapped and cheered for all the singers, but the intensity of the applause would ramp up if you were really, really good, or really, really bad. Jimbo Waczkowski was one such embodiment of really, really bad. His version of "Friends in Low Places" had the crowd on its feet, shouting along in a cacophony of keys and tempos while Rhonda poured whiskey shots for every refrain. It was fine entertainment indeed, but even Jimbo's drunken antics couldn't fully distract Herb from the knowledge that every time someone sang, there was one less person before it was his turn.

"Okay'den everybody!" the KJ announced. "We got a treat for you now. A real celebrity and first-time karaoke'r, this year's bowling champion, Herb Knudsen!"

Suddenly, Lois was pulling him off his stool and blowing him a kiss for luck. Like a piece of driftwood carried to shore by relentless waves, Herb washed up on the small, elevated stage, tripping on the first step despite his vampire grace and almost face-planting on the dingy grey and red carpet. Some good-natured laughs and a, 'More whiskey for this guy!' followed his less than eloquent entrance.

Herb looked at the microphone, momentarily confused by what exactly was supposed to happen next. Uncertainty latched deep inside his chest and squeezed. Herb stood in the headlights of a hundred charging semis, completely transfixed by first fear, then a sudden urge to survive. Fangs *snicked*. One hand gripped the mic so tightly that tiny fractures appeared in the plastic casing, while the other reflexively curled claw-like at his side. The cheers from the crowd soured and curdled in his ears, poured into the cracks in his mind, fed the whispers that boiled their way to the surface.

Hungry eyes glinted in the reflected light bouncing off Jasper's absurd little disco ball. The vampire scanned the pulsing bags of blood, the sounds of the bar reduced to the seductive *thu-thump thu-thump* of scores of hearts waiting to be ripped from shattered ribcages, slashed and torn by his fangs. Herb's legs started to crouch, pistons readying to unleash his lust and fury upon the cattle below, and a low growl rose up from a dark, primal place.

When Herb and Lois's eyes met, it was like a rabid dog reaching the end of its tether, the violent yank almost enough to send him reeling backward into the wall behind him. Caught in her smile, he watched her run a finger across her brow to replace a stray lock of golden blond hair. A shudder ran through Herb as the music began. Eyes never leaving Lois, he began to sing "Long, Cool Woman" by the Hollies.

The voice that came through the speakers surprised a lot of folks, but none more than Herb. For a second he thought Jasper might've been playing a friendly joke, or maybe enacting a carefully devised ploy to protect the crowd from yet another terrible singer, but when Herb turned to look at Jasper, he saw nothing short of awe reflected back at him.

Plunging ahead, he continued with the song. His right foot, heel up and poised to drive his predatory leap into the fray, started to tap, his whole leg now counting rhythm to the Hollies and their classic-cool groove. His previously clawed hand, ready moments ago to rip the life out of anyone in arm's reach, suddenly turned palm-up as his arm tracked across the crowd. Eyes squeezed shut, lost in the song, he swung his head to and fro. Freeing the mic from the stand, he held it close to his mouth while his other hand slapped his thigh, leg still pounding out a rhythm. For the first time in his life, Herb Knudsen *sang*.

The crowd erupted in cheers as guitar riffs cut their way through the speakers, and people started to look appreciatively at Lois. She basked in their attention like a flower drinking in a summer afternoon while the brave and the drunk filled the dance floor. Jasper bumped the volume up, and the music carried into the bowling alley itself. As Herb kicked out lyrics, bowlers stopped mid-approach, and newcomers froze in the act of passing money to Slow Johnson for a pair of shoes. Smiles caught and spread like wildfire, head's started to bob.

Herb could still sense the *thu-thump* of the hearts, but now they all seemed to be pounding in time to the rhythm of his song.

As he cat-walked back and forth across the stage, every pair of eyes that he met was instantly caught up, drawn in, lit to pop like a firecracker, and sent spinning back into the world. The fervor of the crowd was a living thing that writhed and danced on the worn wood of the dance floor and spilled over onto the carpet. Herb dropped to his knees and leaned back, way back, until the back of his head brushed the floor. Both hands squeezing the mic, he unleashed the song like a wild thing long chained set suddenly and joyously free.

Rising up like Dracula from his coffin, Herb faced the crowd again, eyes locked squarely on Lois as he finished the final lines of the song. Sliding the mic back into its stand, Herb felt the song crest, break, and start to recede, a tidal wave performance that had pulled in the unsuspecting, sent them swirling and sweating, and left them bobbing happily after.

The fading music made the thunderous applause crescendo, while cheers of, "Hot damn!" and, "Atta boy, Herby!" filled the bar. Herb barely heard the hollers and shouts. His whole world, every ounce of his attention, was consumed by Lois. Their eyes held as stepped down from the stage, oblivious to the back-slaps and Jasper's eager praise. They held as he crossed the space, slow and certain as the rising sun, held as he took her outstretched hands and stepped into the circle of her arms, widened as she simultaneously moved toward him, finally to close as their lips met.

As they kissed, Herb felt the warmth of the sun on his face. A gentle breeze ruffled his rusty hair, and clear water washed through him. Lois's kiss was balm, surcease, benediction. The cool touch of aloe on a burn, a cracked window in a dark, musty room, the early spring rain on the last bits of snow.

There was a flutter of fear, the tiniest moment of terror. Herb realized there was no way that Lois could possibly feel the same way as he did. His heart bled sorrow through old and heavy scars. This one perfect moment was just that, a moment, one that would end too soon and return him to the unbearable bleakness that was his life before her kiss.

Better to just be done with it, he reasoned. *It's inevitable anyway.*

He opened his eyes to invite the cold shower of reality in and found her staring back.

Still kissing, their eyes met. Lightning struck, thunder sounded, and was that, could that be trumpets, a host of voices raised in celebratory song? At long last, the kiss gave signs of ending. No, not ending, but pausing, allowing the rest of time to catch up, giving the earth permission to spin again, the universe the okay to resume its endless expansion. Their lips separated and Herb drew a deep, shuddering breath. Every feeling that made up the whirling, dancing, joyously laughing dervish in his chest, he saw its measure in her eyes.

The sound of a faraway scuffle was a gnat buzzing by his ear. He whooshed a mental hand at the imagined gnat, hoping it would just go away. Instead, the argument grew louder, claiming more of his attention. Indeterminate noises became words, and words became voices he knew.

First Jasper, reedy and nasally, a coddled child ready to cry for mom. "But you gotta wait your turn. Everybody always waits their turn."

Then Jimbo, marble-mouthed drunk and conciliatory, his voice first loud, then quickly dwindling as he stumbled from the stage. "S'okay. Next time gonna sing. Lovely song. Song-a-long…"

Finally, like a cinder block dropped on a barefoot, a hammer on a thumb, a voice yanked Herb and Lois firmly back to the present moment, a place that had become much less pleasant now that Dallas had taken the stage. "Well, hot damn folks! Helluva night for some kar'oke!"

Had he not been so caught up in Lois, Herb would've smelled him from the parking lot, heard his heavy boot tread as he entered the bowling alley. Instead, Dallas had caught him completely unaware, instantly ruining this most perfect of moments. So Herb didn't feel too terribly bad when he exclaimed, "Oh for fuck's sake. What's *he* doing here?"

The bar fell silent, looking from Dallas to Herb and back again. People didn't cut in line at karaoke. That was just *rude*. But people also didn't just toss around F-bombs in public, either. That was also rude. Heads swiveled as the crowd tried to suss out just who the worse offender was in a situation like this. Herb felt vindicated when he saw more and more faces turn disapproving scowls toward Dallas. It really was rude to cut the line at karaoke. Even Herb, a total newbie, understood that.

Drunk, determined, and oblivious to the crowd's ire, Dallas wrapped a paw around the mic and barked at Jasper to queue up some Roky Erickson.

"Who?" Jasper asked. "Ropey who?"

"Roky, not ropey. Rhymes with pokey." Dallas growled. "Okey doke artichokee? Get on now and play some Roky!"

Jasper shrugged, shook his head.

"You can spell, can't ya? R-O-K-Y. Roky Erickson. Song's called 'Night of the Vampire!'" Dallas exclaimed with exasperation.

Jasper flicked his eyes nervously at the still-speechless crowd watching the exchange on the small stage. "Vampire? But Dallas, it ain't even kind of close to Halloween yet. I don't got my spooky song discs..."

For every action, there is an equal and opposite reaction. For example, when Dallas leaned in and seemed to grow bigger, Jasper leaned back and seemed to shrivel as he stammered, "I'm s-sorry Dallas, I ain't never heard of no Ropey or Roky Erickson or no vampire tonight song."

"Okay, you little piss-ant. Slayer, then. 'At Dawn they Sleep.' You've got that, right?" Dallas asked, looked at Jasper hopefully. "'At Dawn they Sleep!' That's the title. You don't got that in your machine?"

Sweat running freely down his face, Jasper again shook his head.

Dallas started to pace, dragging the mic back and forth. "Um... oh yeah! 'Bela Lugosi's Dead,' Bauhaus. Frickin' Bauhaus! Everyone knows that one. 'Undead, undead, undead,'" Dallas sang.

"Sorry Dallas,"

"Alice Cooper. 'Welcome to My Nightmare.'"

"Nope."

"Um, how about 'Werewolf of London?' I can change the words. To like, vampire. Of Trappersville."

"Uh-uh. I told you, I don't got my Halloween discs here tonight."

The crowd was transfixed by the strange drama. Lois was visibly mortified, while Herb was wracked by fear and rage. Every song Dallas shouted into the mic made more hairs rise on the back of his neck, made him instinctively want to flee. But the thought of Dallas outing him like this at a karaoke bar, and doing so when he was on his first and, so far, really, really good date with Lois... It was unthinkable. Unforgivable.

"Neil Young!" Dallas barked. "If this is any kind of real kar'oke, you gotta have Neil Young."

Jasper saw his possible salvation dangling from a thread. "Oh, hell yeah, Dallas. I got lots of Neil Young. Lemme guess. You're a 'Cinnamon Girl' fan, right? One for the ladies?"

Despite being dunk and agitated, Dallas was still quick as a cobra. In a flash, he'd gathered the front of Jasper's shirt and yanked his face in so close their noses were touching. Rhonda's gasp of fear for her only, favorite, and well-mulleted son snapped the silence like a broken piano string, but it was quickly replaced by a deeper, tenser silence. Everyone in the room knew Dallas and usually liked him well enough, but they also knew he had a short fuse and genuinely enjoyed punching things from time to time.

"Not. Cinnamon. Girl," he said, voice grinding like the rusty tracks of an old bulldozer. "You will play 'Vampire Blues.' It's a vampire song about a god damned vampire, and I'm gonna sing it whether you got it in your damn book or not. I ain't doin' this for fun. I'm making a point. A god damned public service announcement." He paused to slam a fist to his chest, standing straighter with noble purpose. "So look up the damn song."

Jasper riffled through his books again, crowed triumphantly, and grabbed a shiny CD. "Yes! Best K-J ever. I got it, Dal. I got it. You don't gotta hit me now."

As Jasper frantically queued up the song, Dallas turned his whiskey-soaked gaze back to the bar, bloodshot eyes roaming sullenly through the crowd until they found Herb and Lois.

Herb vibrated with dangerous anger, but Dallas was too drunk, pissed off, and self-righteous to notice. He glared right back down at Herb from over the mic and said in his false-hearty voice, "Well, Herb! I'll be damned. Who'da thunk I'd see you here. Guess I'd better dedicate this next number to my best friend, my bestest buddy. My compadre, Herbert Knudsen. You like Neil Young, right Herb?"

Jasper, ever the professional, started the song at that exact moment. As it started, Herb's fury was momentarily diverted. Listening to the opening chords, he was sure Jasper had made a mistake. A Neil Young song? It sounded more like Muddy Waters, Bo Diddley, maybe. But when Dallas started to sing in his loud, drunken, almost on key voice, Herb's icy fright and red-hot rage returned, turning his gut into a maelstrom of emotion.

Dallas was getting into it, hunched forward, the mic stand pushed over the edge of the platform at a sharp angle. His eyes shifted from Herb's to Lois's, who still stood in shock, one arm wrapped tight across her midsection and her other hand pressed over her mouth as if she was about to gag on a foul taste in her mouth.

As he belted out the words about a vampire and sucking blood, Dallas brought the mic stand back upright. One hand pointed straight at Herb, indictment plain for all to see. His other hand reached into a pocket, pulled something out, and threw it Rollie Fingers style straight at Herb. When the bulb of garlic hit him in the forehead, Herb lost it. No longer able to just stand and fume, he pounced. His body sailed across the small dance floor, arms outstretched, hands clawed. His face was contorted with hatred and rage right up until the moment it met a meaty fist, swung by an arm that was made for heavy labor and bar brawls. The force of the punch pushed his trajectory off target. Instead of slamming bodily into his intended victim, Herb tripped and careened past Dallas into the heavy felt curtain covering the back wall. Growling and spinning, Herb lashed out with his own fist, the glancing blow sending Dallas backward off the platform. Recovering from the fall, Dallas dusted off the front of his jeans, cracked his knuckles, and settled into a classic boxer's pose: knees bent, elbows in, fists up, and wide, drunk, and angry eyes glaring over almond-sized knuckles.

"C'mon, you hell spawn! That the best you got?" he challenged as the crowd quickly made room for the impending brawl.

Herb squatted on the edge of the karaoke stage like a gargoyle, arms splayed and fangs bared. He let loose something part growl and part curse in response to Dallas's challenge. Leaping down from the platform to the dance floor, the two forces collided. Herb was inhumanly strong and fast, but Dallas was a former football player and current bar brawler. The result was a pretty even match-up, with neither man gaining the advantage.

"What the hell is wrong with you, Dallas?" Herb yelled as he swung.

"Me? You're the goddamned vamp!" Dallas ducked, slipped, kicked out a booted foot.

"Both of you stop it! Stop it right now!" Lois's shrill scream distracted Herb for a split second, and Dallas's kick caught him in the shin. Falling, he shot a hand out, caught the tail of Dallas's untucked flannel.

"I'm somebody now! People like me. They like me!"

Herb wrenched on Dallas's shirt, pulled him to the floor. Dallas continued the momentum and rolled on top of Herb, wrapping his hands around Herb's neck.

"Like you? Who the hell are you kidding? You're a damn loser! And now you kill people! You think people are gonna like you if you drink their blood?"

A fist hammered down piston-like. Herb jerked his head to the side at the last moment and heard Dallas's knuckles crack hard against the floor, followed by a sharp intake of breath as he pulled his bruised fist back.

"What are you talking about, Dallas?" Lois screamed from the front of the growing crowd of on-lookers. "Herb hasn't killed anyone! Are you crazy?"

"...just called the cops, you assholes! So you'd better get the hell outta here, both of you!" Rhonda yelled from behind the bar, phone still in hand.

"Say it, Herb. Tell her! Tell her how you killed that guy in the woods. Probably Helen and them other folks, too. How you tried to kill me. How you tried to kill her!"

Dallas still had one hand squeezing Herb's neck. With a violent thrust, Herb shoved him back and up. The blow lifted Dallas off the floor, sent him reeling backward toward the pool table in the corner. Dallas hit the rail with a grunt and a curse. Reaching behind him, he grabbed a pool cue and swung right as Herb was charging.

"I didn't try to kill Lois!" Herb blocked the swing, the pool cue snapping in half as it cracked against his forearm. Barreling into Dallas, he screamed, "I love her!"

Shocked silence followed as Herb and Dallas embraced. For a moment, it looked like the two had decided a good hug would settle everything. Herb heard the gasps and someone whisper, "Holy crap. Did you see his teeth?" Leaning back, he pulled his open mouth away from the side of Dallas's neck. As he shifted his weight back, he was caught by a strange cold-hot sensation emanating from his chest. Someone's hand caught his as he stumbled back.

Mouth agape, fangs on full display, Herb looked at Dallas. His best friend gaped in wide-eyed, horrified amazement, his breath coming in short, sharp puffs, his hand still holding the haft of the broken cue.

Head feeling like it was dangling from a palsied puppeteer's hand, Herb looked haltingly down. The strange, unidentifiable sensation in his chest slowly resolved as his eyes followed the broken cue extending from Dallas's hand to its terminus in his own increasingly bloody shirt. His head lolled to one side, and he saw it was Lois who'd caught his hand, who was helping him fall back as gently as possible to the floor, surrounded by fading whispers and a growing cacophony of voices.

"Oh god, oh Herb! Someone... someone help!" Lois pleaded, looking around frantically at the confused, scared faces of the crowd.

"But what the hell's wrong with his teeth?" he heard someone say.

Another voice chimed in with, "Dallas said he killed a guy? That guy they found in the woods?"

"For real?" someone else gasped. "He ate someone?"

"What's wrong with you? He needs an ambulance! He needs help!" Lois screamed back, sobbing.

"All them vampire songs," another voice added. "Holy shipyards. Dallas is right. He's a vamp. An honest-to-god vamp'er. Right here in Wisconsin!"

"Hey, did you see that guy? I think it was that guy from that movie. He was just over there, in the corner. Where'd he go?" a woman asked.

"Geezuz, he's burning up! Wait, no. More like smoldering...." another voice added.

"Call an ambulance! Dallas, someone, please call an ambulance!" Lois screamed again, eyes frantic and wide.

"You say Herb's a vampire?" someone a little slower on the uptake asked.

"Vamps can't be bowling champions, right? We gotta redo the finals, right?" Fancy Dan's distinctive voice chimed in from somewhere near the back.

"Christ! He's burning up like embers in a fire, he is. No, don't get too close," another voice cautioned. "That shirt could be polyester, and it'll melt right to your skin."

Herb tried to listen to the words, but someone was cramming cotton into his ears and filling his chest with molten lava. His neck was a noodle, his head too heavy to lift. Eyes roaming, he saw the fear, the disbelief, and the blossoming anger in the faces leaning closer and closer. All the old faces that had become new friends after they saw him bowl, ate his food, listened to him sing. They liked him, they really liked him.

Don't they? he wondered. Why were they so angry now?

There, towering in the center of the tightening circle, was Dallas, his mouth moving, repeating something over and over.

He's sorry? Herb thought distantly. *He should be. Stabbing me with a pool cue. What a jerk.*

Then, an angel. Radiant, beautiful, looking down at him from a great height. Strands of hair like sunlight floating in a halo around her face. Mascara-blackened tears fell and sizzled against his skin as she drew closer.

I love you, Lois. His mouth moved without sound. Sound required breath, but breath belonged to the living.

He smiled. It hurt to smile, but he wanted to give her something, and he had nothing else to give. The burning had spread from his chest to his gut, his arms and legs, tendrils of heat wrapping up around his scalp and pulling at his forehead, crawling up his throat and melting his teeth. Beneath the fire was a growing darkness, eating everything up. His vision narrowed to a blurry circle framing her face, now inches above his own. As the burning darkness spread, he tried one last time to say her name.

The Final Chapter

*W*HERE DO VAMPIRES GO *when they die?*

Herb's question floated unanswered through the darting minnows of disco ball light. He looked around, surprised by his strange vantage point near the dimpled acoustic tiles of the bar's ceiling. Below, Dallas stood frozen, choking on a mixture of consternation and remorse. Lois knelt beside his body, face streaked with tears. Reaching for his hands, his face, her fingers met only smoldering dust. While Rhonda screamed into the phone for an ambulance, the locals turned and turned, a confused sea with a constantly shifting tide, drawing closer to Herb's body, then pulling away. The frantic activity below buffeted and jostled Herb's awareness. He floated like a plastic bag on a fickle breeze, first one direction, then another, up and away from the charred and melting vessel below.

He knew in an abstract sort of way that he was dying, that soon all the pieces of him would fall away and there'd be nothing left of him in this world. As he floated above the confused, macabre scene below, memories fell and sparkled diamond-like on the dingy carpet below. There, Dallas punching Joey O'Connell in the girl's bathroom, Herb watching in stupefied appreciation. And there, Stanley waving his umbrella at a group of kids as they *oohed* and *aahed* about his abduction. Another sparkle, and he remembered watching Super Bowl XXXI, convinced he wouldn't be sober for a week. Sparkle, and he felt Helen's breasts brushing against his arm, Jenni's nails across his back.

Piece after glimmering piece, the memories fell as Herb turned and twisted in the invisible breeze. Running the table at Stein's. Drinking beers in Dallas's back yard. People chanting his name as he bowled a perfect game. Sparkle after sparkle, memories fell while Herb watched and relived and smiled before they were gone.

Some of the gems had a darker cast, rubies and sapphires, garnets and opals. These memories hurt to look at, like poking old bruises on his soul. Bo the retriever barking in the back of a pickup truck. The sound of a spinal cord snapping in the night. Candy's lifeless eyes looking to him for an explanation. Lady, the unfortunate pug, sequined collar coated in gore. These darker memories were plentiful, stretching back and back to when he was young. As each glistened and faded, he felt lighter, freer, moving up through the ceiling of the bar and seeping into the night air. The sky opened above him, so full of stars he could hardly see the darkness between.

The memories fell faster now, raining like welder sparks on the world below. Fangs piercing veins, duct taping a rusted hole in the Pinto, arm wrestling with Dallas, running through the night like the summer wind itself. Each memory sparked, lit up his world, fizzled, and was gone as what was Herb bled away into the night.

Memories of his Maker shook loose and glinted the moment Herb recognized him. Perched on a fencepost near the woods, a gentle wind stirring his short cape, the vampire gazed up at the starscape spanning the horizons. Despite being nothing more than a pile of ash in a bowling alley bar and this gossamer-thin awareness, Herb still had a sense of *self*, and was rather surprised to find his Maker looking directly at him.

It ends this way for most of my children, Herb heard his Maker... speak? Think? He couldn't tell, but the words were not without kindness. *For what it's worth, at the end you were loved. Very few of our kind are so fortunate. Go now, Herbert Knudsen, who makes pretty good French toast. Go now and remember what it was to be loved.*

As his Maker commanded, so it was. The brightest sparkles of all fell like tears turned to snowflakes, catching the moonlight with a radiance no words could ever describe. A hundred thousand memories lit up the world around him as he rose, rose, rose into the night. And while each sparkling, burning memory was as unique and beautiful as the snowflakes they reminded him of, they were all the same. *Lois, Lois, my Lois.*

Memories finally gone, there was very little left of Herb, just the tiniest piece of consciousness that every person has at their center. That bare essence once known as Herb was still aware, though. Aware enough to wonder with gratitude that he was rising up, up toward the limitless stars above.

Heaven? he wondered, basking in the starlight.

His Maker's final thought reached him just as the stars fell away. It sent Herb plummeting. The wind became a freight train roar, and the pristine sky turned to jaundice and rot. As the darkness and scorching pain embraced him, his Maker's last words seared him like a brand.

Nope. Sorry. You're a vampire, remember?

. . . ● . ● . ● . .

AUTHOR'S NOTE

Oh no! Poor Herb! That's just awful. And Dallas? What a jerk, right? The absolute worst. He's not going to get away with that, is he? Is he?!?

The adventure continues in **Northwoods Wolfman**. Dallas learns a little sympathy for the devil, Lois discovers something surprising about herself, and Stanley might actually be the smartest guy in town.

And maybe we haven't seen the last of our dearly departed vampire friend, Herbert Knudsen...

. . . ● . ● . ● . .

If you like paranormal comedy, sign up for my once-a-month newsletter, **The Paranomedy Pint** and get a **FREE short story**! Each month, I share a great book to read, a fun show to watch, a tasty drink to drink, and a little paranormal weirdness, too.

· · · ● · ● · · ·

THE END

Did you have fun?

I had a heck of a good time writing this book. If you enjoyed reading it, I hope you'll take a moment to share a rating or even a review! Ratings and reviews for authors are like tips for bartenders. We love 'em. They also help others who stumble across the book decide if they should give it a try.

Use these QR codes to easily post a review on your preferred site(s):

Amazon 

Goodreads

BookBub

When Being a Vampire Sucks

Most pop culture casts vampires as either awesome or terrible (or sparkly, but don't get me started on that). If they aren't dangerously irresistible and fulfilling some dark prophecy or other, they're a nightmarish beast wreaking bloody havoc at every turn.

That can't be it, though. There has to be more. There have to be vampires that oversleep, watch infomercials, forget to pay the electric bill, and can't remember where they left their keys. Vampires for whom being a vampire isn't all that awesome. Vampires for whom being a vampire actually kind of sucks.

I had that little epiphany when I was rewatching *Interview with the Vampire.* I had moved to Los Angeles, CA in the early 2000s and popped a copy in the old VCR. That's right—a Video Cassette Recorder. If that brings you back, you're welcome. If you have no idea what I'm talking about, Google it and learn some history, for Pete's sake. Anyway, back to the movie. Kirsten Dunst played Claudia, a destitute and sickly child. Louis and Lestat turn little Claudia into a vampire and—boom!—she's perfect. Her curling locks shine, her pale skin glows, and she's fit as a fiddle.

I'd read the book and watched the movie before. Not once had I stopped and thought, *Wait a second...* It wasn't until that rewatching in my late 20s that I was really bothered by Claudia's turning. Was it that easy for everyone? What about the other guys? The regular guys. The slightly below average guys. The guys that can barely match their socks. What would becoming a vampire be like for them?

I didn't realize it until much later, but that is when *Wisconsin Vamp* was born. Actually, the movie *Interview with the Vampire* was firmly in mind as I wrote it. Fun fact: Herb's maker is Lestat. Well, not Lestat Lestat. That'd get me sued. He was **ahem** heavily influenced by the idea of a vampire that shares many of the same qualities and circumstances as Lestat. Please don't sue me.

Anywho...

Once I started thinking about average, everyday folks becoming monsters, I couldn't stop. Questions rattled around my skull incessantly. Do werewolves pee on trees? Does Dramamine help sea-sick mermaids? Do zombies hang out with zombies because it's nice to have people around without having to make small talk? Ever since I started writing *Wisconsin Vamp,* I've been enamoured with ordinary monsters.

So, let's raise our glasses and toast the ordinary... and how extraordinary that can be.

A Bit About Scott

People say you should write what you know. That's damned good advice, so Scott writes about ordinary Midwesterners making an extraordinary mess of things. Hey, if the flannel fits...

Oh, one more thing. "Ordinary" totally includes vampires, werewolves, zombies, witches, shapeshifters, aliens and more!

Find Scott on:

www.swbauthorblog.wordpress.com

www.facebook.com/swbuthor

www.instagram.com/swbauthor

www.goodreads.com/swbauthor

www.bookbub.com/authors/scott-burtness

and in bars and bowling alleys up in the Midwest.

FREE Short Story

Get *Five Stars*, a FREE demonic horror comedy short story, when you sign up for **The Paranomedy Pint**, Scott's once-a-month email featuring a great book to read, a fun show to watch, something terrific to drink, and a little paranormal weirdness to enjoy!!

Beer-Fueled Urban Fantasy by Scott Burtness

SCOTT BURTNESS

ODDS 'n' ENDS

A is for All the Monsters We Can't Stand: A Hilarious Mon-
ster-Themed Coloring Book for Grownups

Story and poems by Scott Burtness | Illustrations by Harold Torres